P9-CEC-773

YORICK AND BÖNES

Friends by Any Other Name

YORICK
AND
BÖNES

Friends by Any Other Name

JEREMY TANKARD
AND HERMIONE TANKARD

Quill Tree Books
Imprints of HarperCollinsPublishers

HARPER
alley

Quill Tree Books is an imprint of HarperCollins Publishers.
HarperAlley is an imprint of HarperCollins Publishers.

Yorick and Bones: Friends by Any Other Name
Copyright © 2021 by Jeremy Tankard
All rights reserved. Printed in Spain.
www.harperalley.com
ISBN 978-0-06-285433-9 — ISBN 978-0-06-285434-6 (paperback)
The artist used Clip Studio to create the digital illustrations for this book.
Typography by Chris Dickey
21 22 23 24 25   EP   10 9 8 7 6 5 4 3 2 1

First Edition

Jeremy: For Theo and Heather

Hermione: For my dad, because he is the BEST!!!! Oh my goodness
I love him so much. He is talented and very, very clever. Wow.
What would I do without such an amazing inspiration? He's
just so cool! How did I get so lucky? Beats me. He definitely did
not type this dedication himself when I wasn't looking. So, in
conclusion: this book is dedicated to him (my amazing father).

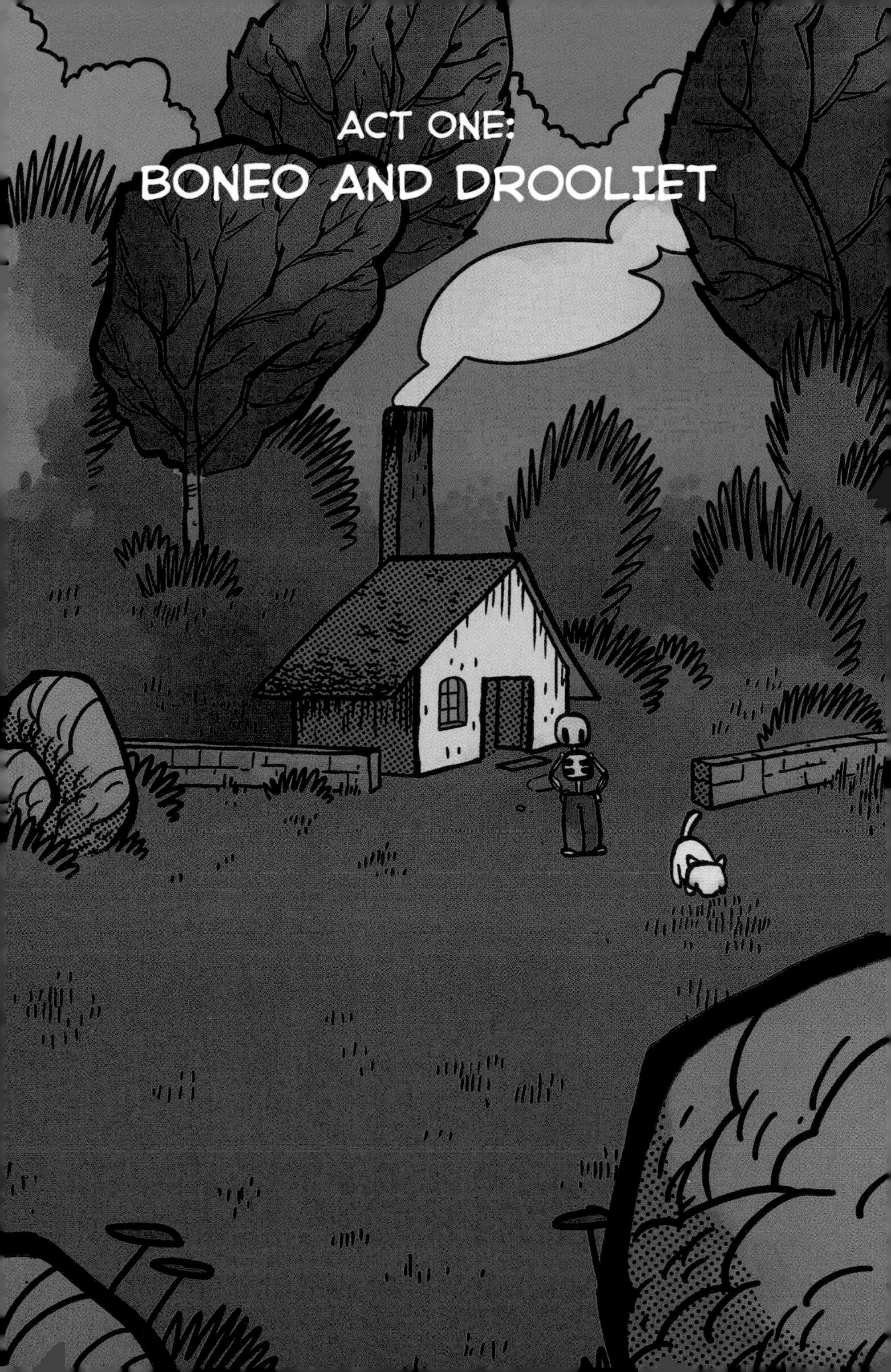
ACT ONE:
BONEO AND DROOLIET

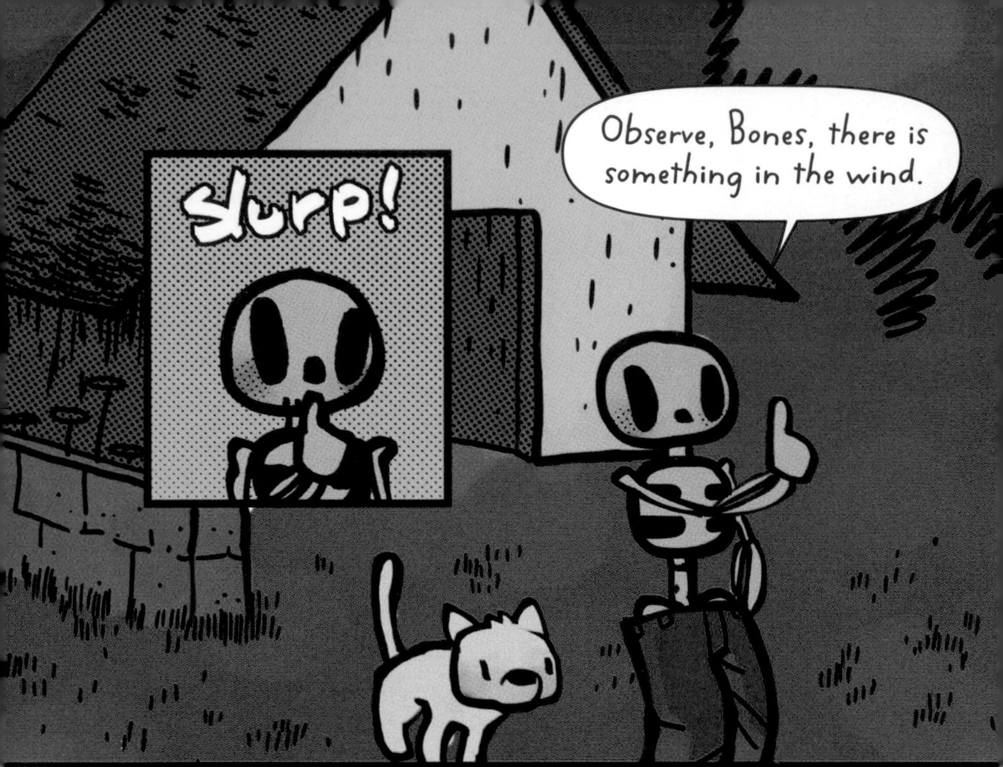
Slurp!
Observe, Bones, there is something in the wind.

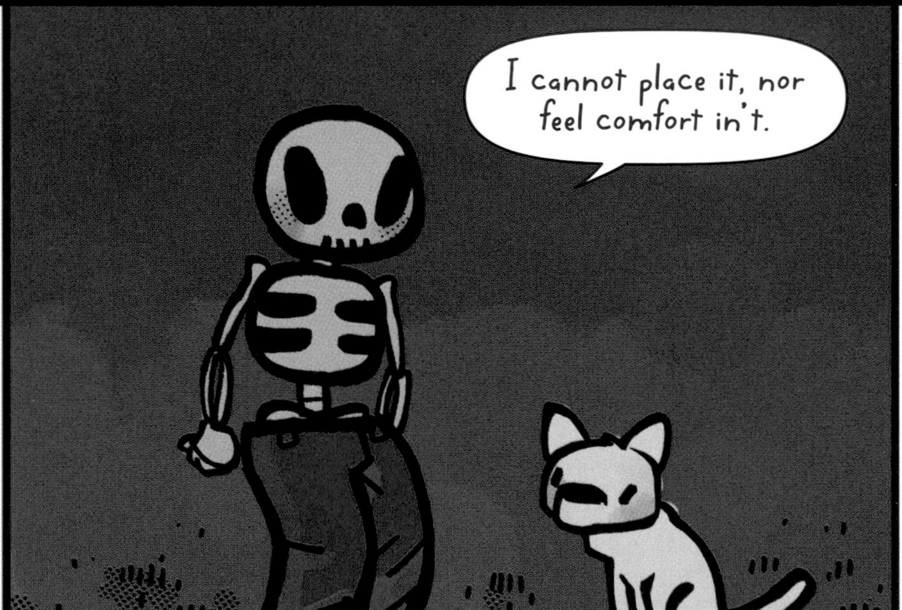
I cannot place it, nor feel comfort in't.

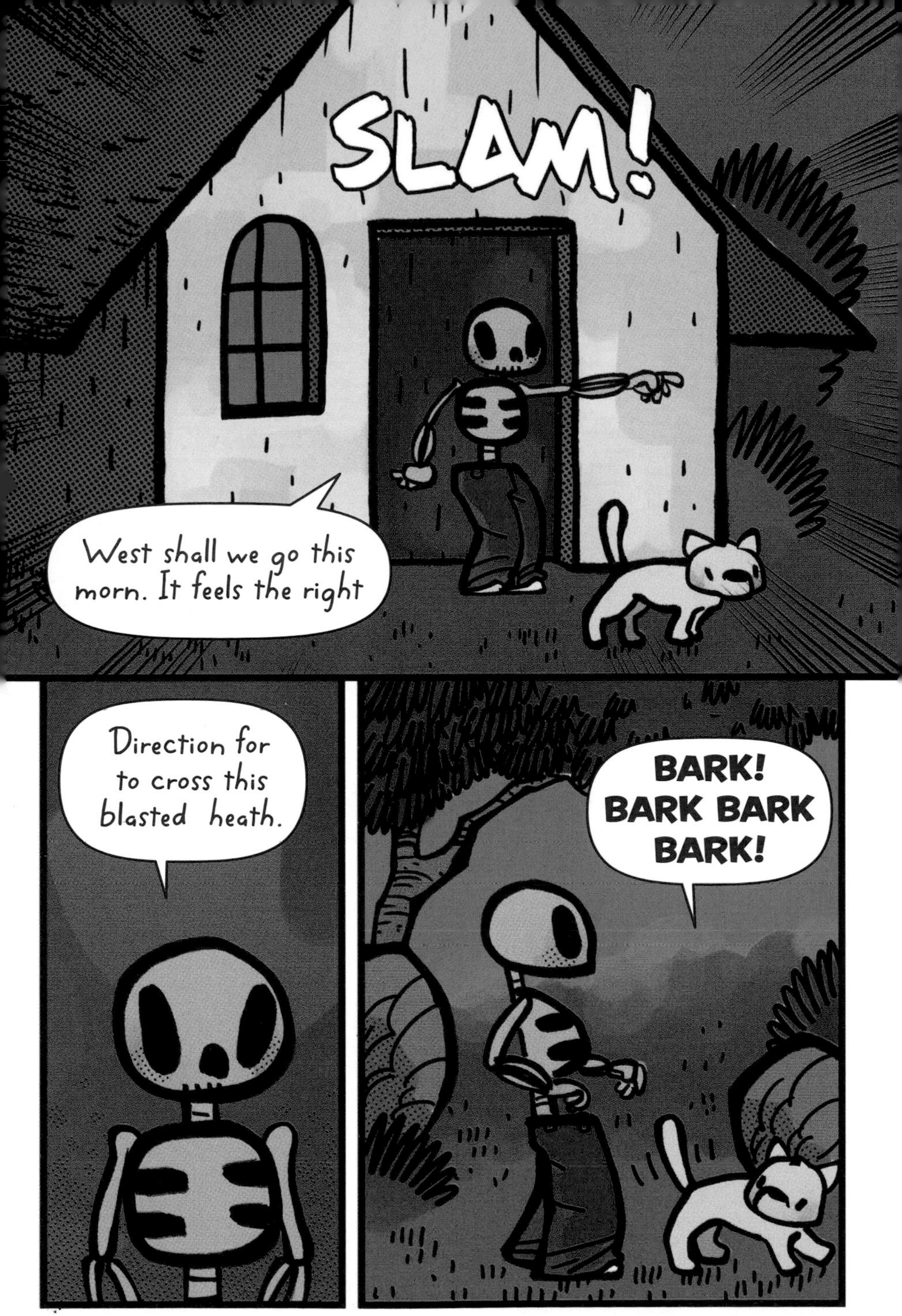
SLAM!
West shall we go this morn. It feels the right
Direction for to cross this blasted heath.
BARK! BARK BARK BARK!

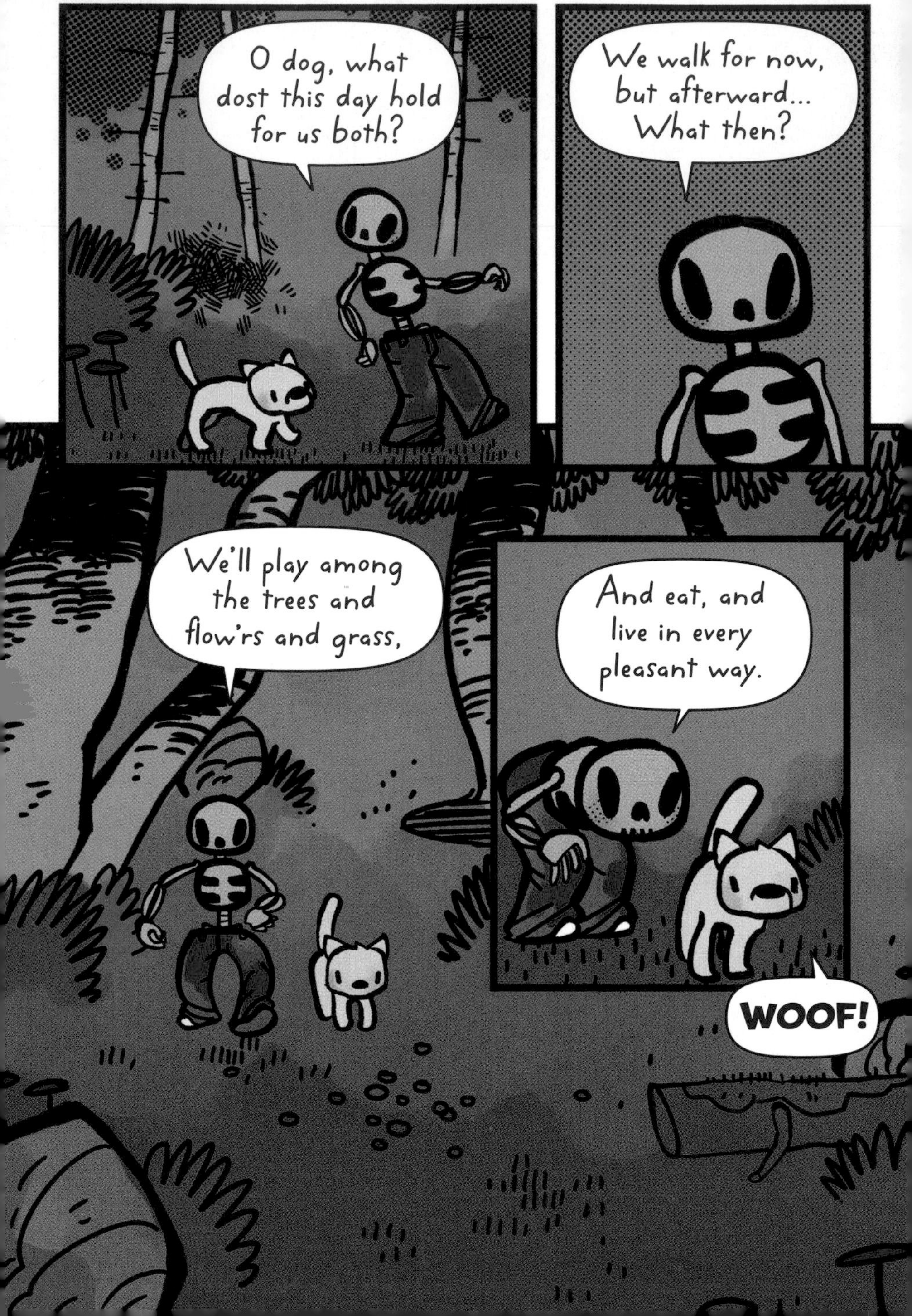
O dog, what dost this day hold for us both?
We walk for now, but afterward... What then?
We'll play among the trees and flow'rs and grass,
And eat, and live in every pleasant way.
WOOF!

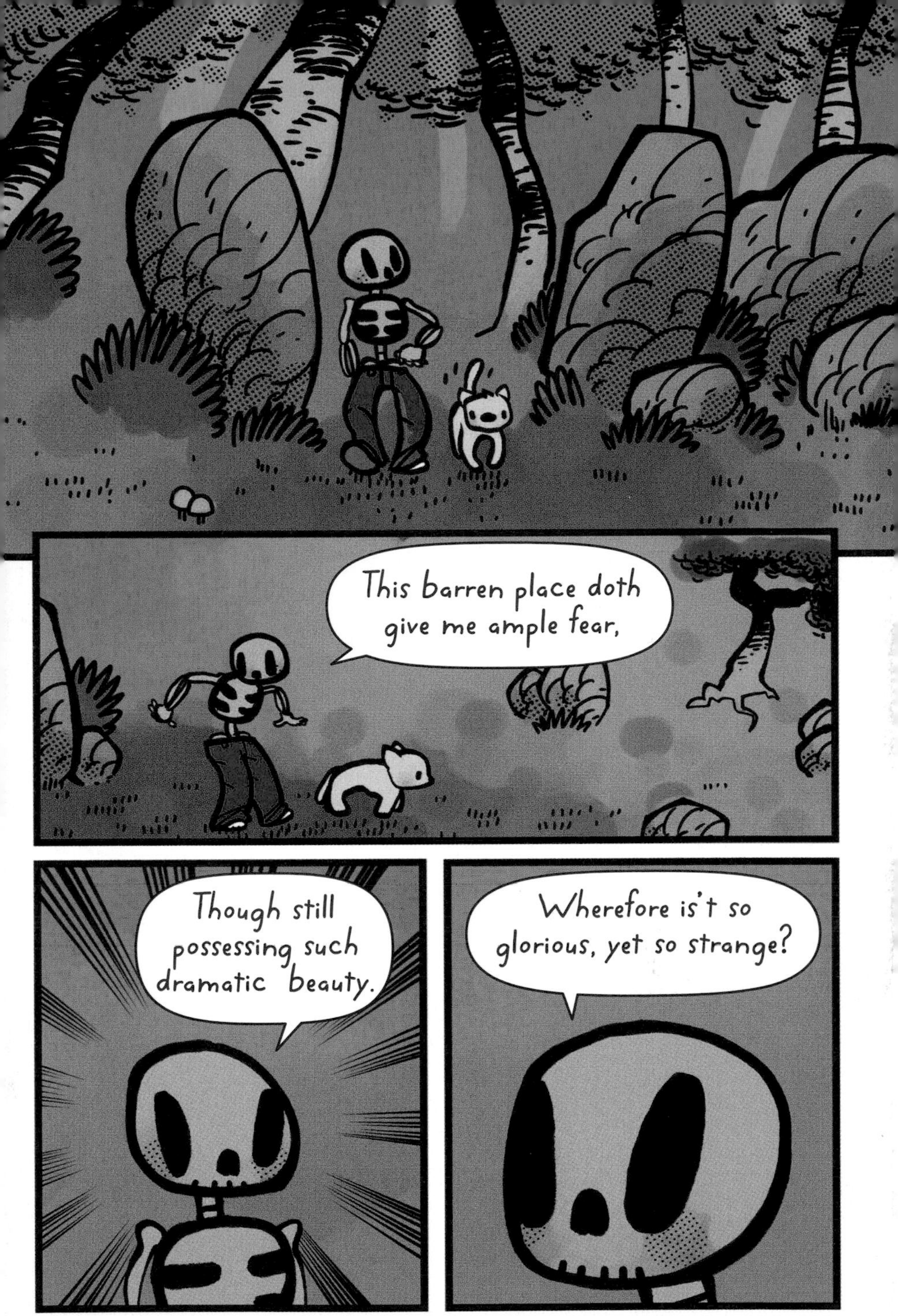
This barren place doth give me ample fear,
Though still possessing such dramatic beauty.
Wherefore is't so glorious, yet so strange?

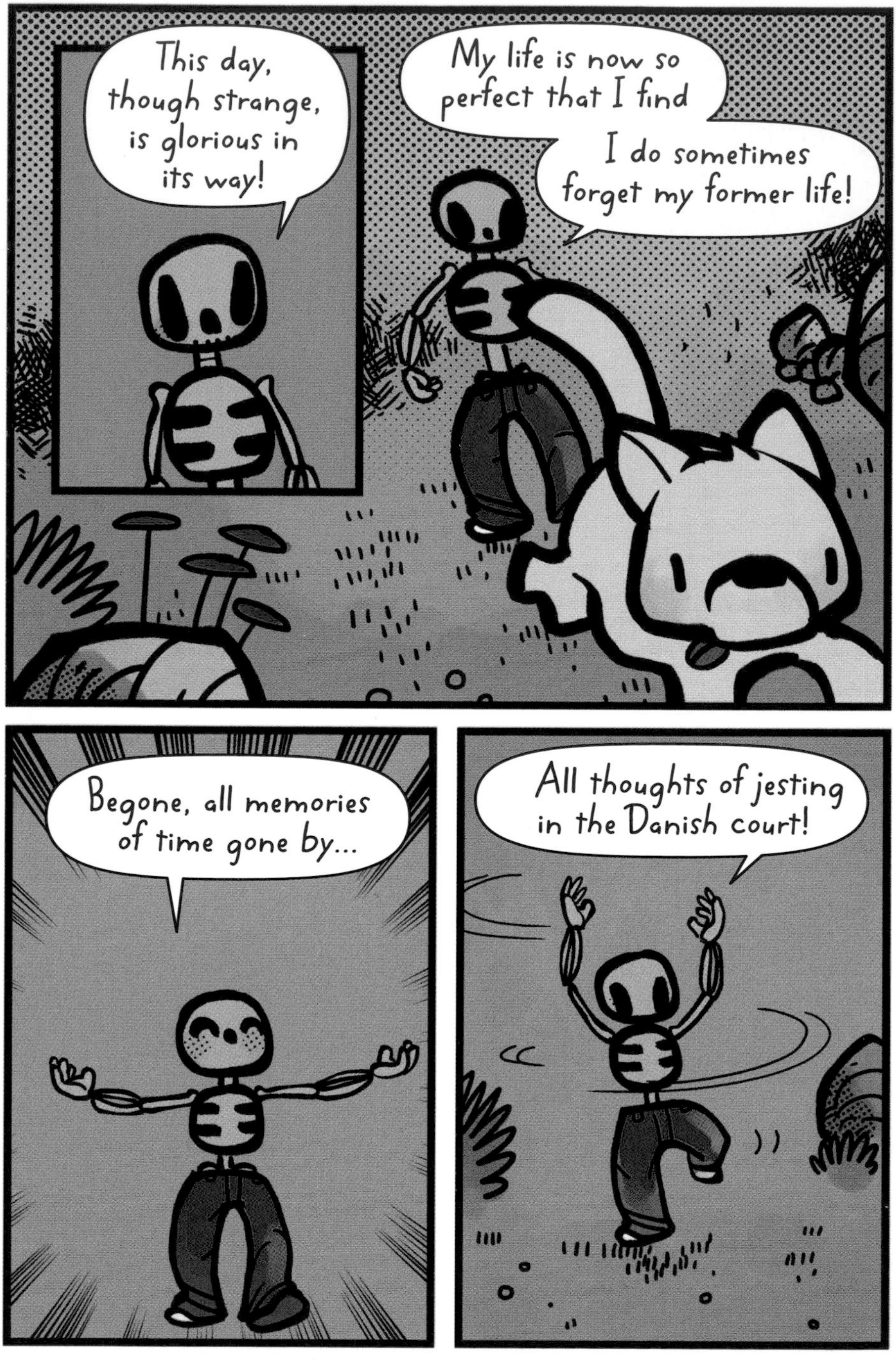
This day, though strange, is glorious in its way!
My life is now so perfect that I find
I do sometimes forget my former life!
Begone, all memories of time gone by...
All thoughts of jesting in the Danish court!

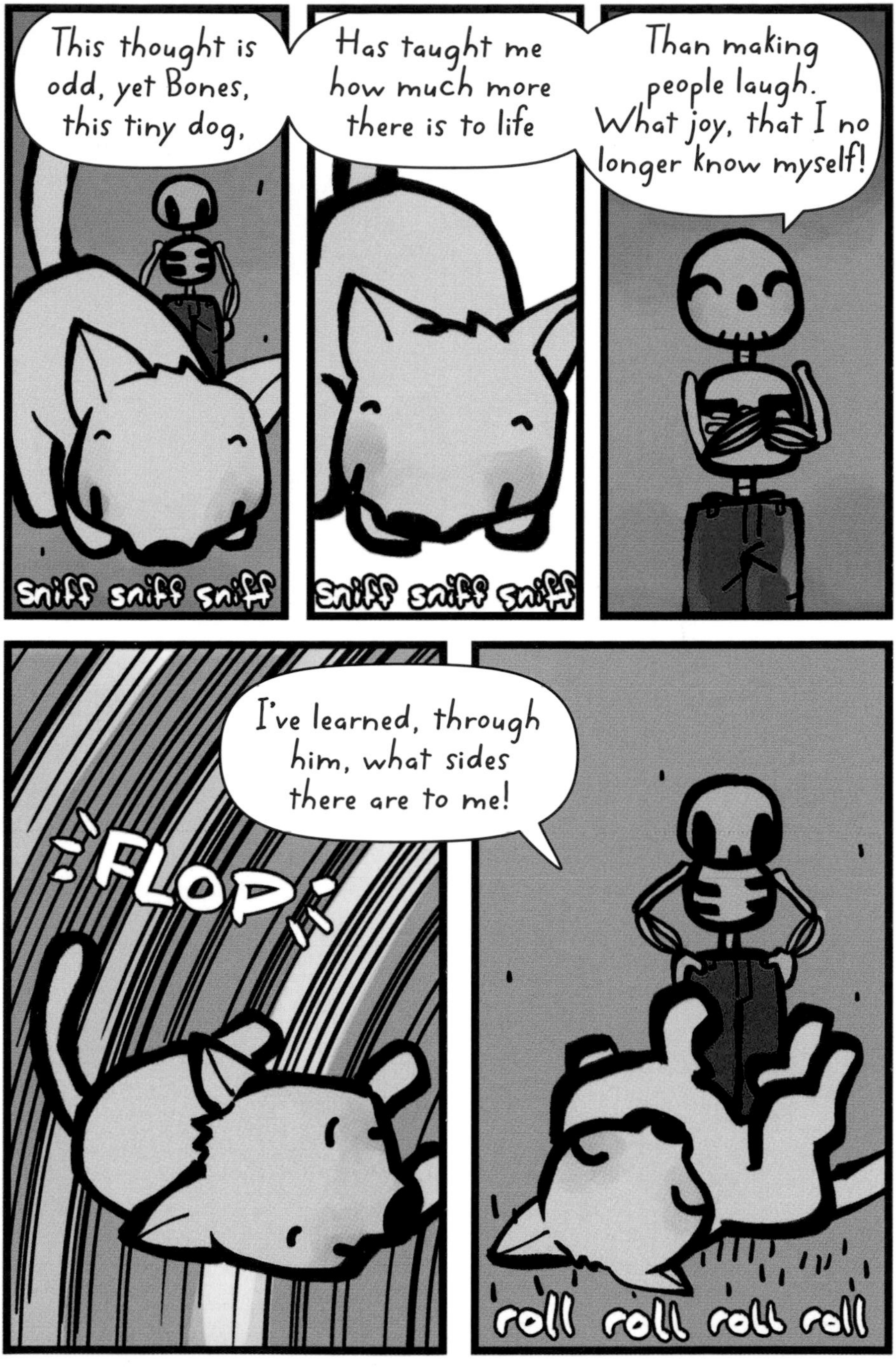
This thought is odd, yet Bones, this tiny dog,
sniff sniff sniff
Has taught me how much more there is to life
sniff sniff sniff
Than making people laugh. What joy, that I no longer know myself!
FLOP
I've learned, through him, what sides there are to me!
roll roll roll roll

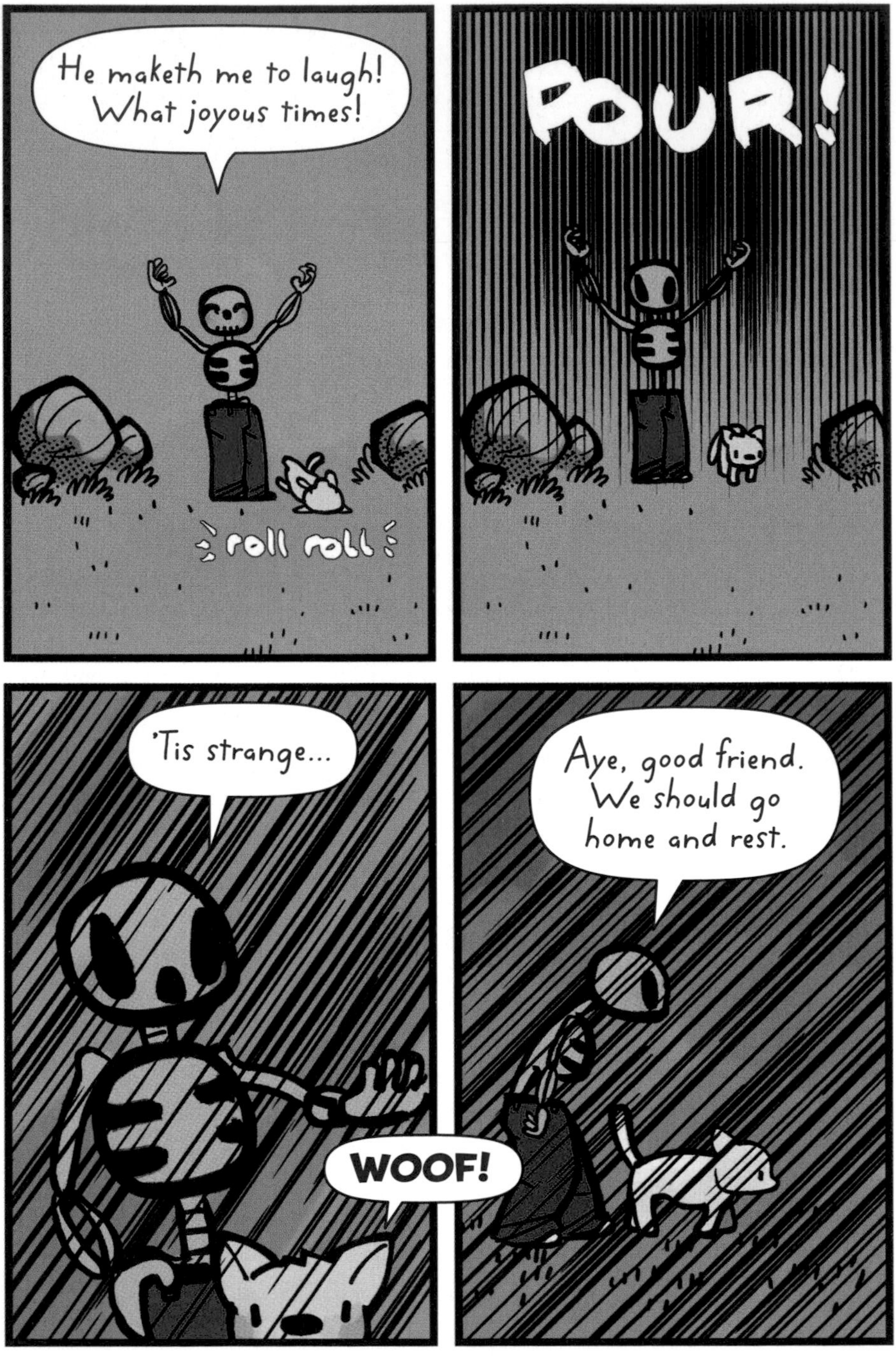
He maketh me to laugh! What joyous times!
roll roll
POUR!
'Tis strange...
WOOF!
Aye, good friend. We should go home and rest.

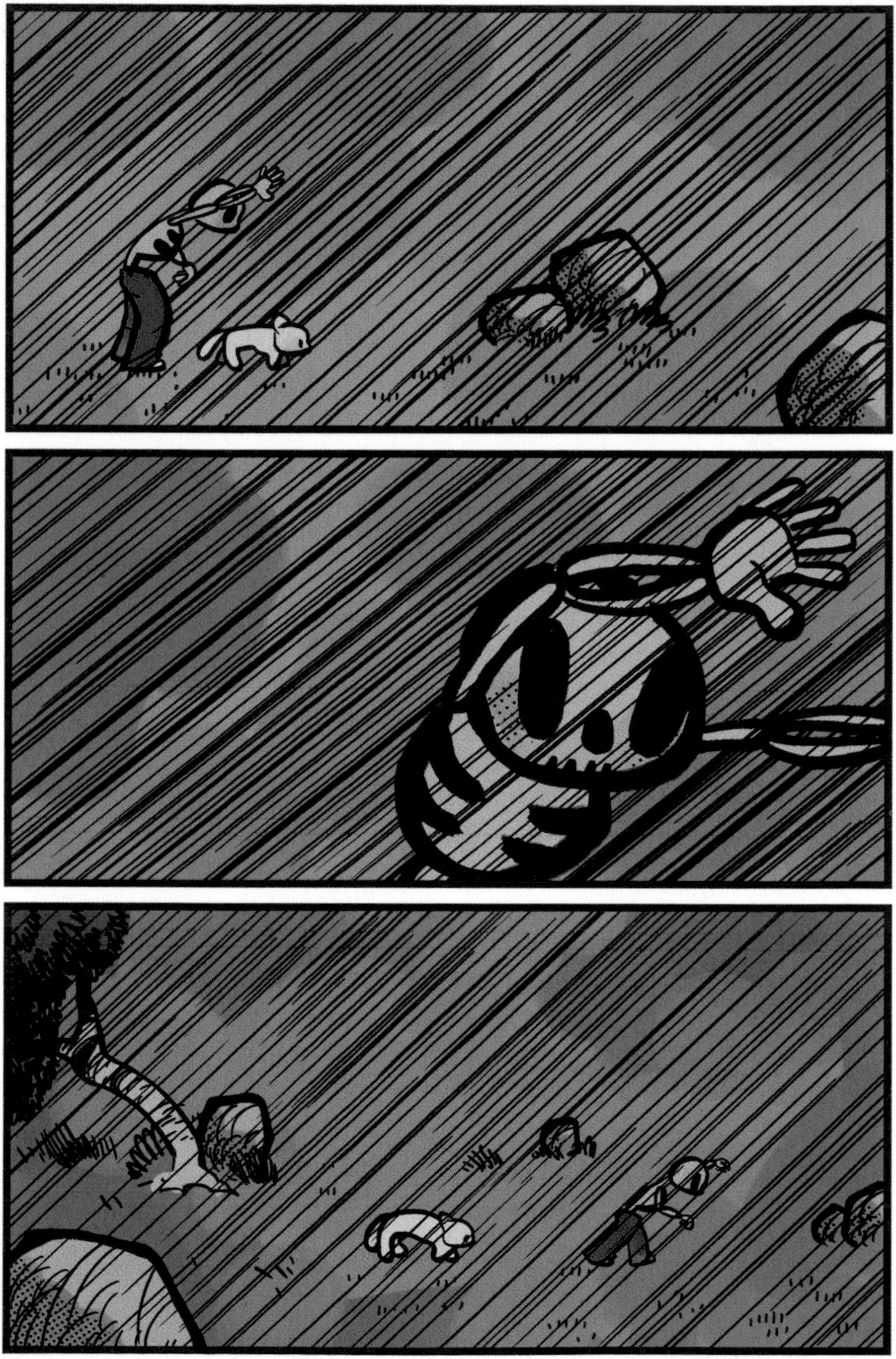

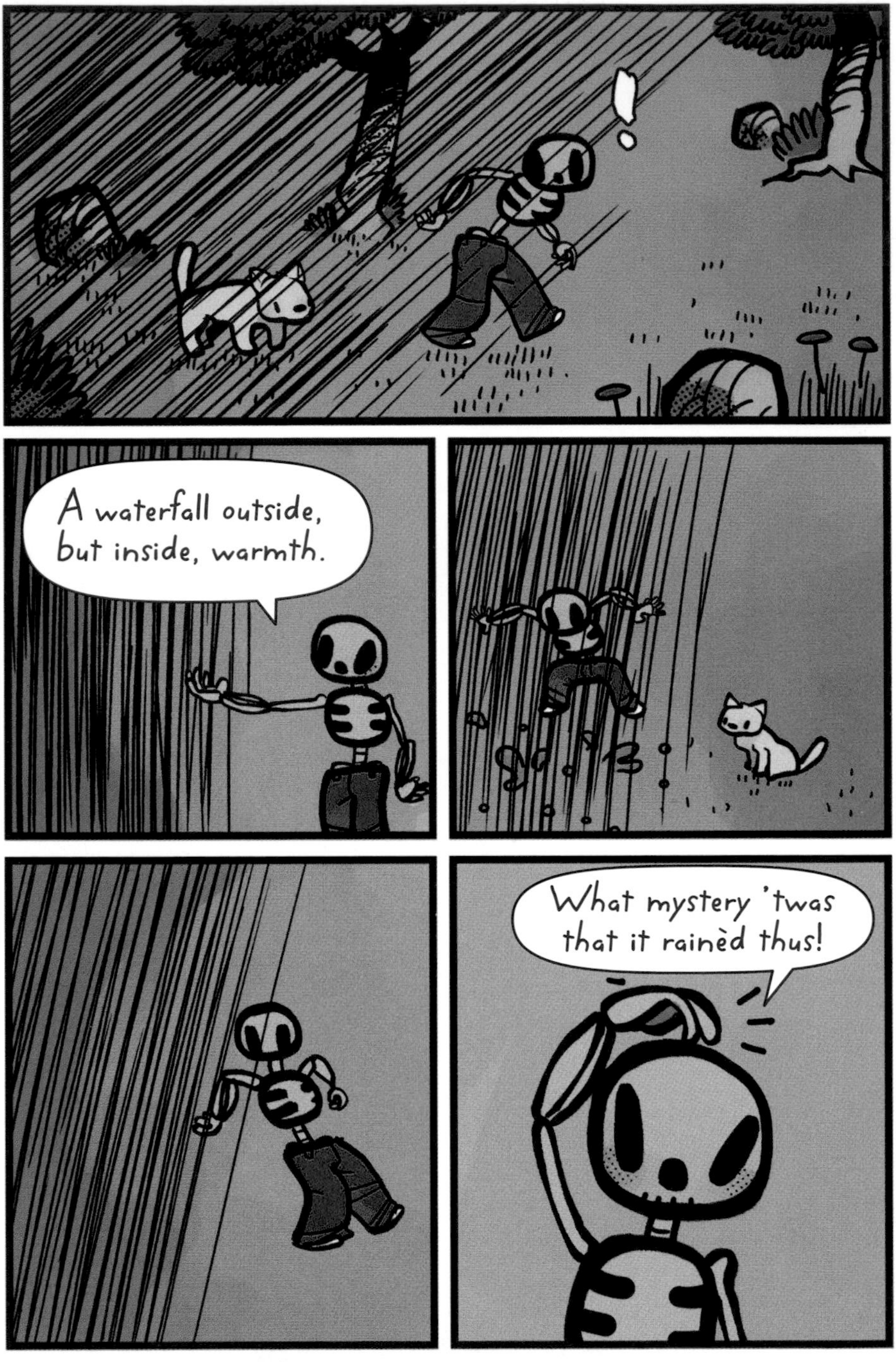
A waterfall outside,
but inside, warmth.
What mystery 'twas
that it rainèd thus!

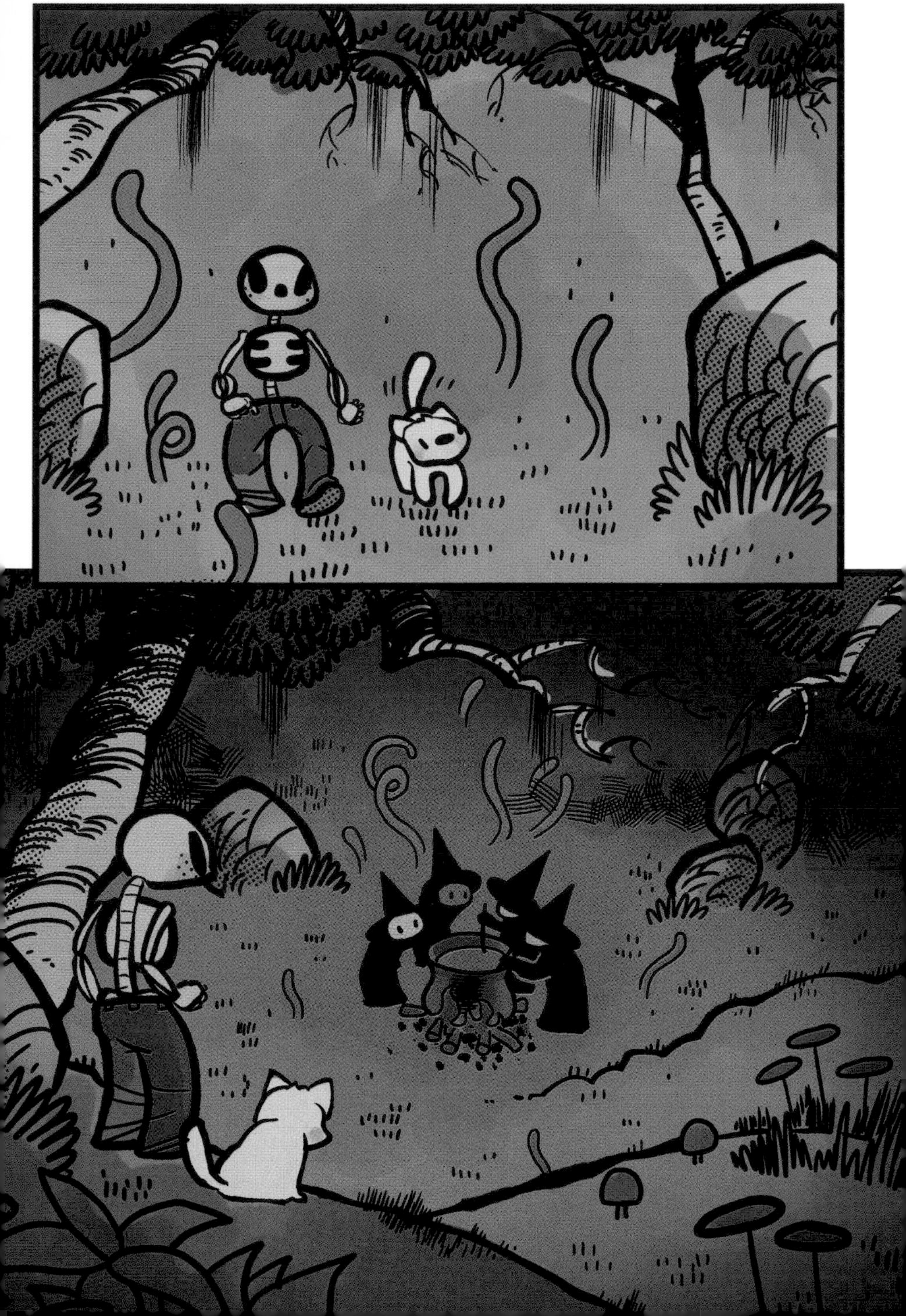

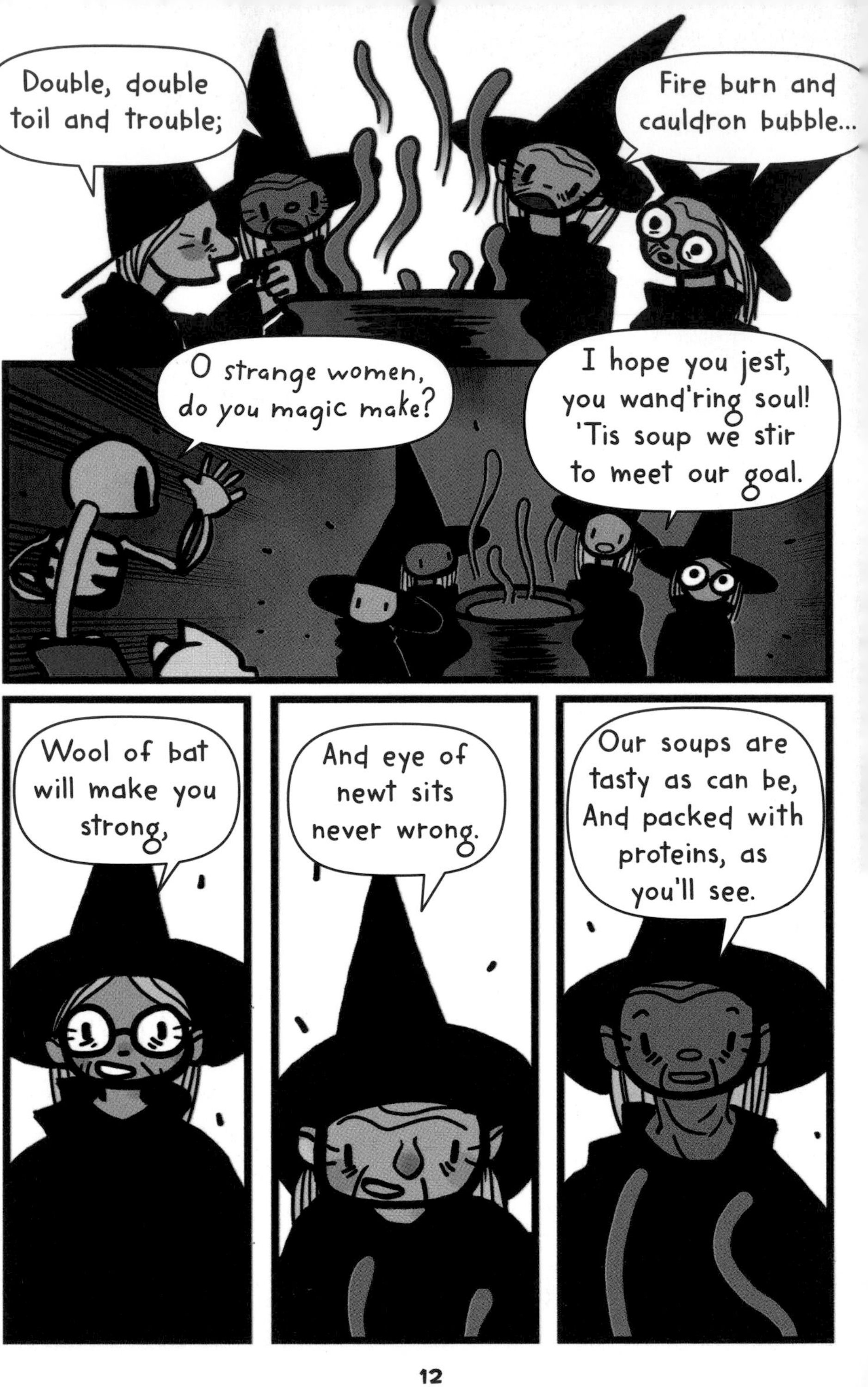

Double, double toil and trouble;
Fire burn and cauldron bubble...
O strange women, do you magic make?
I hope you jest, you wand'ring soul! 'Tis soup we stir to meet our goal.
Wool of bat will make you strong,
And eye of newt sits never wrong.
Our soups are tasty as can be, And packed with proteins, as you'll see.

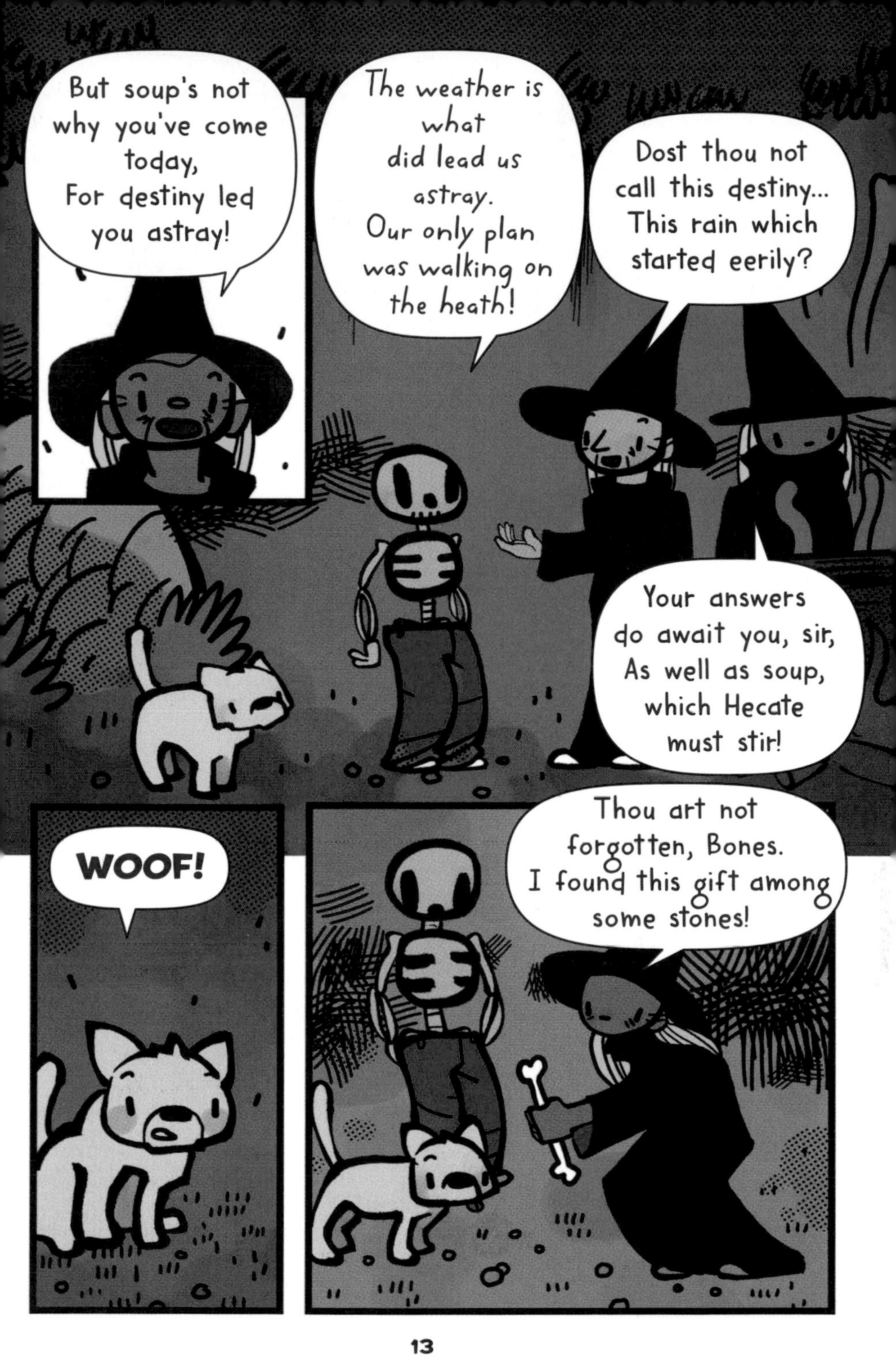
But soup's not why you've come today, For destiny led you astray!
The weather is what did lead us astray. Our only plan was walking on the heath!
Dost thou not call this destiny... This rain which started eerily?
Your answers do await you, sir, As well as soup, which Hecate must stir!
WOOF!
Thou art not forgotten, Bones. I found this gift among some stones!

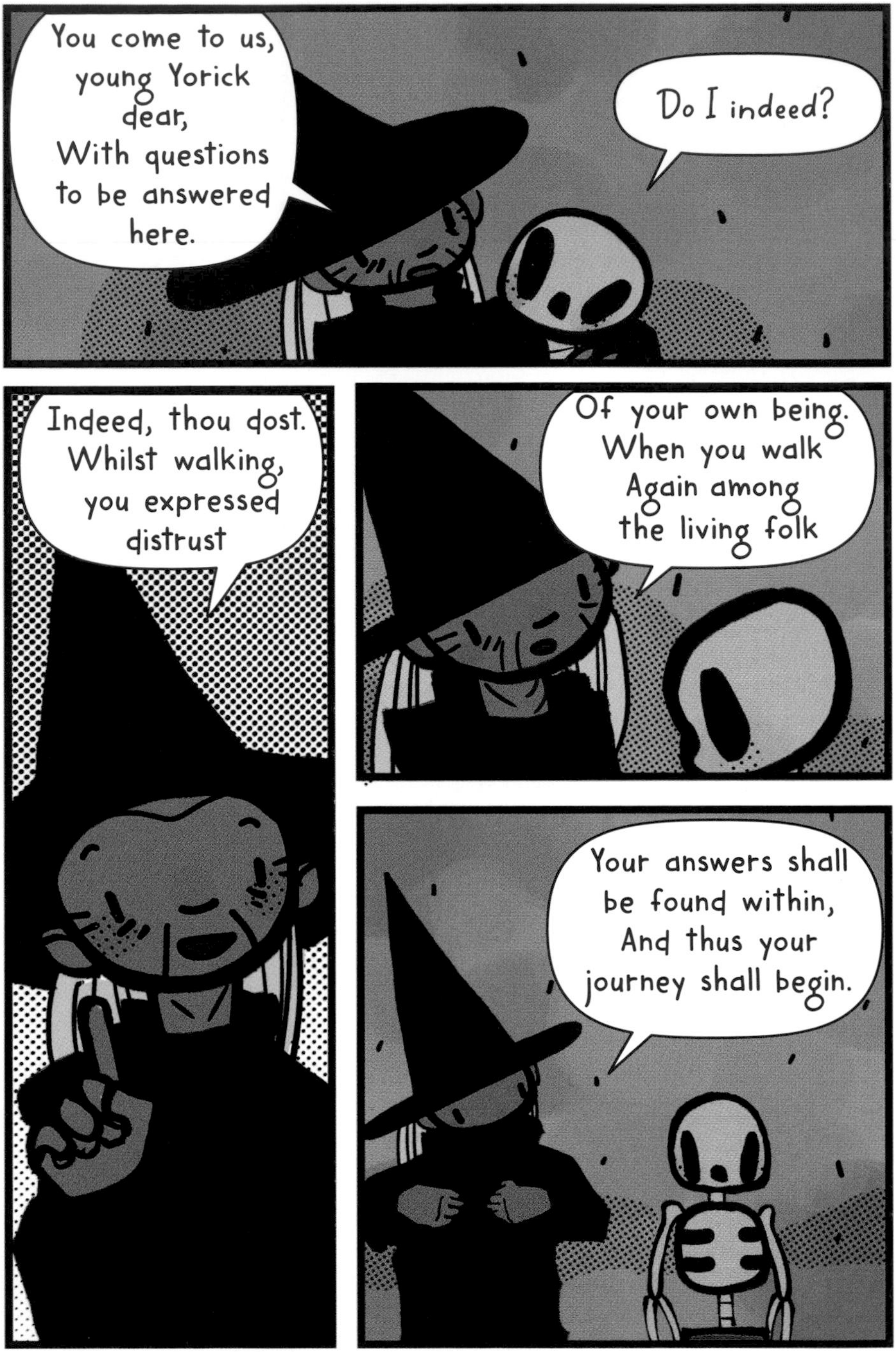
You come to us, young Yorick dear, With questions to be answered here.
Do I indeed?
Indeed, thou dost. Whilst walking, you expressed distrust
Of your own being. When you walk Again among the living folk
Your answers shall be found within, And thus your journey shall begin.

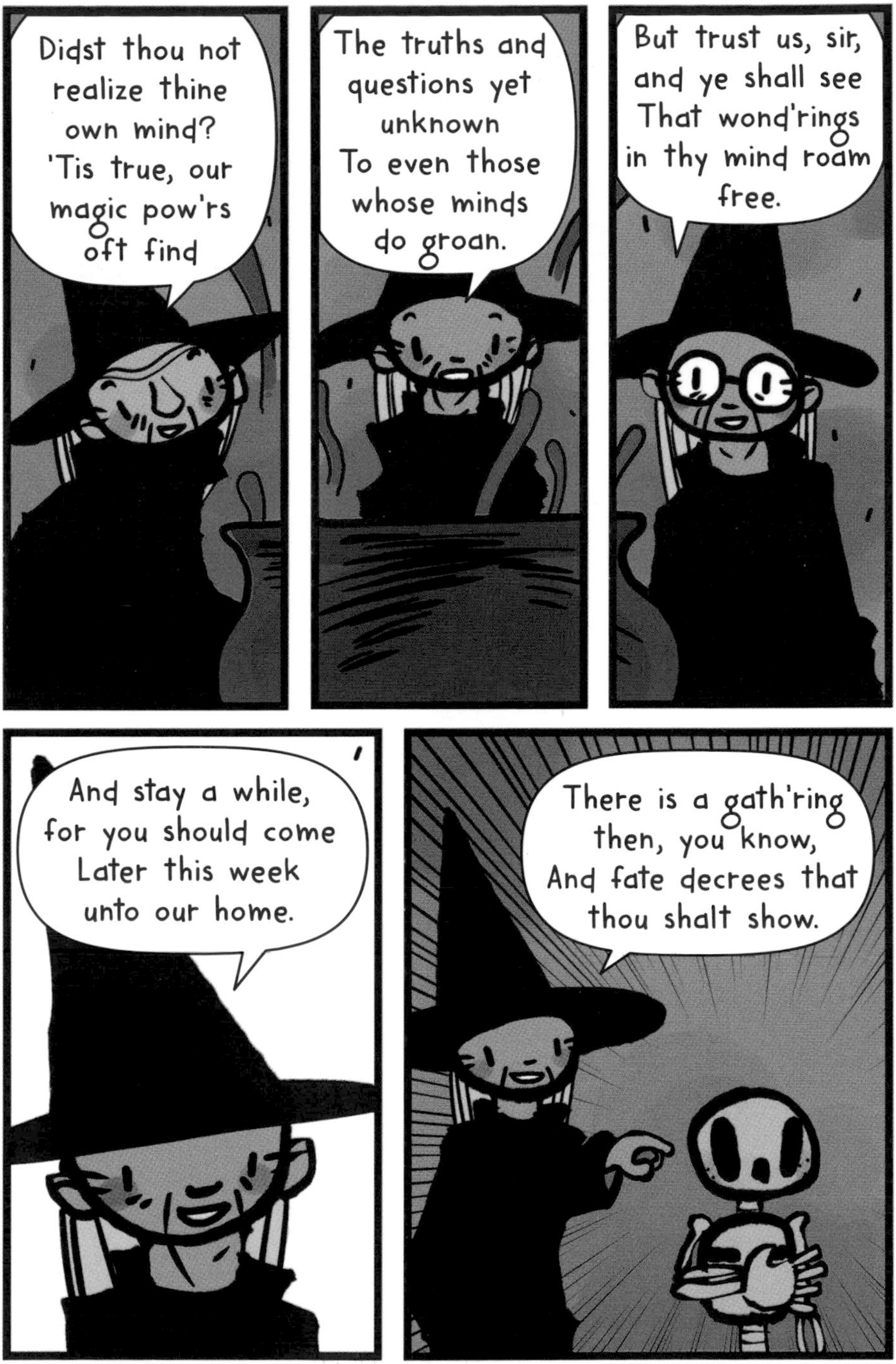
Didst thou not realize thine own mind? 'Tis true, our magic pow'rs oft find
The truths and questions yet unknown To even those whose minds do groan.
But trust us, sir, and ye shall see That wond'rings in thy mind roam free.
And stay a while, for you should come Later this week unto our home.
There is a gath'ring then, you know, And fate decrees that thou shalt show.

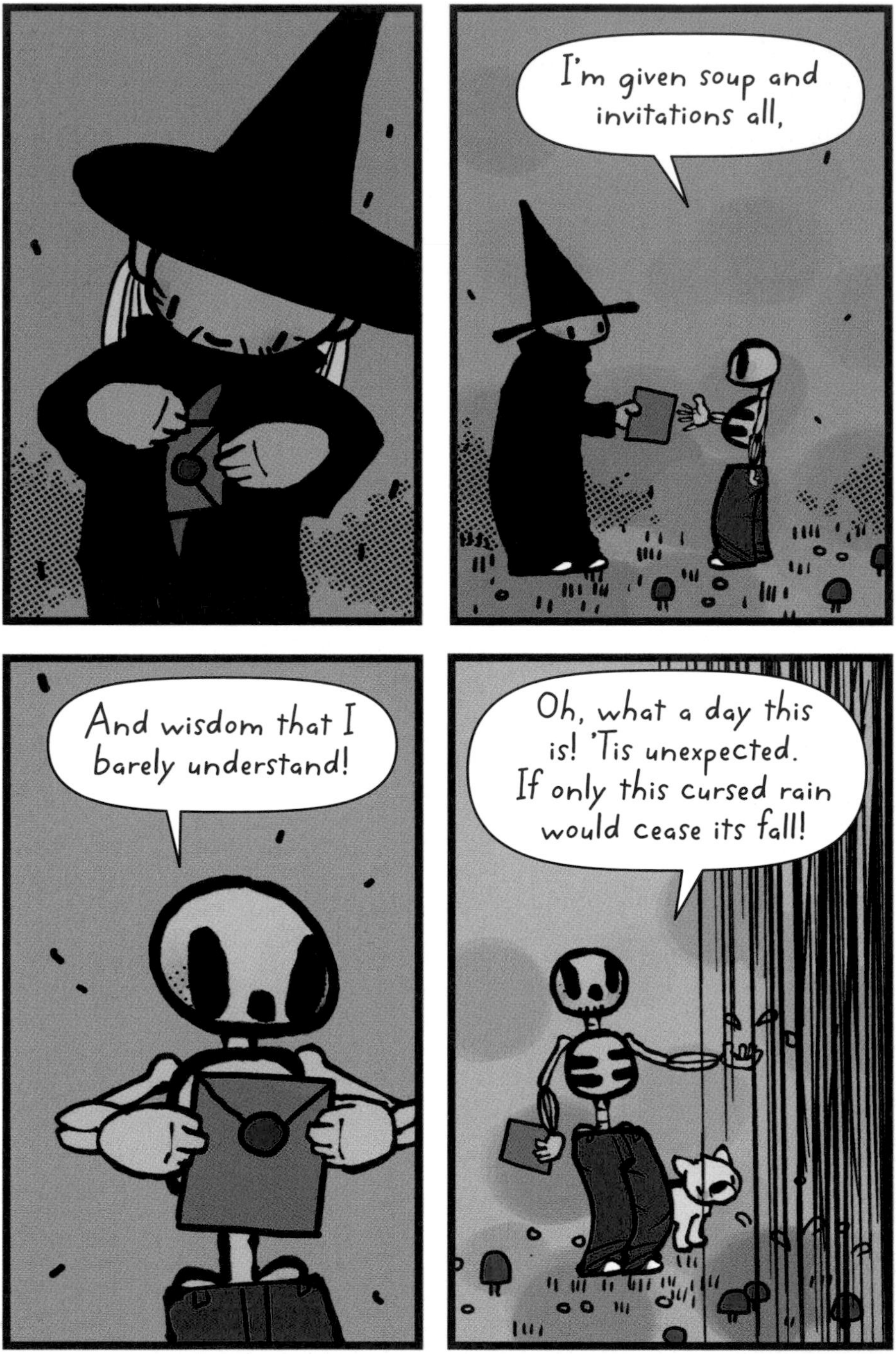
I'm given soup and invitations all,
And wisdom that I barely understand!
Oh, what a day this is! 'Tis unexpected. If only this cursed rain would cease its fall!

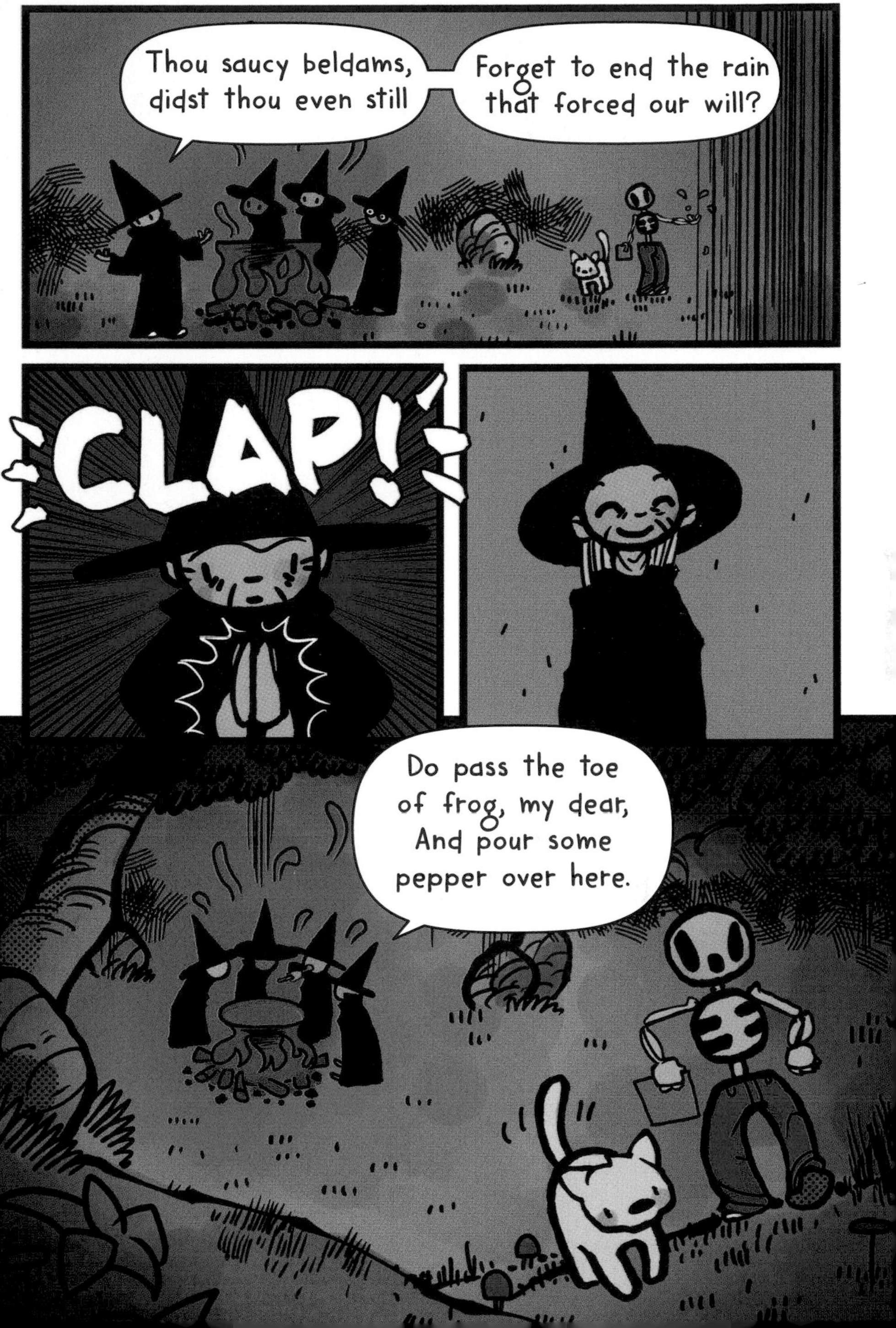
Thou saucy beldams, didst thou even still
Forget to end the rain that forced our will?
CLAP!
Do pass the toe of frog, my dear, And pour some pepper over here.

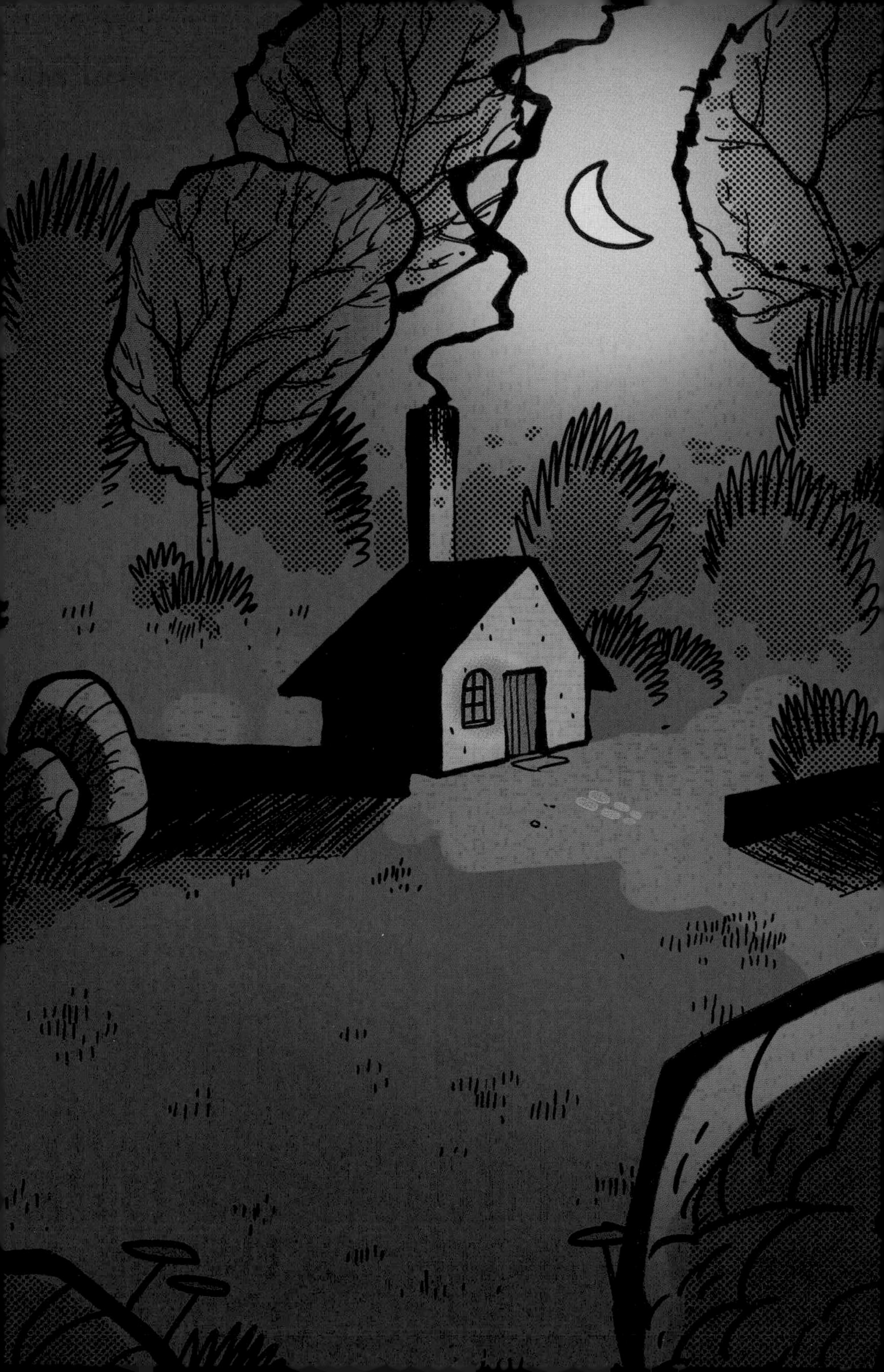

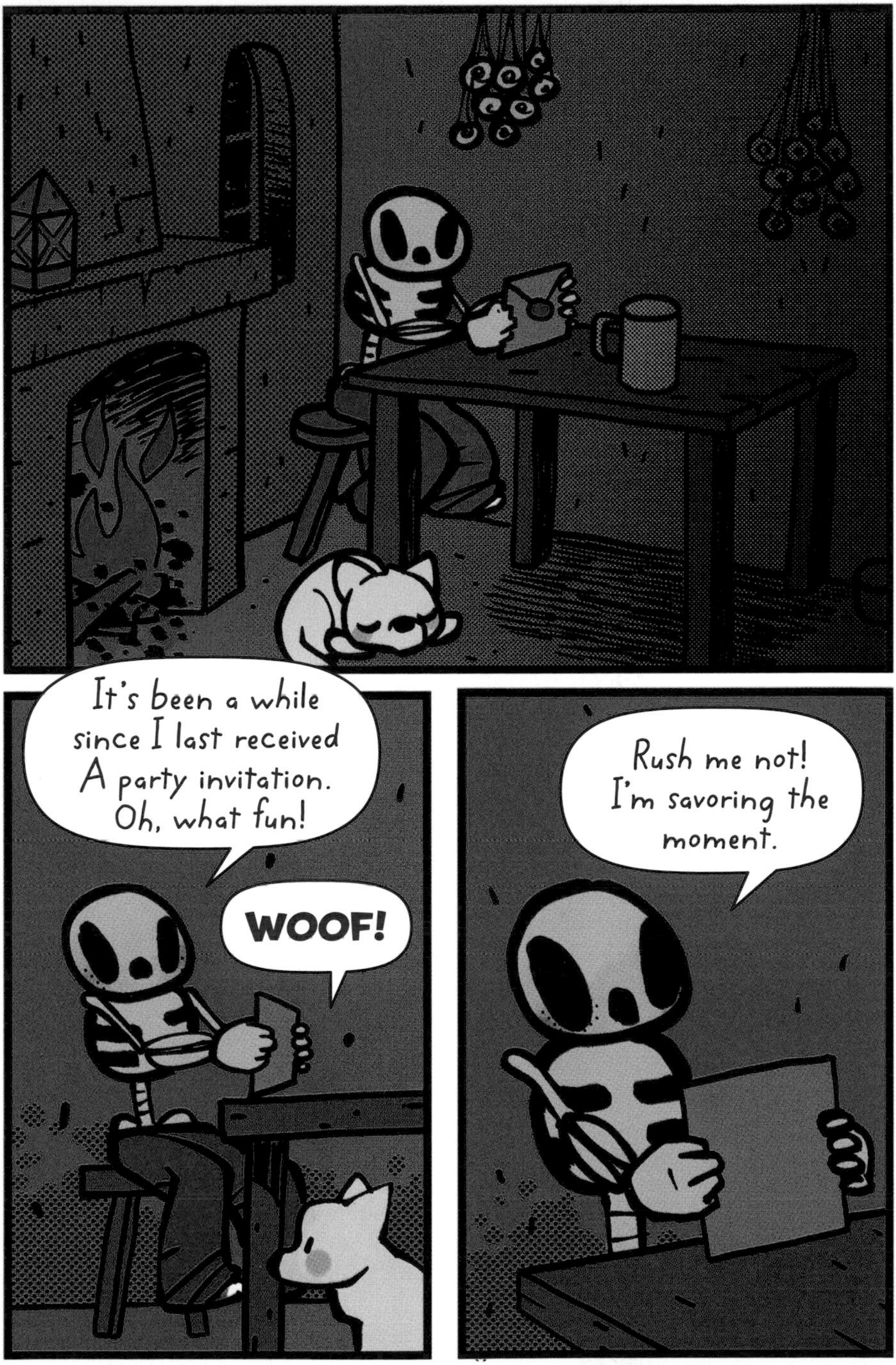
It's been a while since I last received A party invitation. Oh, what fun!
WOOF!
Rush me not! I'm savoring the moment.

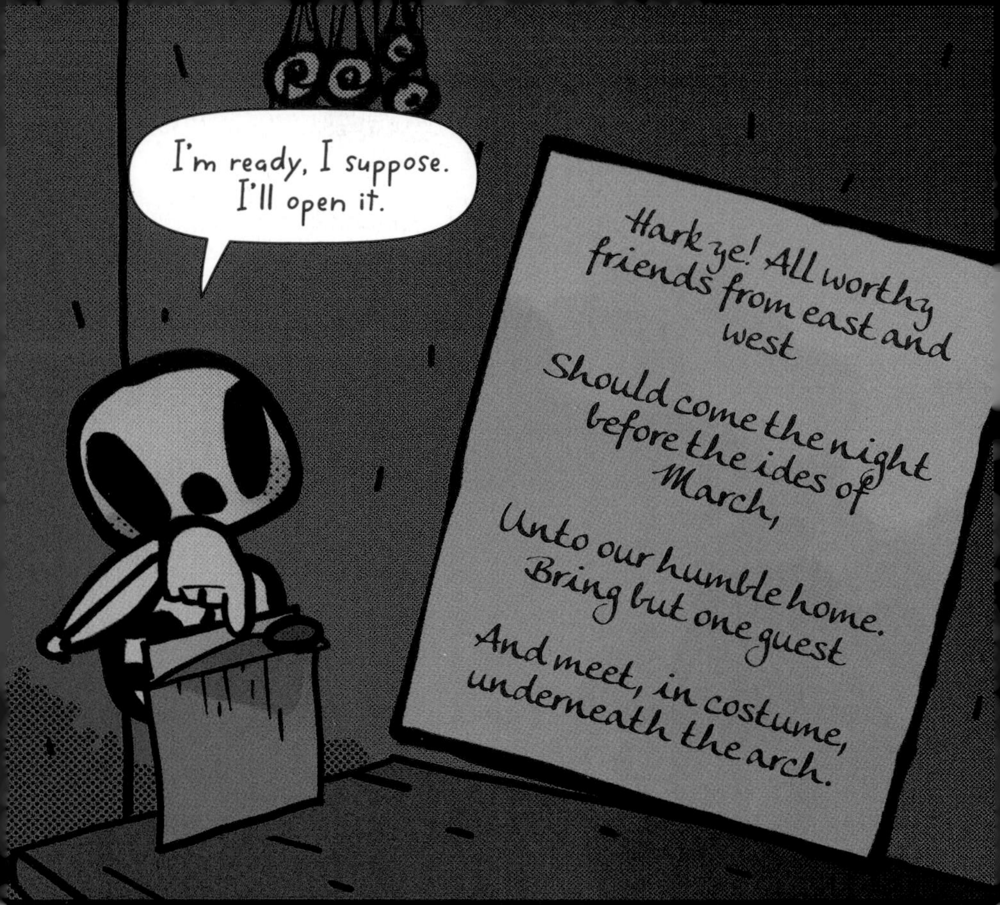
I'm ready, I suppose. I'll open it.
Hark ye! All worthy friends from east and west
Should come the night before the ides of March,
Unto our humble home. Bring but one guest
And meet, in costume, underneath the arch.

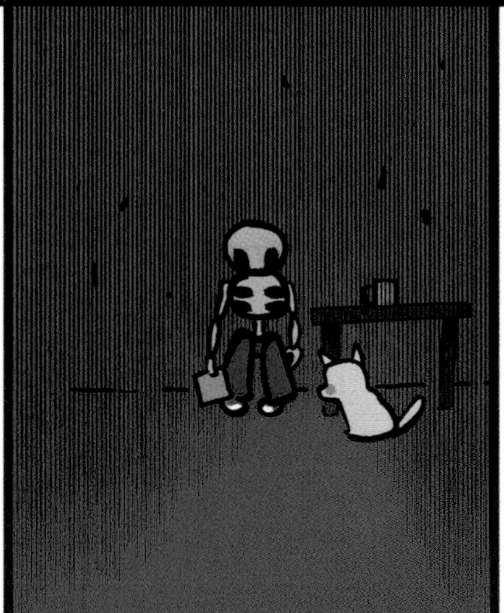

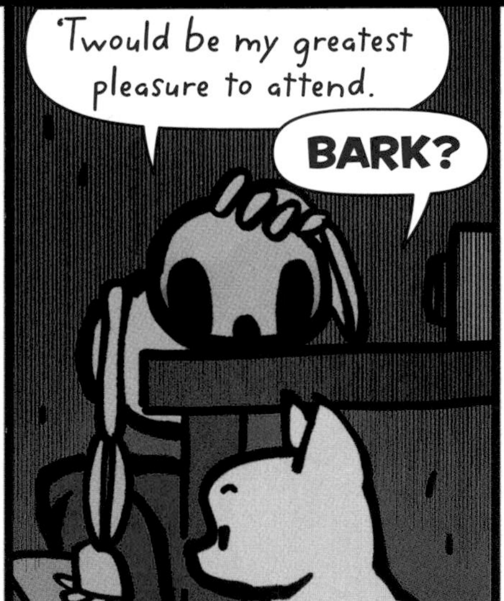
'Twould be my greatest pleasure to attend.
BARK?

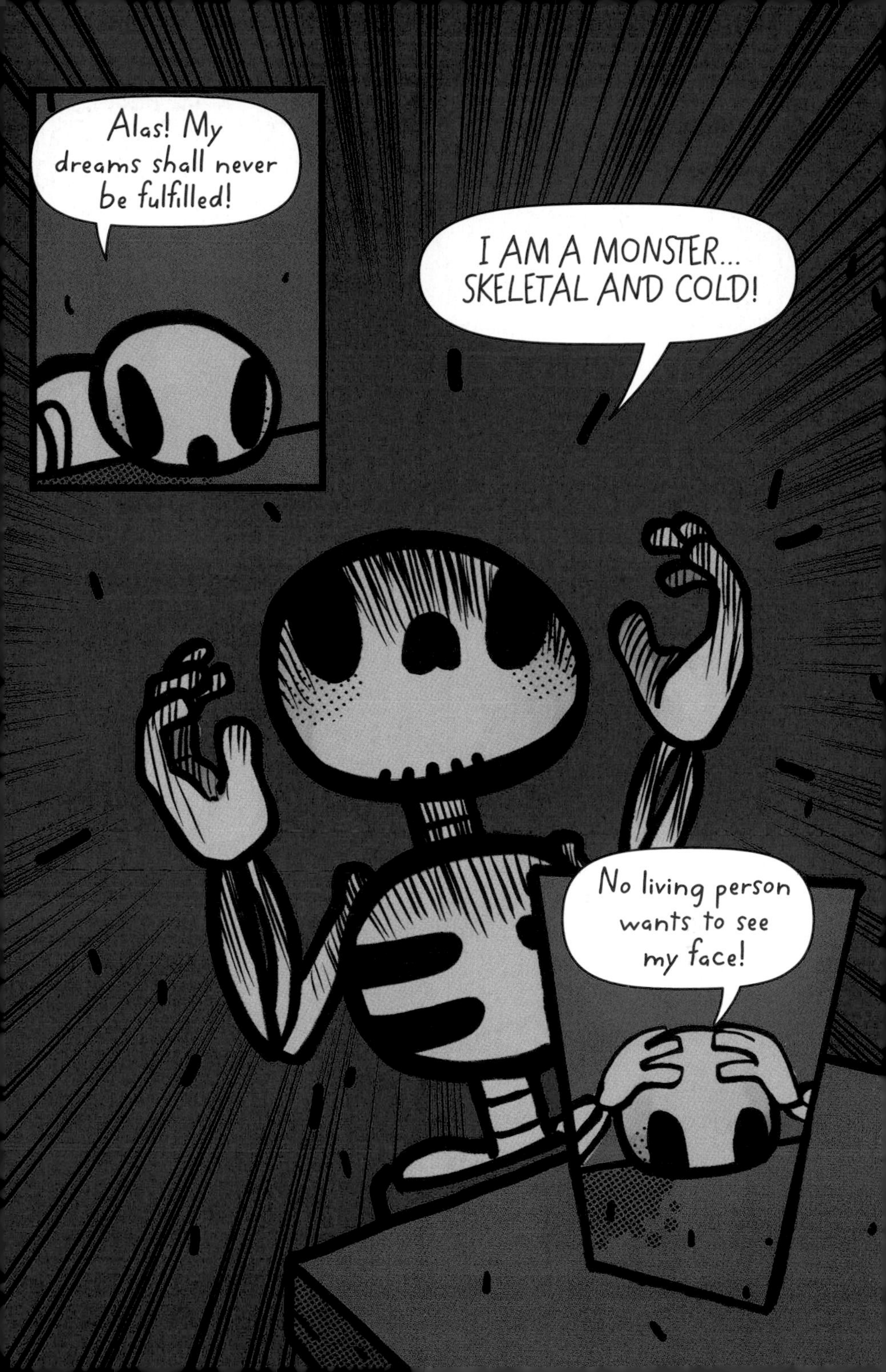
Alas! My dreams shall never be fulfilled!
I AM A MONSTER... SKELETAL AND COLD!
No living person wants to see my face!

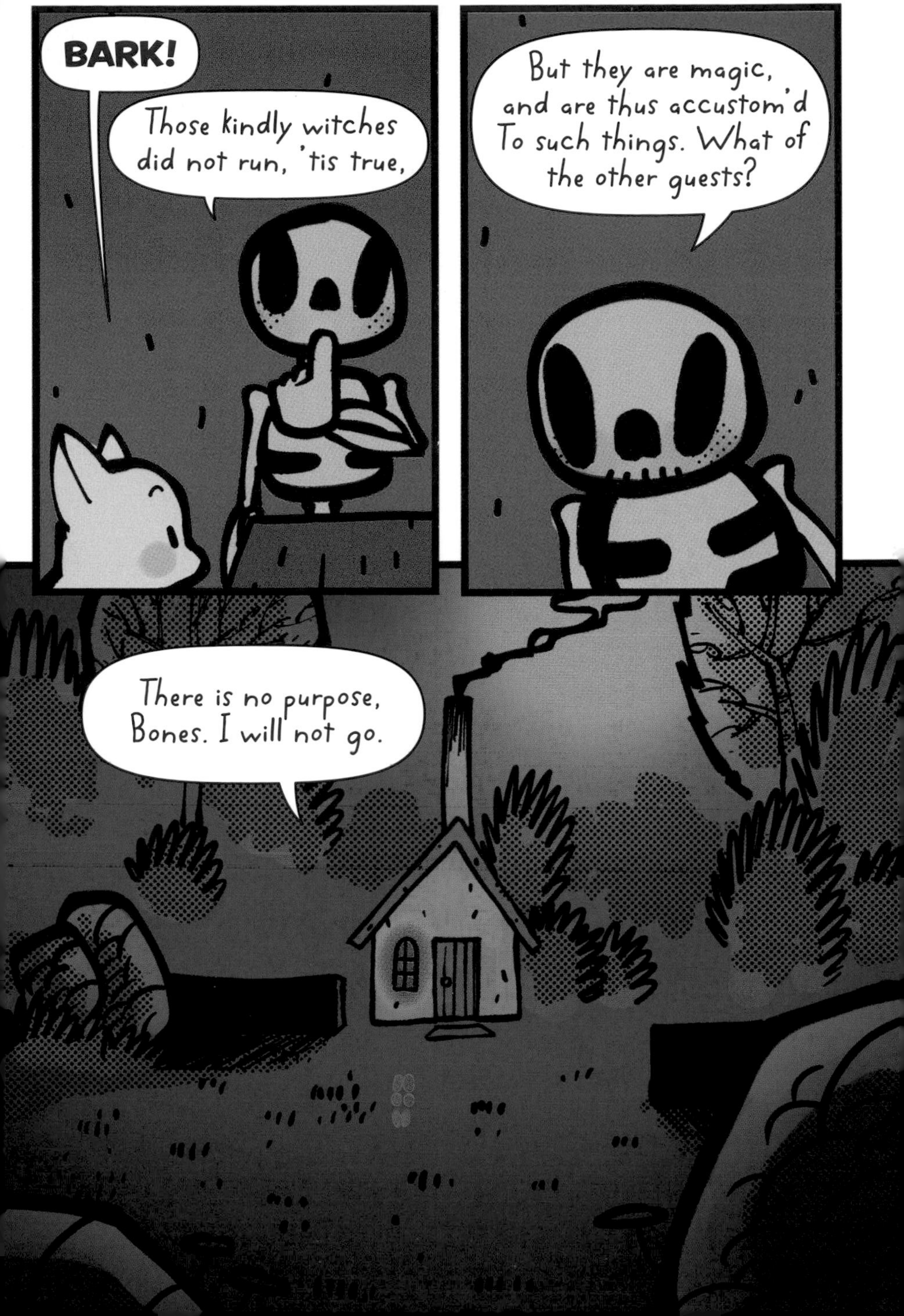
BARK!
Those kindly witches did not run, 'tis true,
But they are magic, and are thus accustom'd To such things. What of the other guests?
There is no purpose, Bones. I will not go.

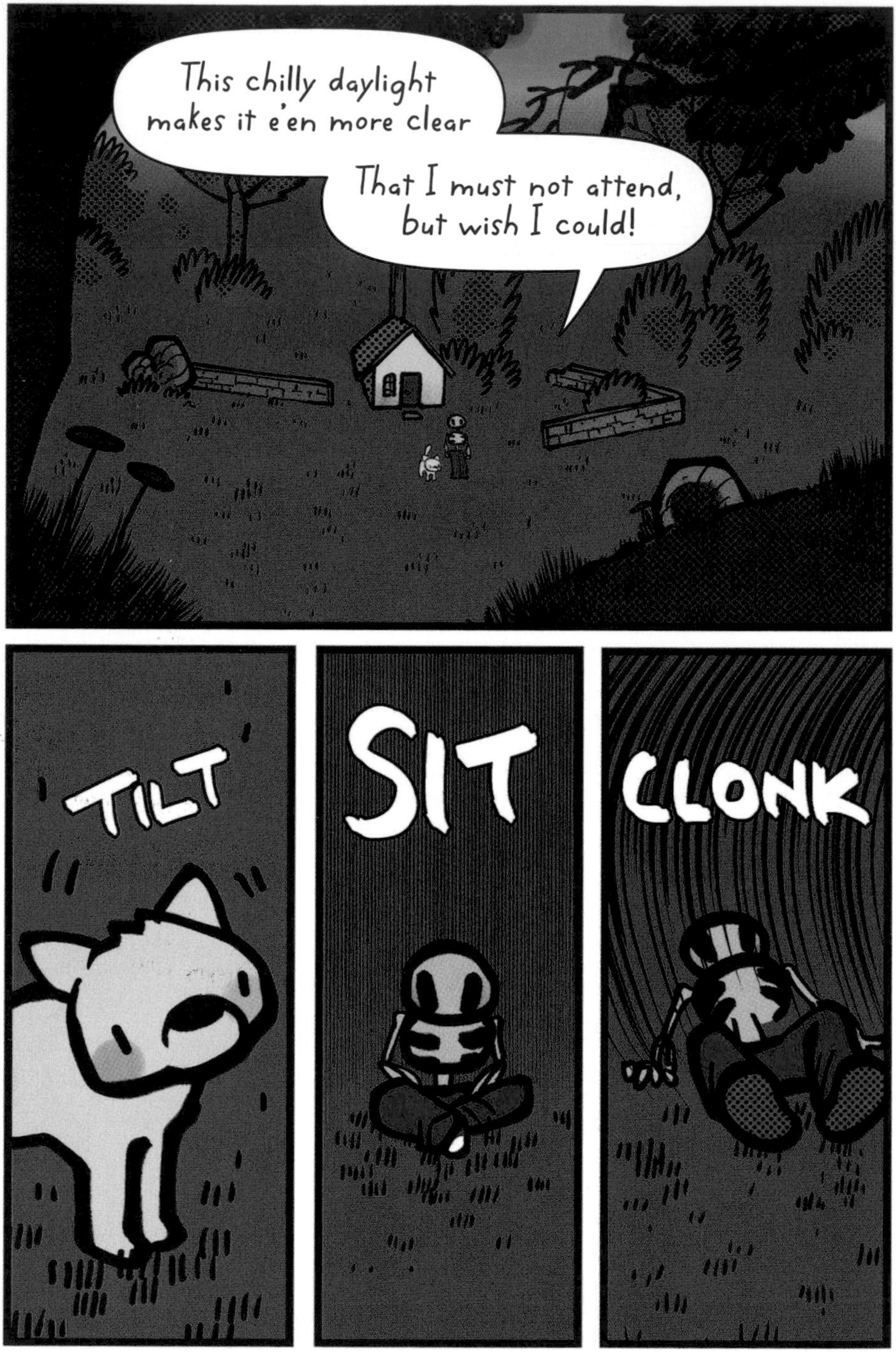
This chilly daylight makes it e'en more clear
That I must not attend, but wish I could!
TILT
SIT
CLONK

WHOOSH
drag drag drag
BARK! BARK! BARK!

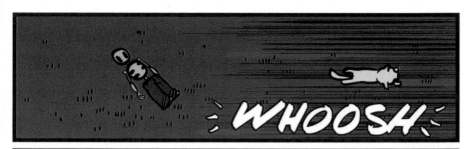

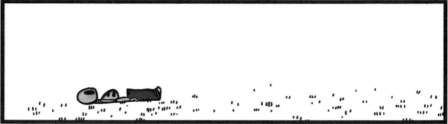

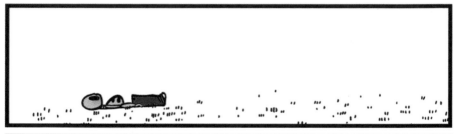

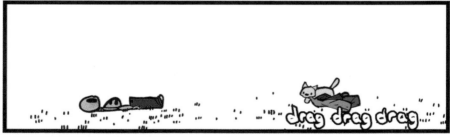

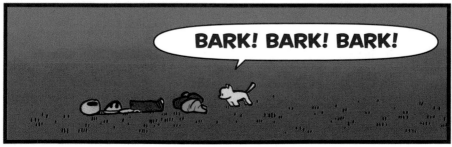

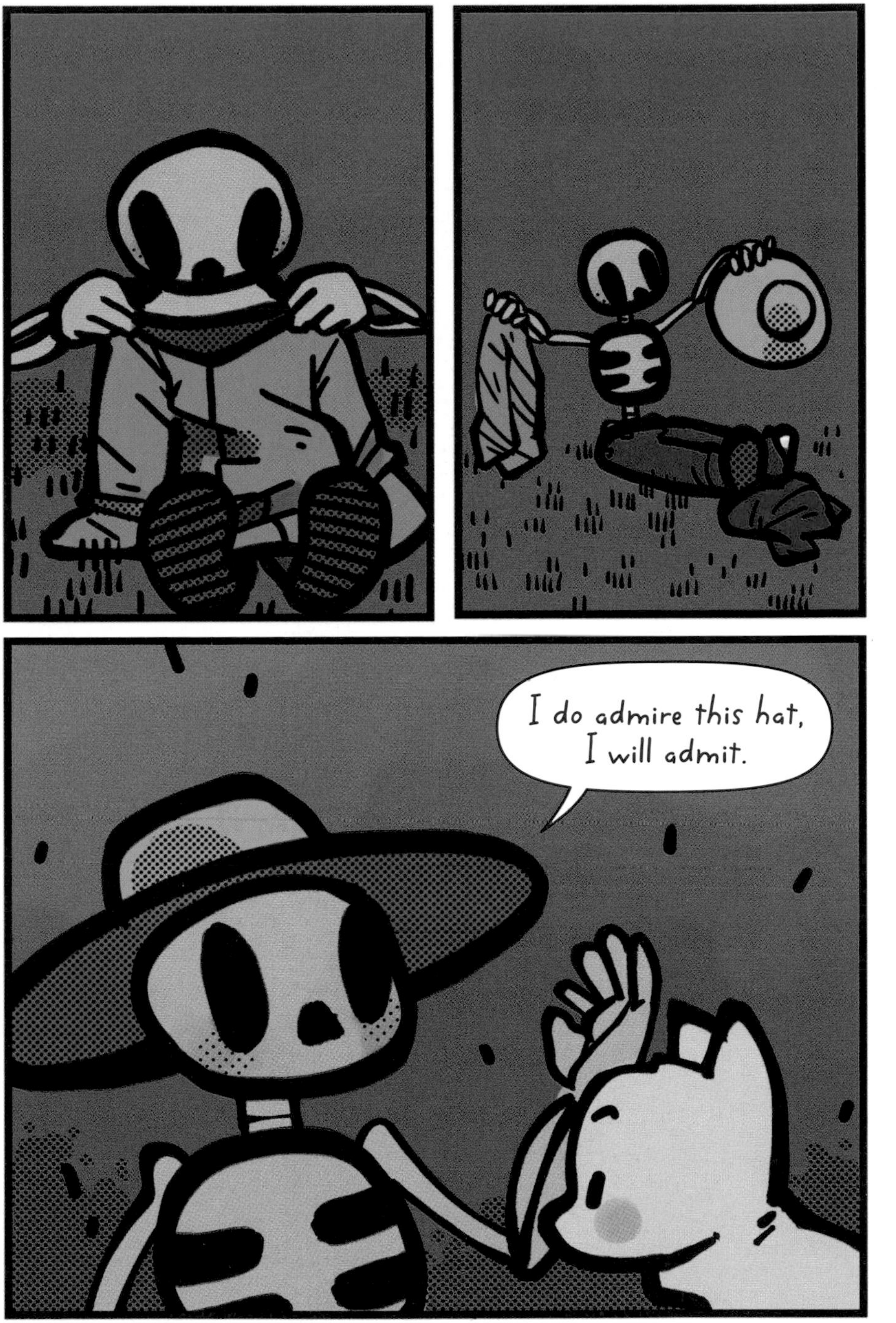
I do admire this hat,
I will admit.

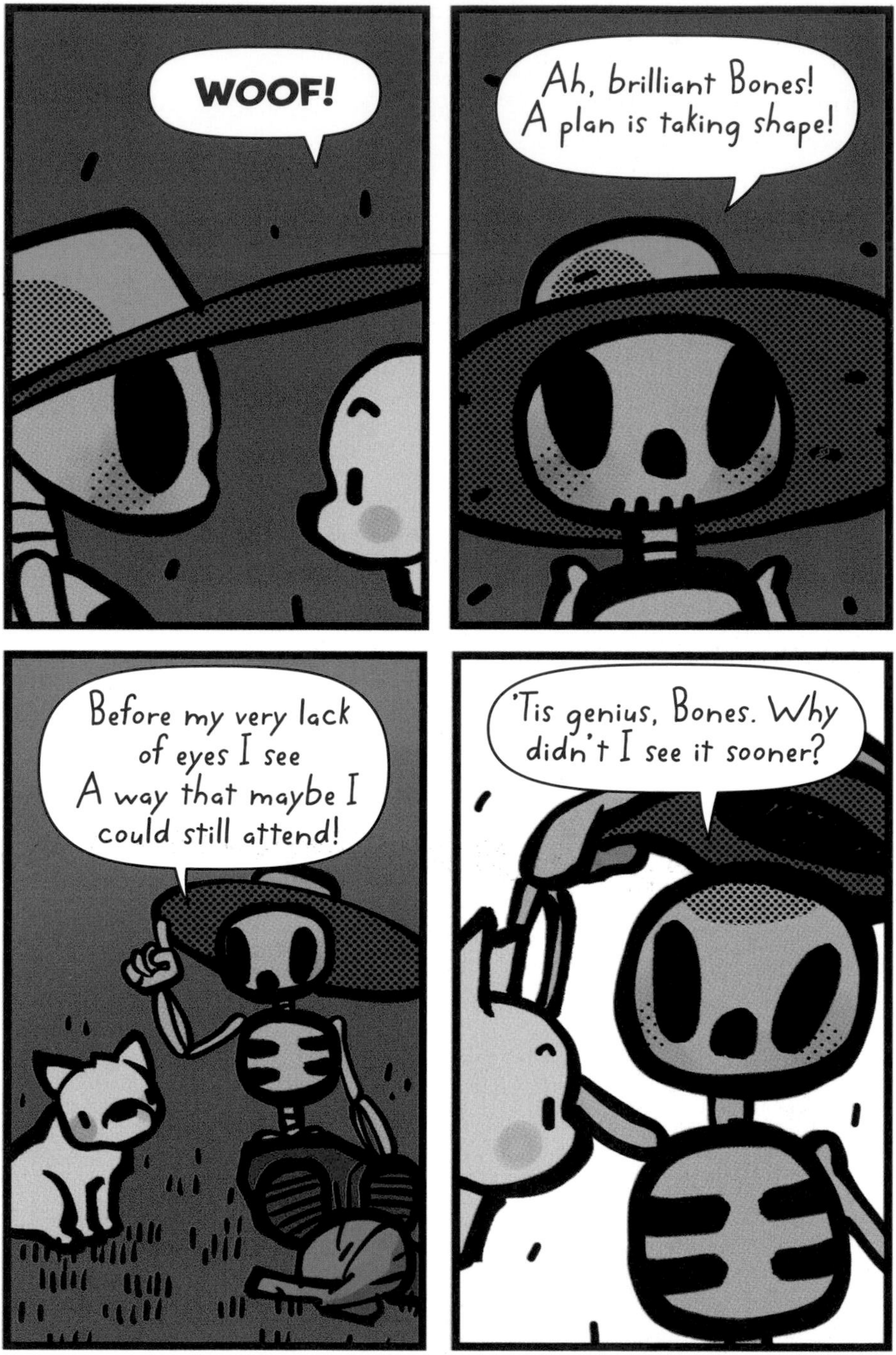
WOOF!
Ah, brilliant Bones! A plan is taking shape!
Before my very lack of eyes I see A way that maybe I could still attend!
'Tis genius, Bones. Why didn't I see it sooner?

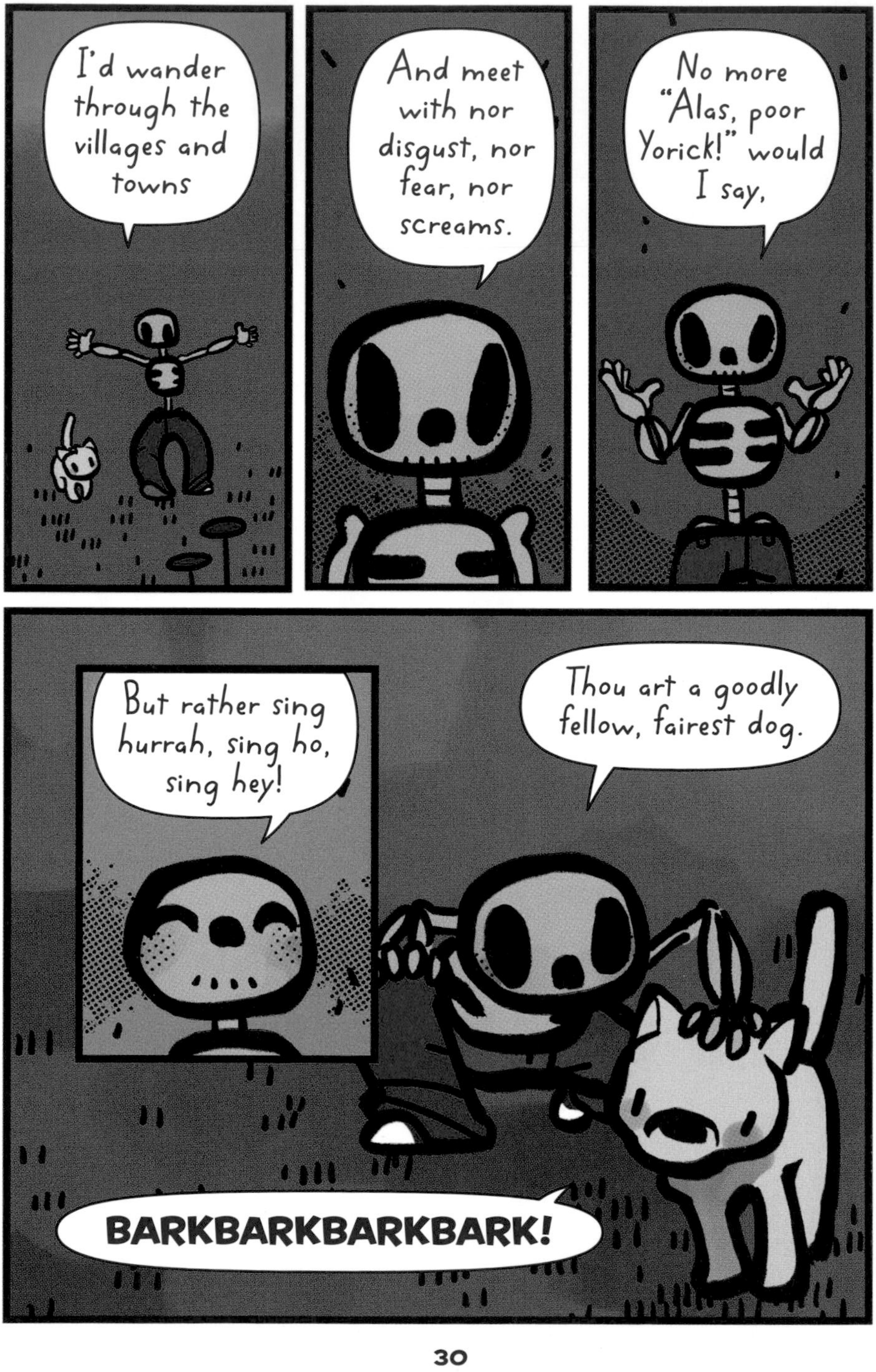
I'd wander through the villages and towns
And meet with nor disgust, nor fear, nor screams.
No more "Alas, poor Yorick!" would I say,
But rather sing hurrah, sing ho, sing hey!
Thou art a goodly fellow, fairest dog.
BARKBARKBARKBARK!

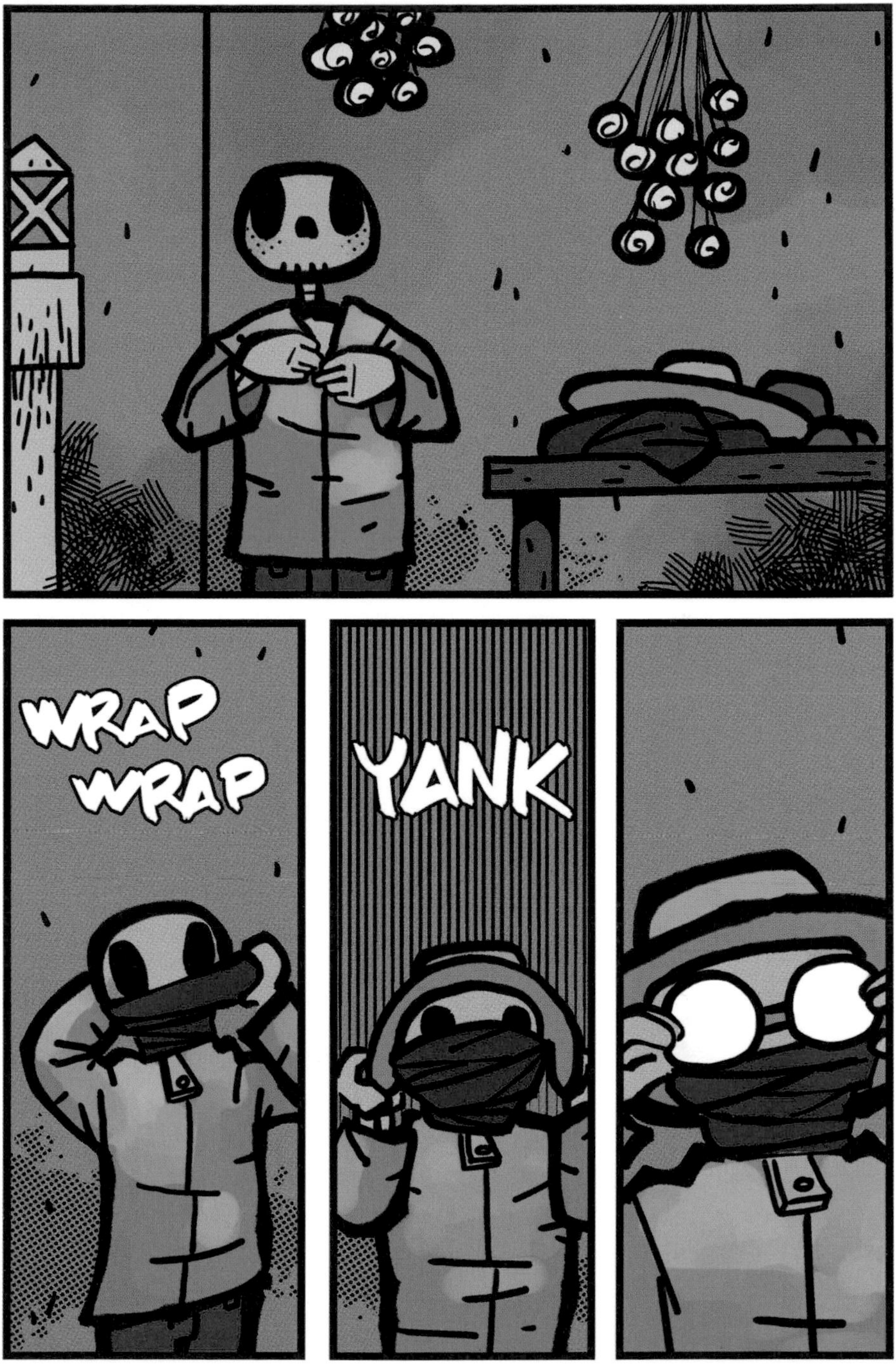
WRAP
WRAP
YANK

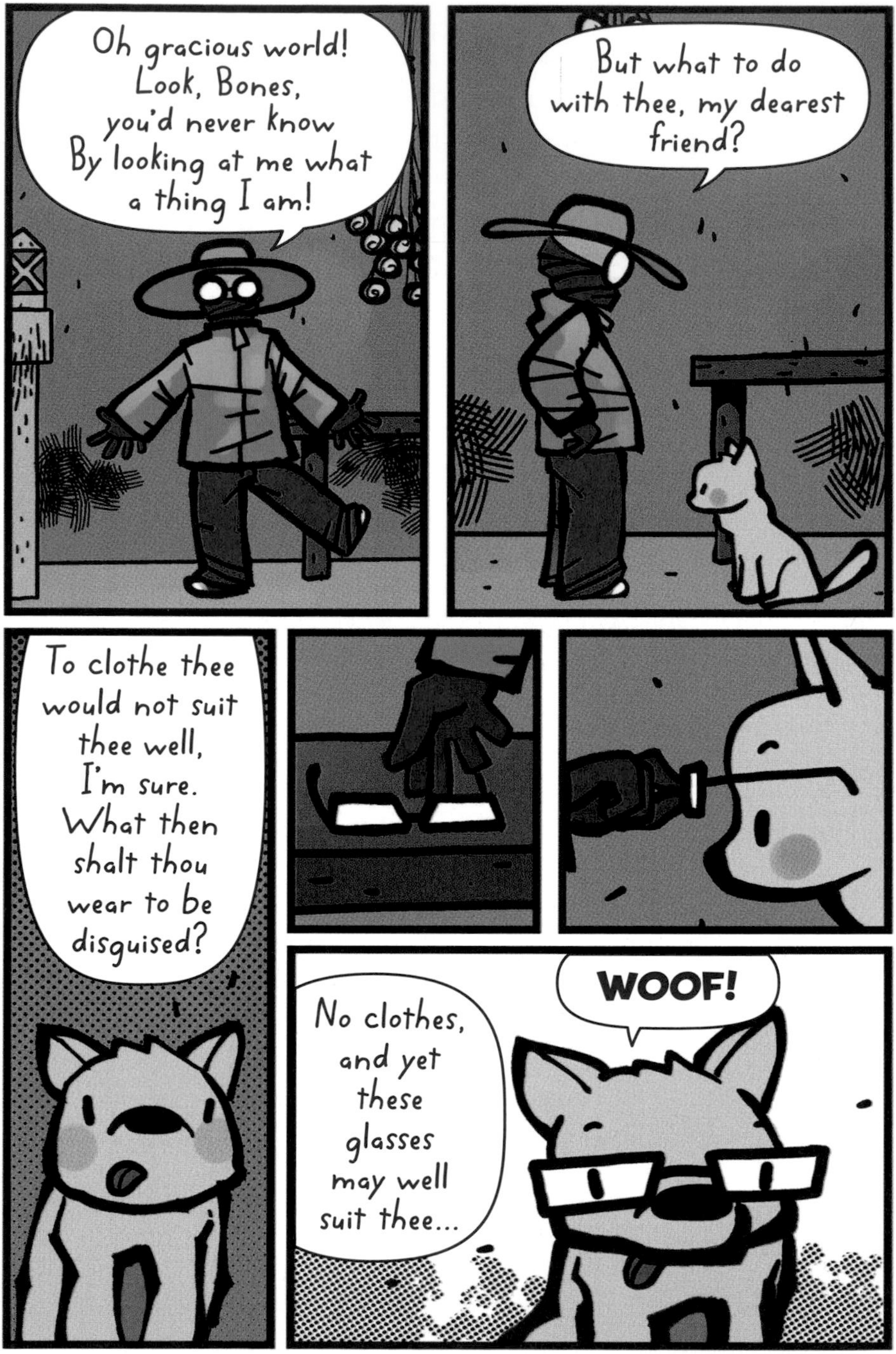
Oh gracious world! Look, Bones, you'd never know By looking at me what a thing I am!
But what to do with thee, my dearest friend?
To clothe thee would not suit thee well, I'm sure. What then shalt thou wear to be disguised?
No clothes, and yet these glasses may well suit thee...
WOOF!

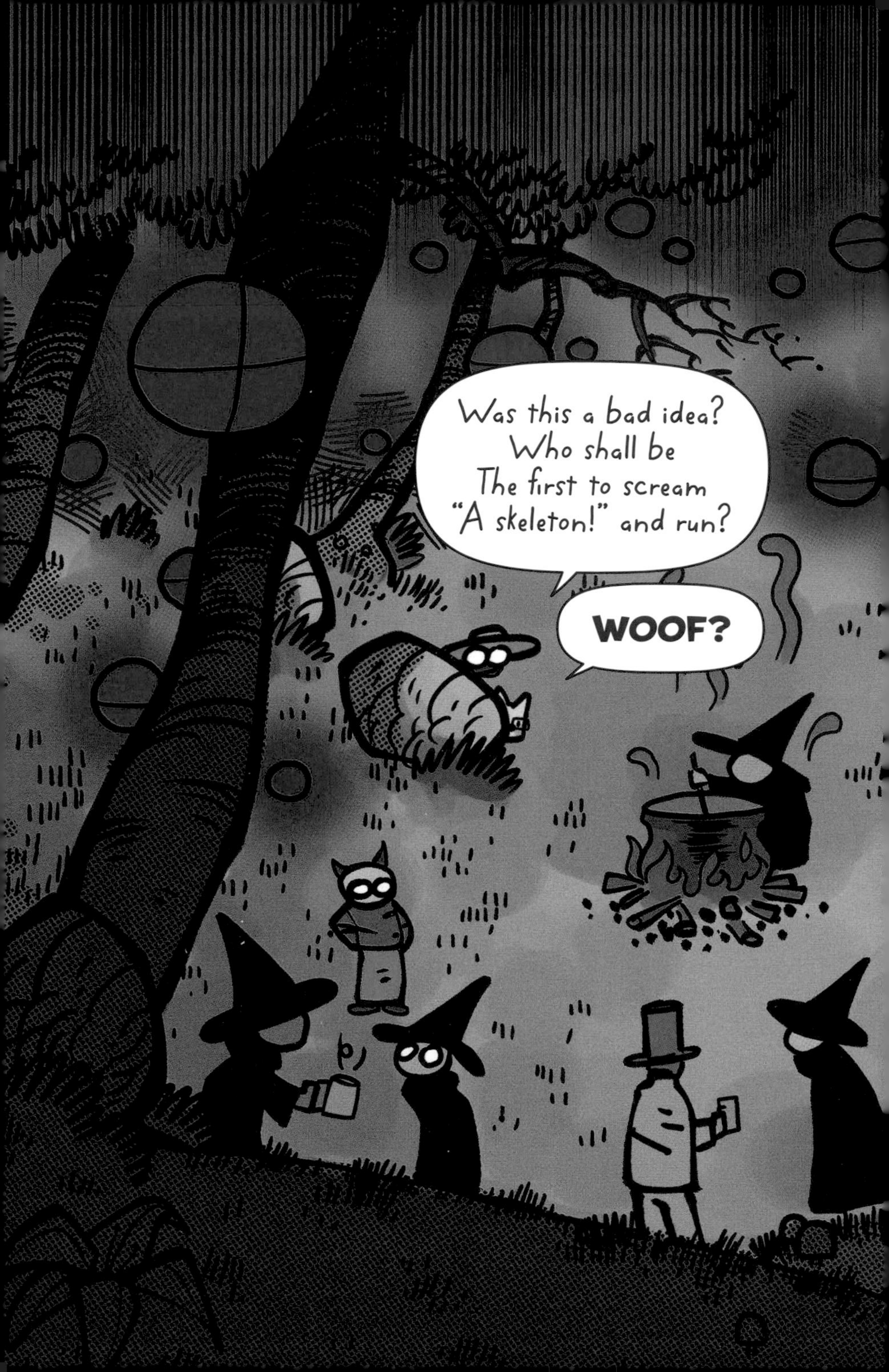
Was this a bad idea? Who shall be The first to scream "A skeleton!" and run?
WOOF?

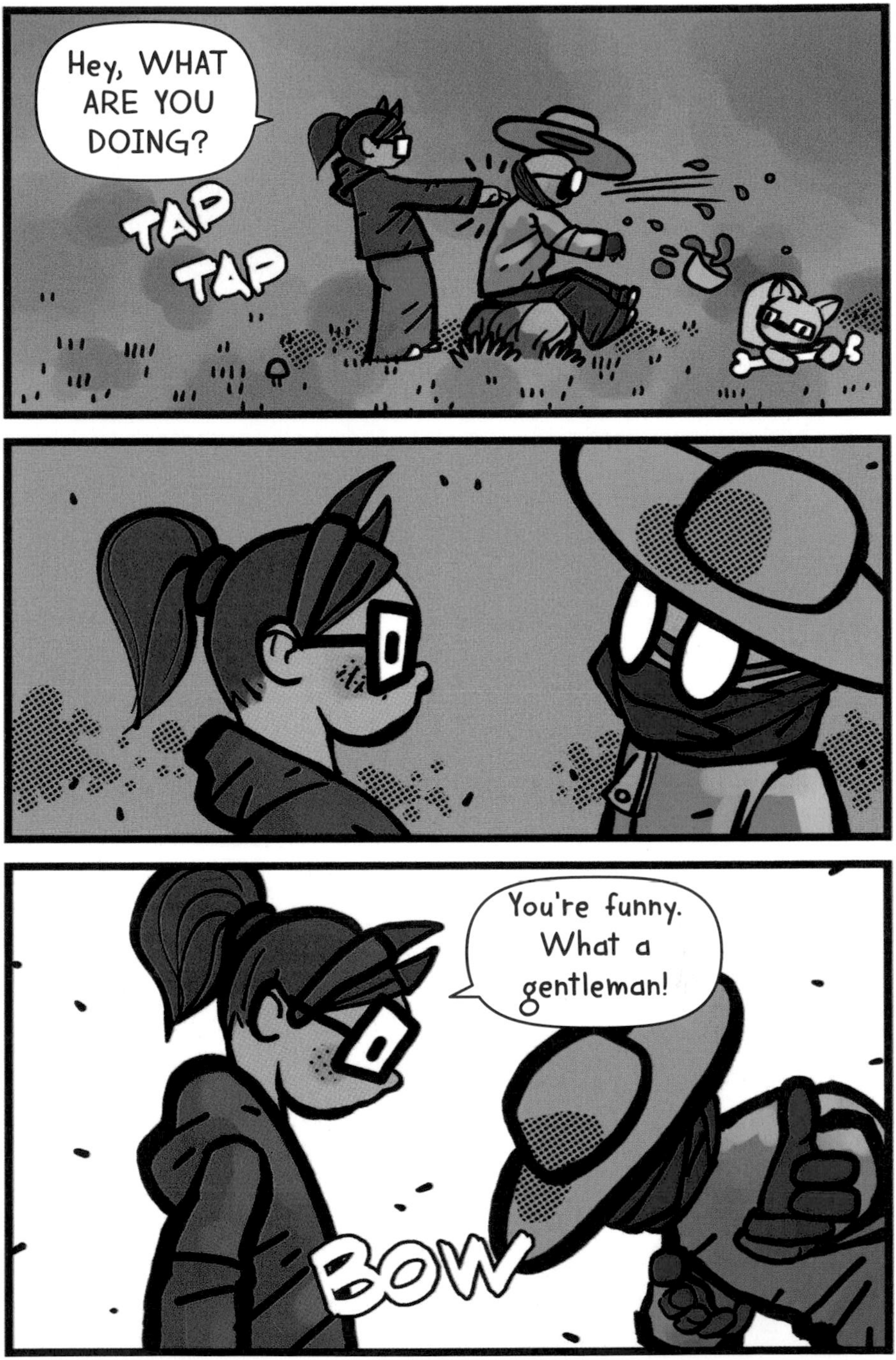
Hey, WHAT ARE YOU DOING?
TAP
TAP
You're funny. What a gentleman!
BOW

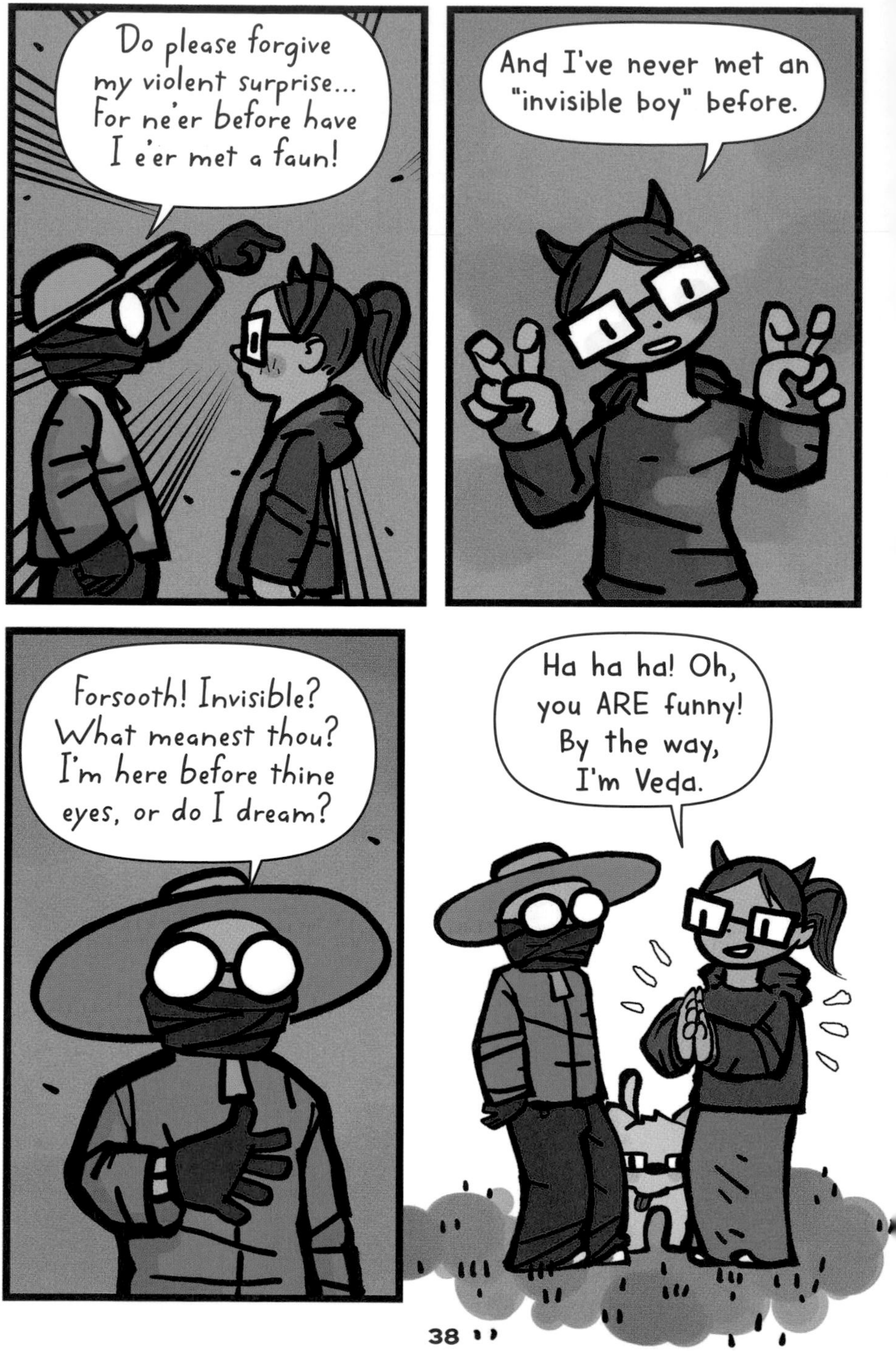
Do please forgive my violent surprise... For ne'er before have I e'er met a faun!
And I've never met an "invisible boy" before.
Forsooth! Invisible? What meanest thou? I'm here before thine eyes, or do I dream?
Ha ha ha! Oh, you ARE funny! By the way, I'm Veda.

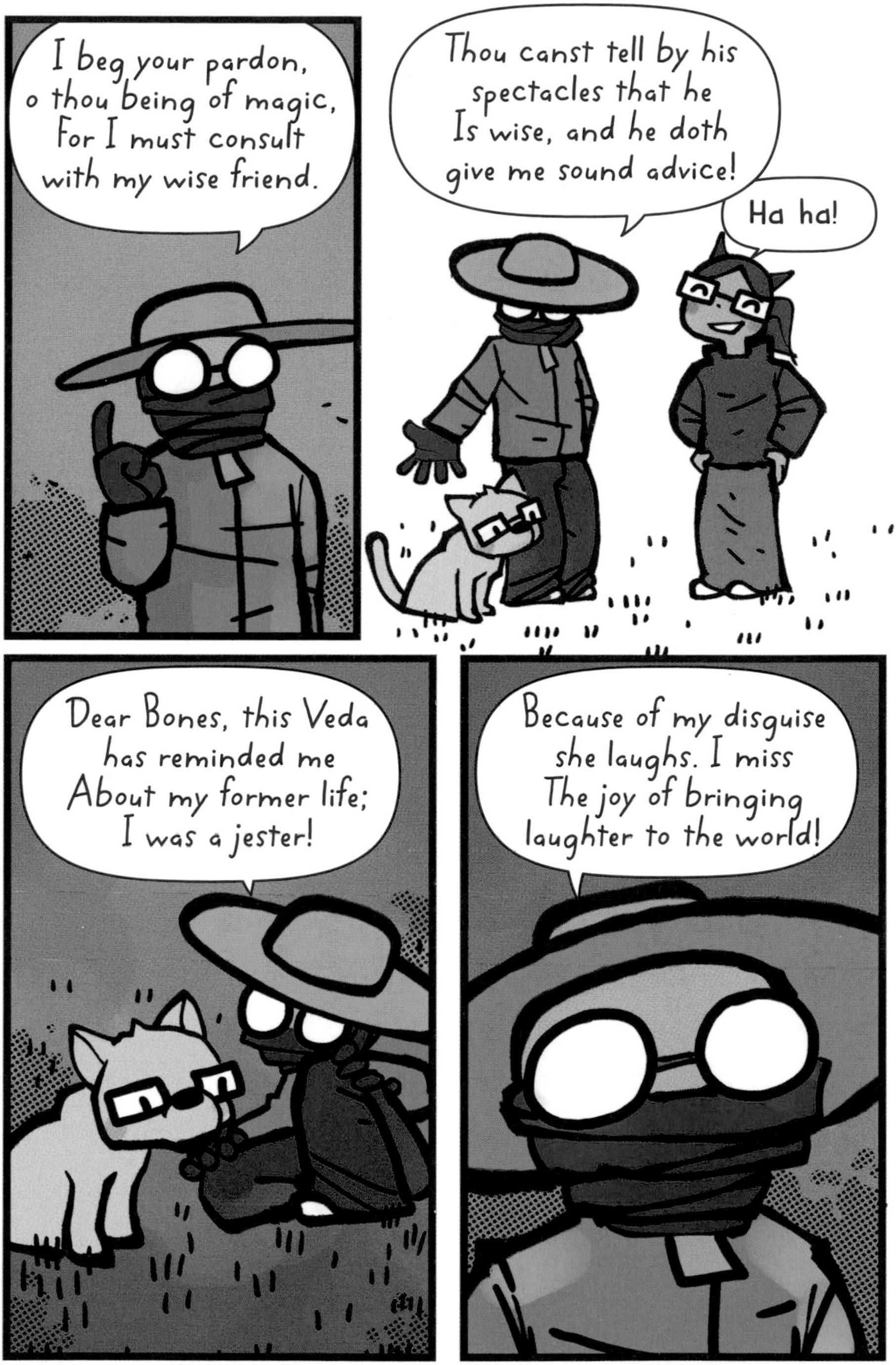
I beg your pardon, o thou being of magic, For I must consult with my wise friend.
Thou canst tell by his spectacles that he Is wise, and he doth give me sound advice!
Ha ha!
Dear Bones, this Veda has reminded me About my former life; I was a jester!
Because of my disguise she laughs. I miss The joy of bringing laughter to the world!

41

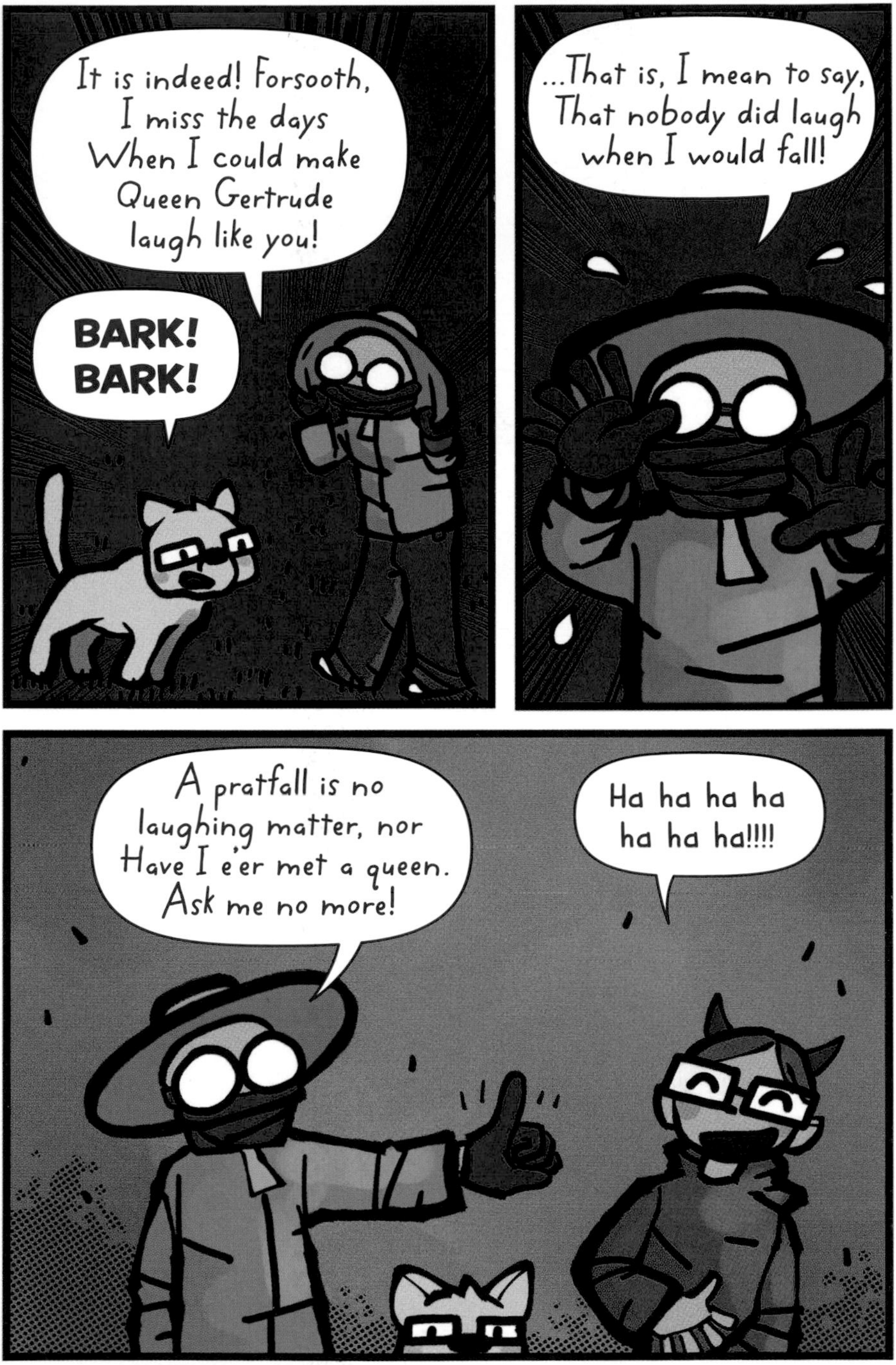
It is indeed! Forsooth, I miss the days When I could make Queen Gertrude laugh like you!
BARK! BARK!
...That is, I mean to say, That nobody did laugh when I would fall!
A pratfall is no laughing matter, nor Have I e'er met a queen. Ask me no more!
Ha ha ha ha ha ha ha!!!!

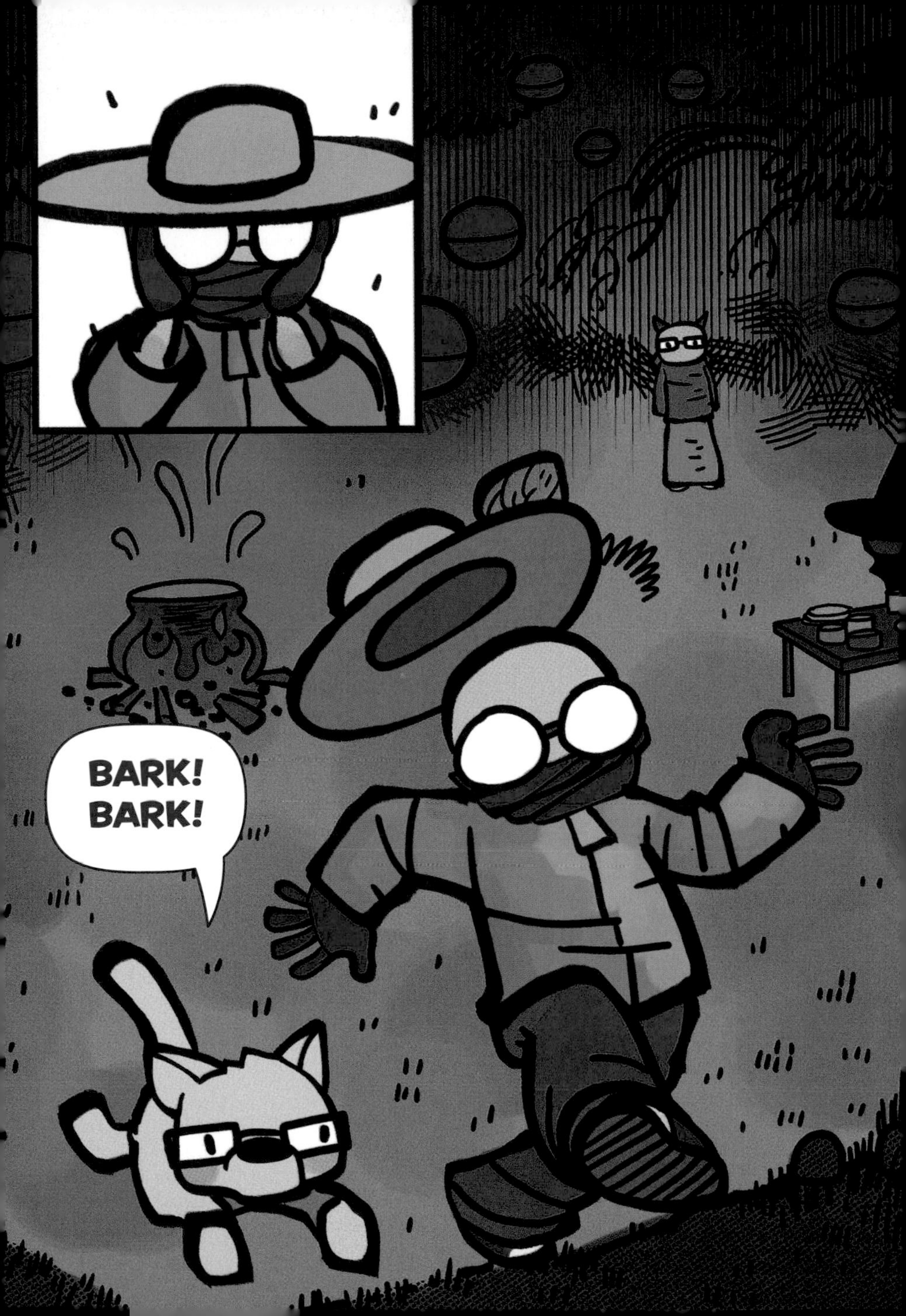
BARK! BARK!

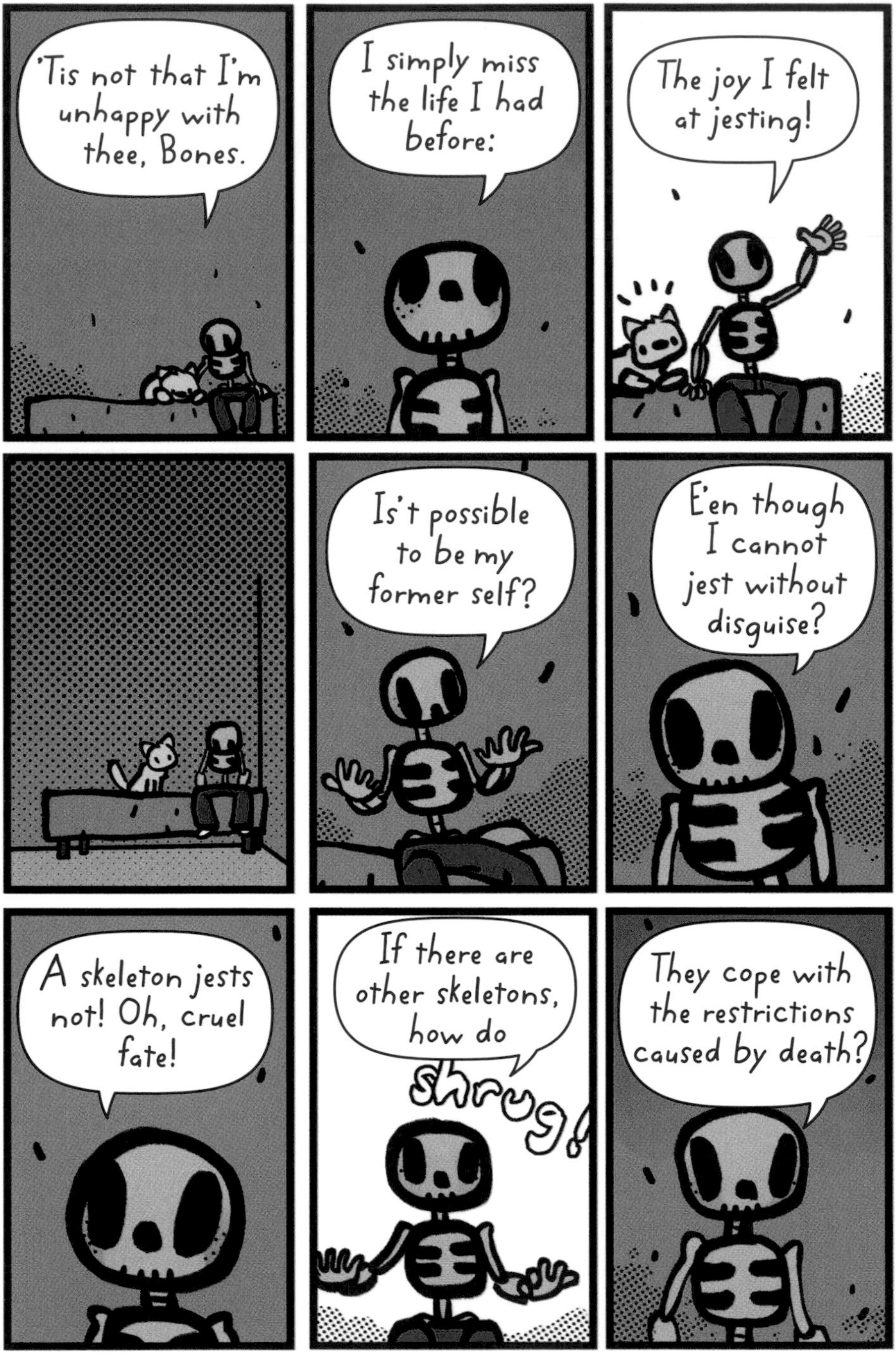
'Tis not that I'm unhappy with thee, Bones.
I simply miss the life I had before:
The joy I felt at jesting!
Is't possible to be my former self?
E'en though I cannot jest without disguise?
A skeleton jests not! Oh, cruel fate!
If there are other skeletons, how do
shrug!
They cope with the restrictions caused by death?

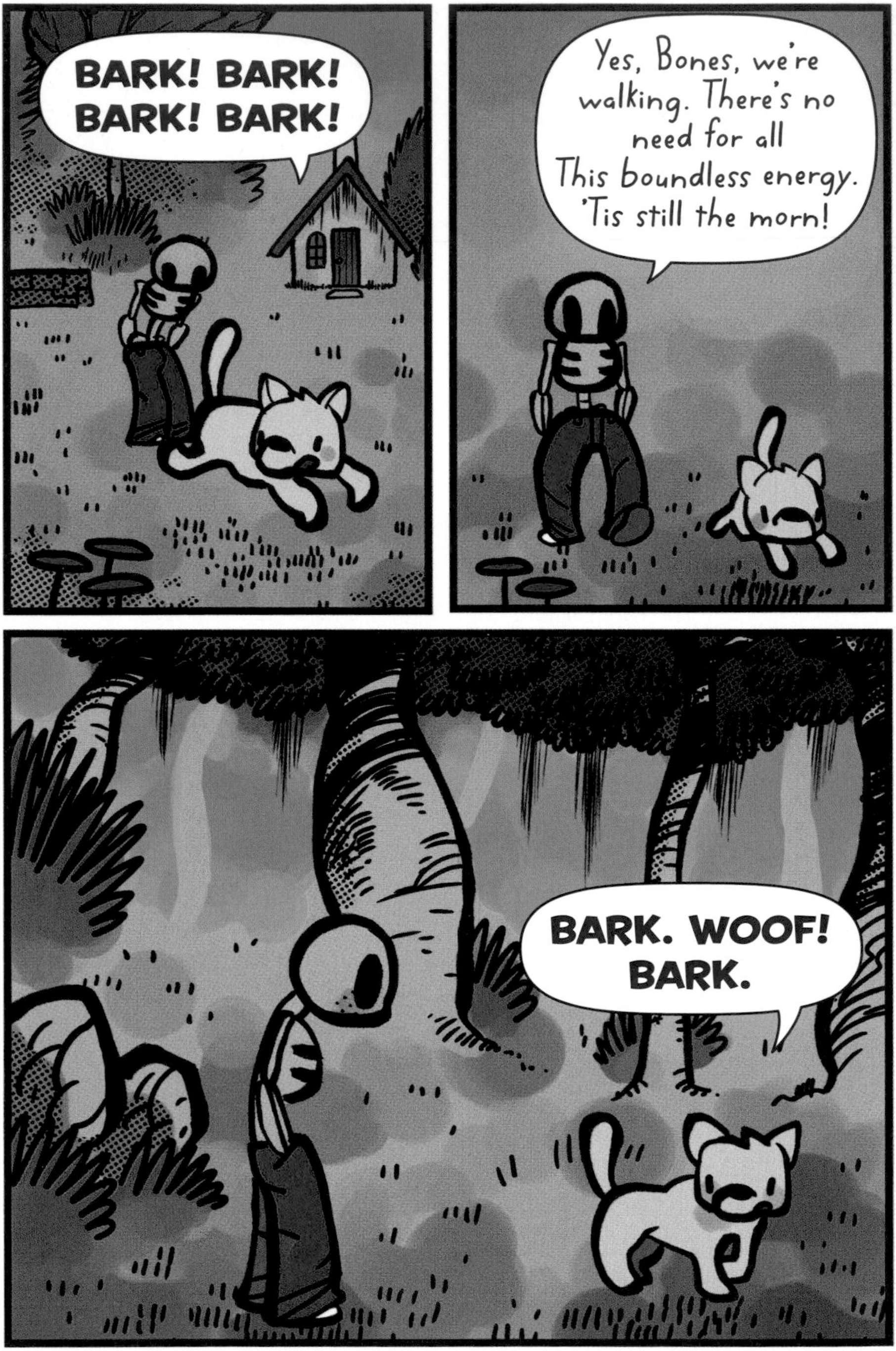
BARK! BARK! BARK! BARK!
Yes, Bones, we're walking. There's no need for all This boundless energy. 'Tis still the morn!
BARK. WOOF! BARK.

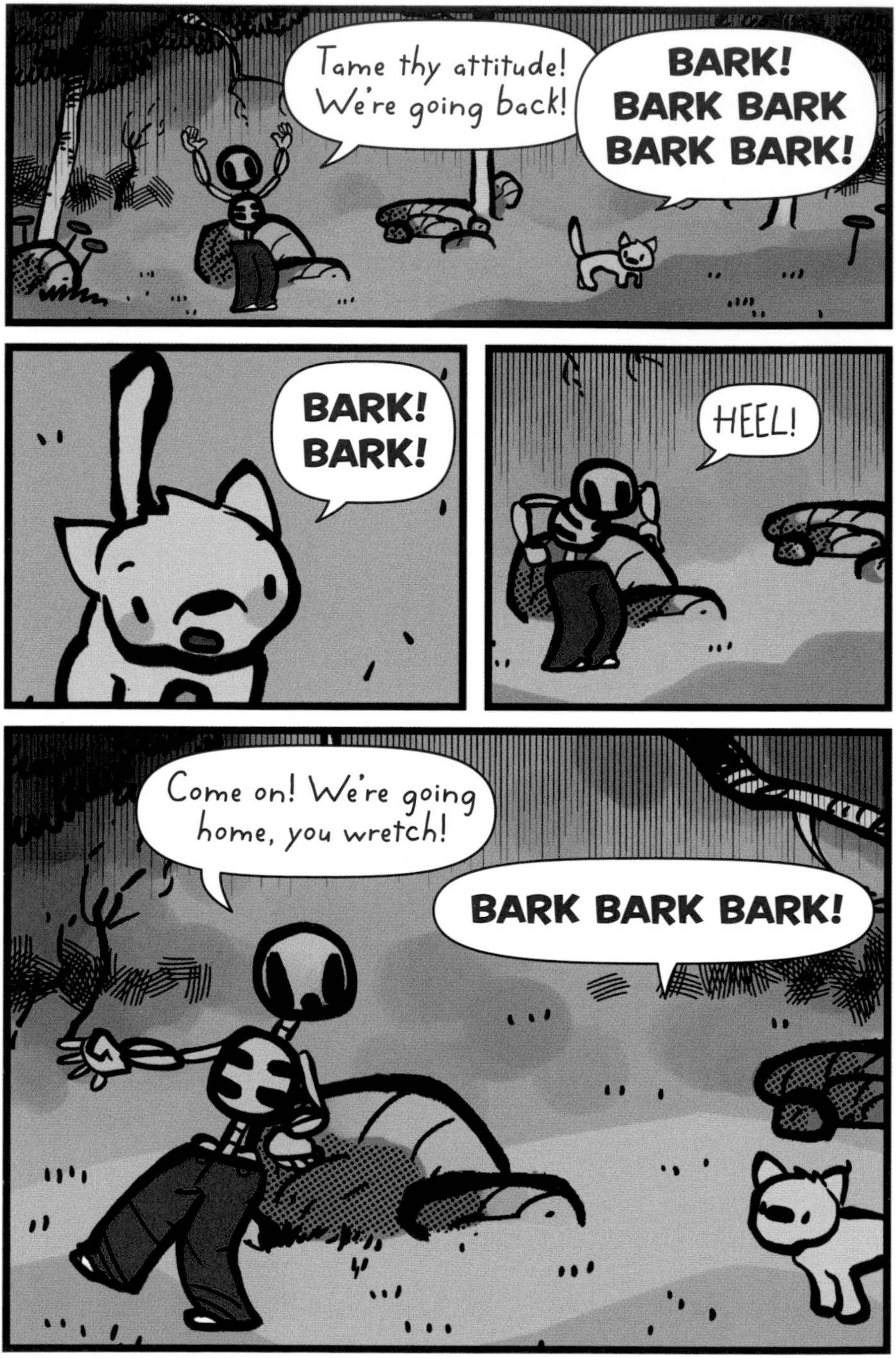
Tame thy attitude! We're going back!
BARK! BARK BARK BARK BARK!
BARK! BARK!
HEEL!
Come on! We're going home, you wretch!
BARK BARK BARK!

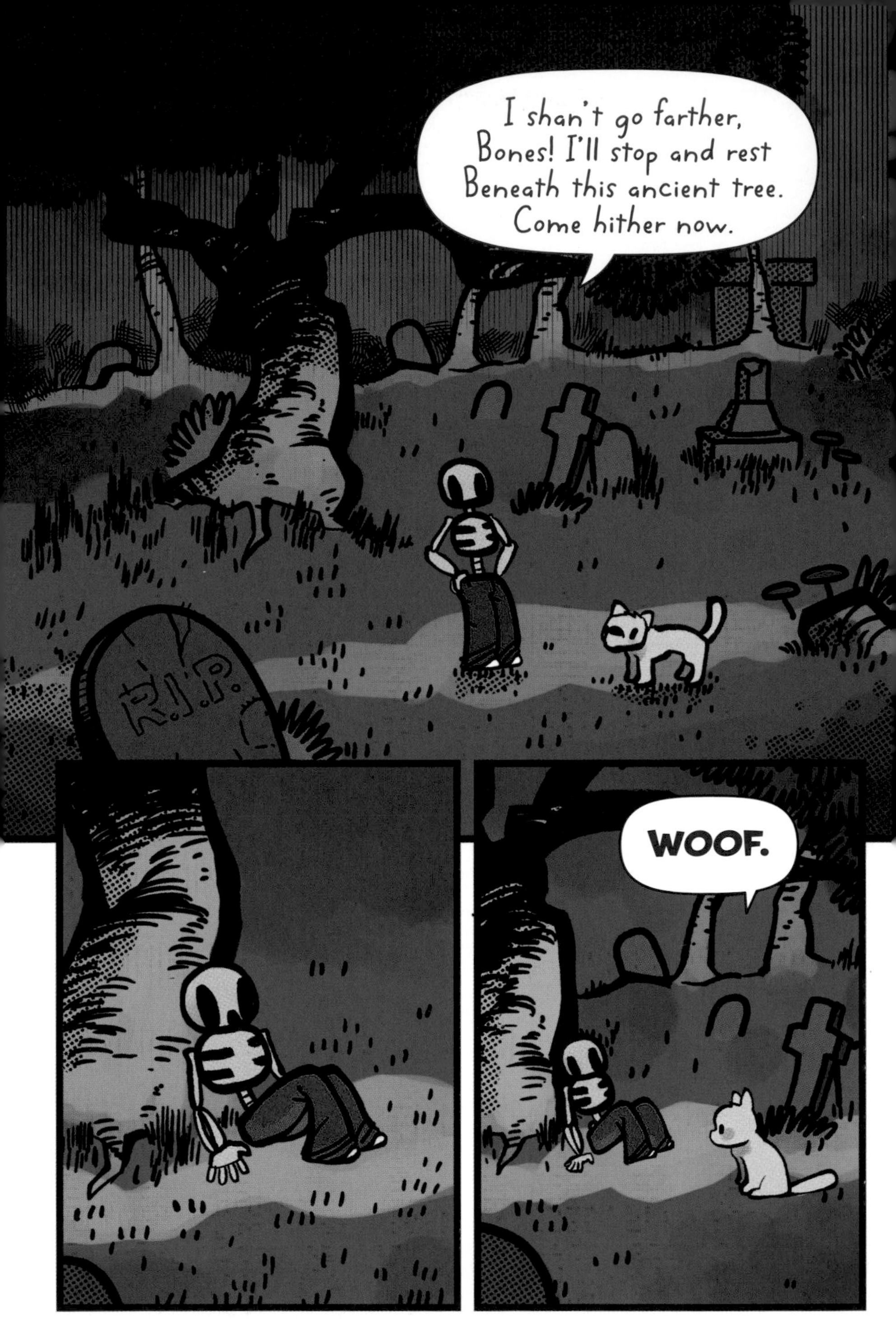
I shan't go farther, Bones! I'll stop and rest Beneath this ancient tree. Come hither now.
R.I.P.
WOOF.

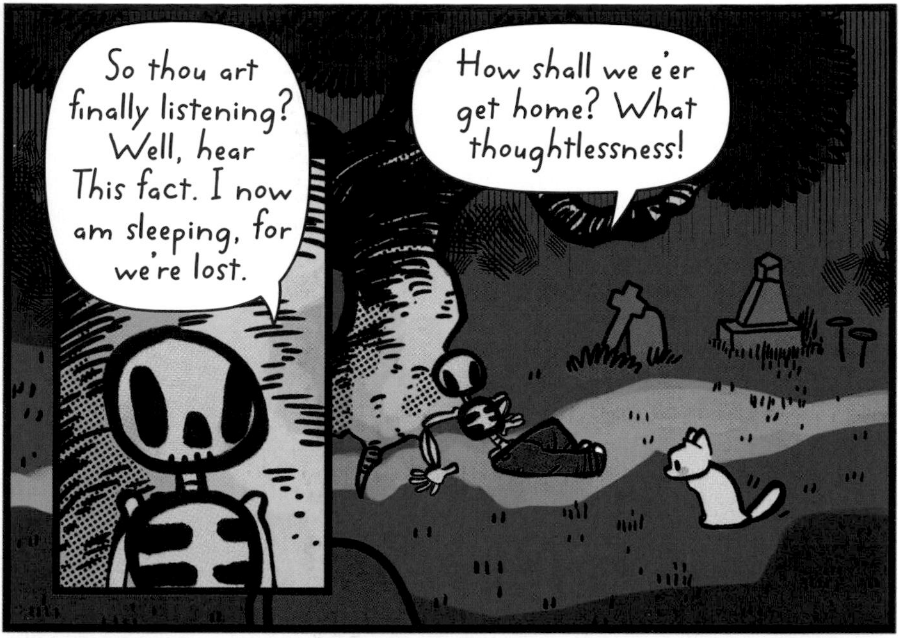
So thou art finally listening? Well, hear This fact. I now am sleeping, for we're lost.
How shall we e'er get home? What thoughtlessness!

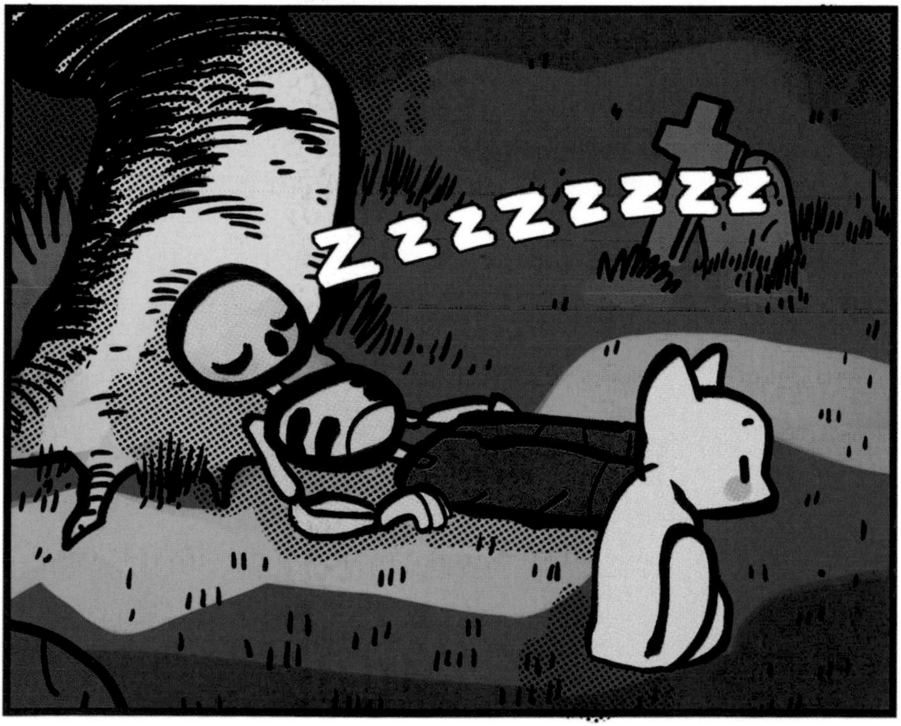
ZZZZZZZZ

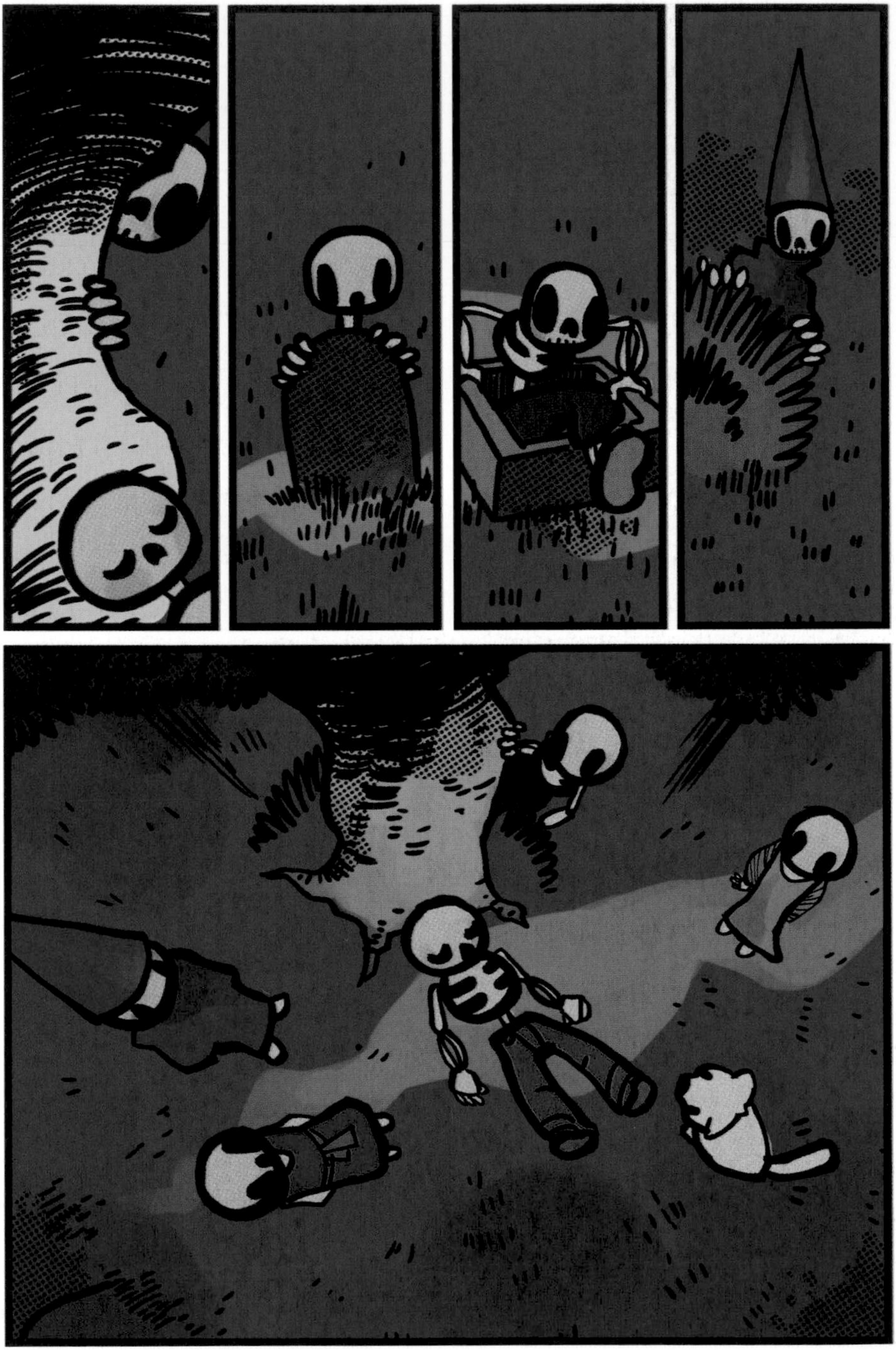

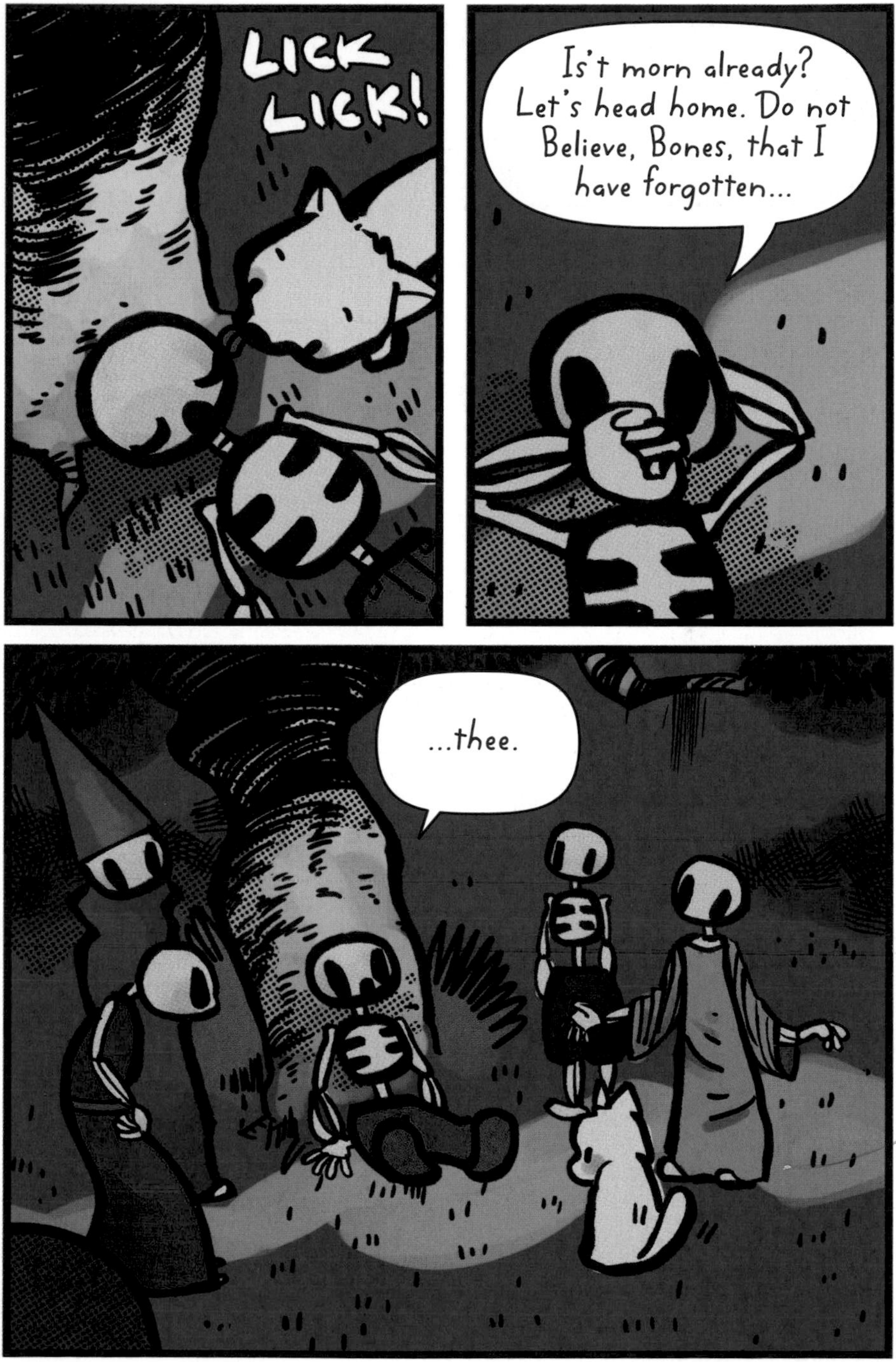
LICK LICK!
Is't morn already? Let's head home. Do not Believe, Bones, that I have forgotten...
...thee.

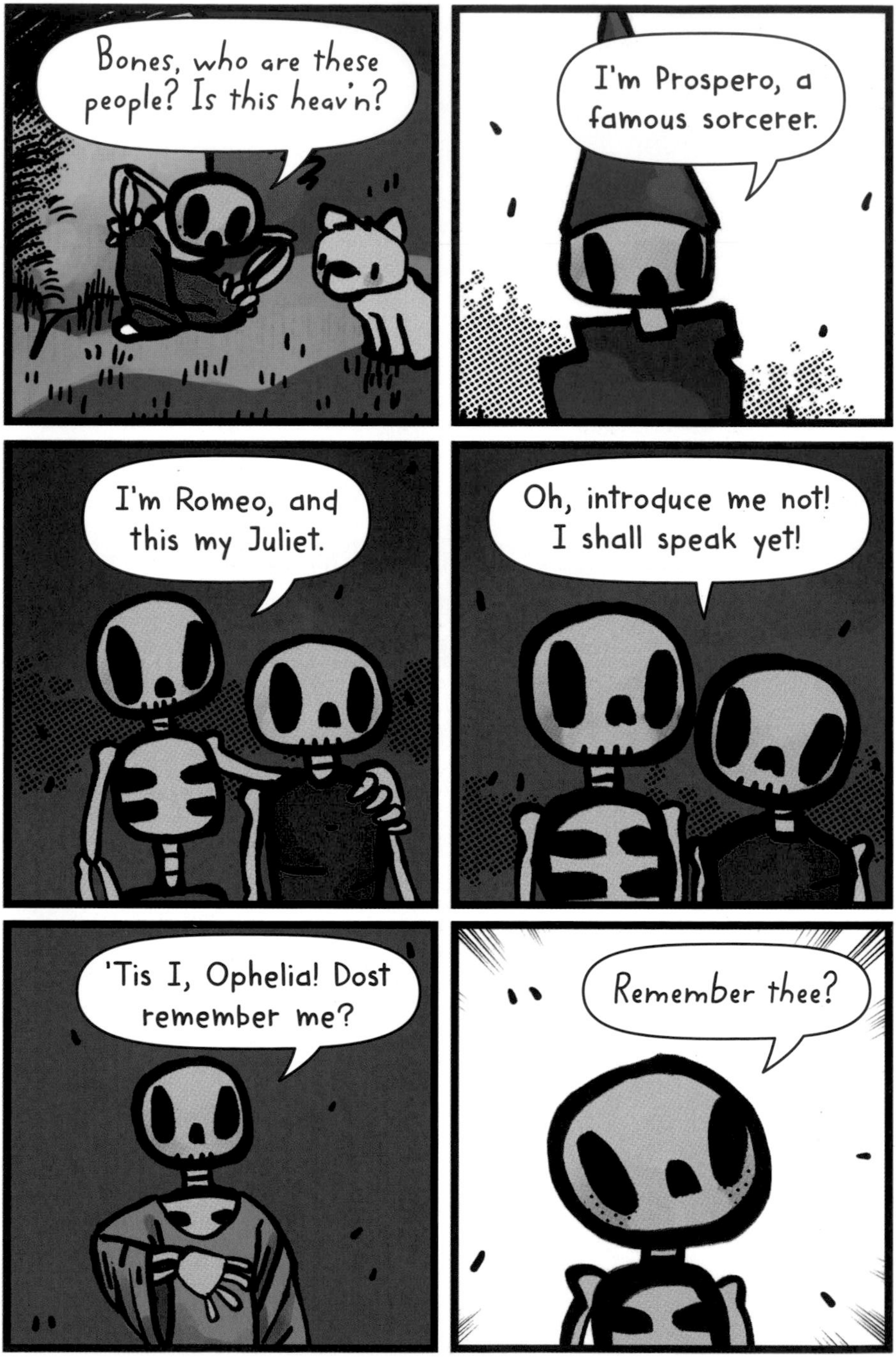
Bones, who are these people? Is this heav'n?
I'm Prospero, a famous sorcerer.
I'm Romeo, and this my Juliet.
Oh, introduce me not! I shall speak yet!
'Tis I, Ophelia! Dost remember me?
Remember thee?

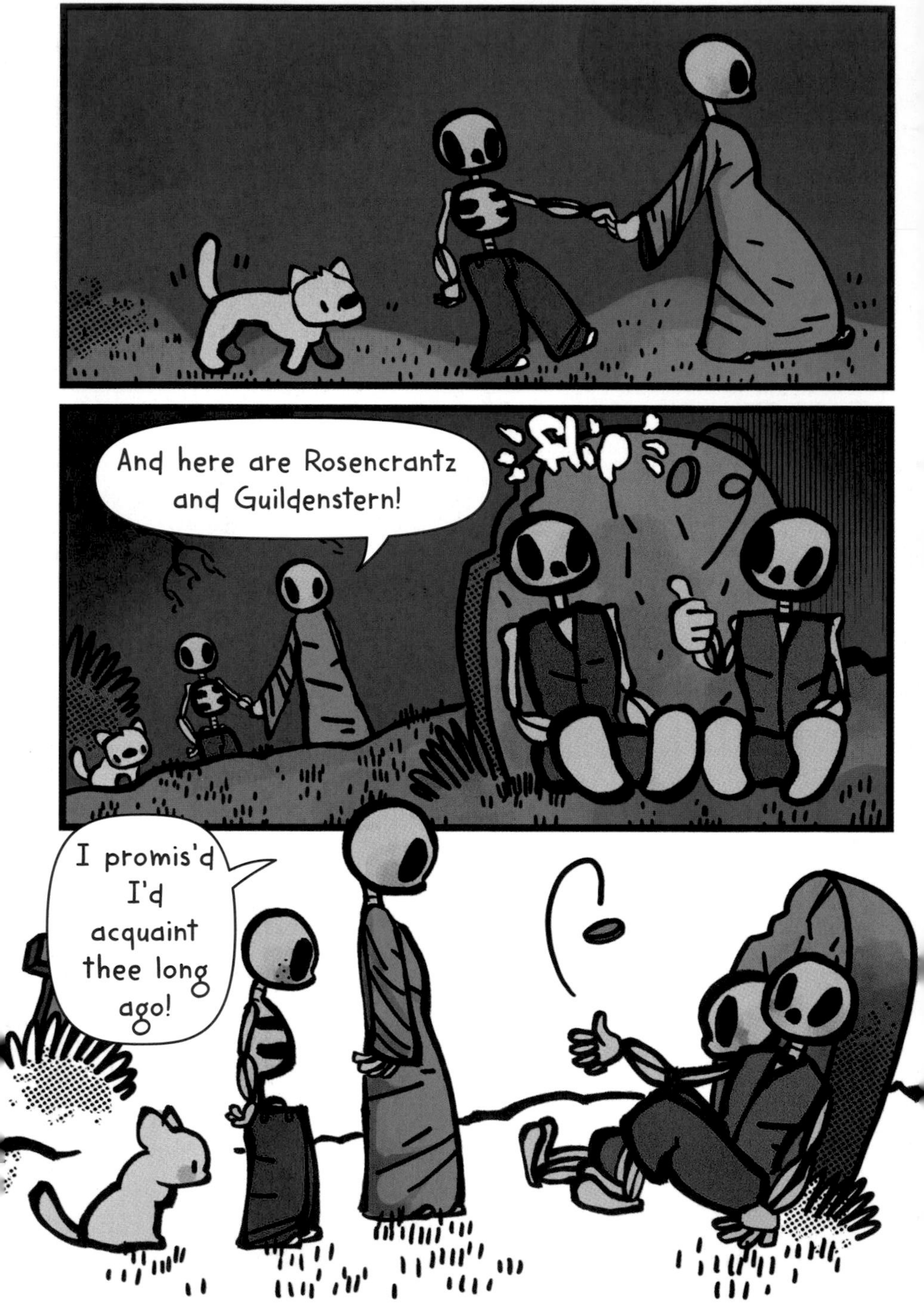

And here are Rosencrantz and Guildenstern!
FLIP
I promis'd I'd acquaint thee long ago!

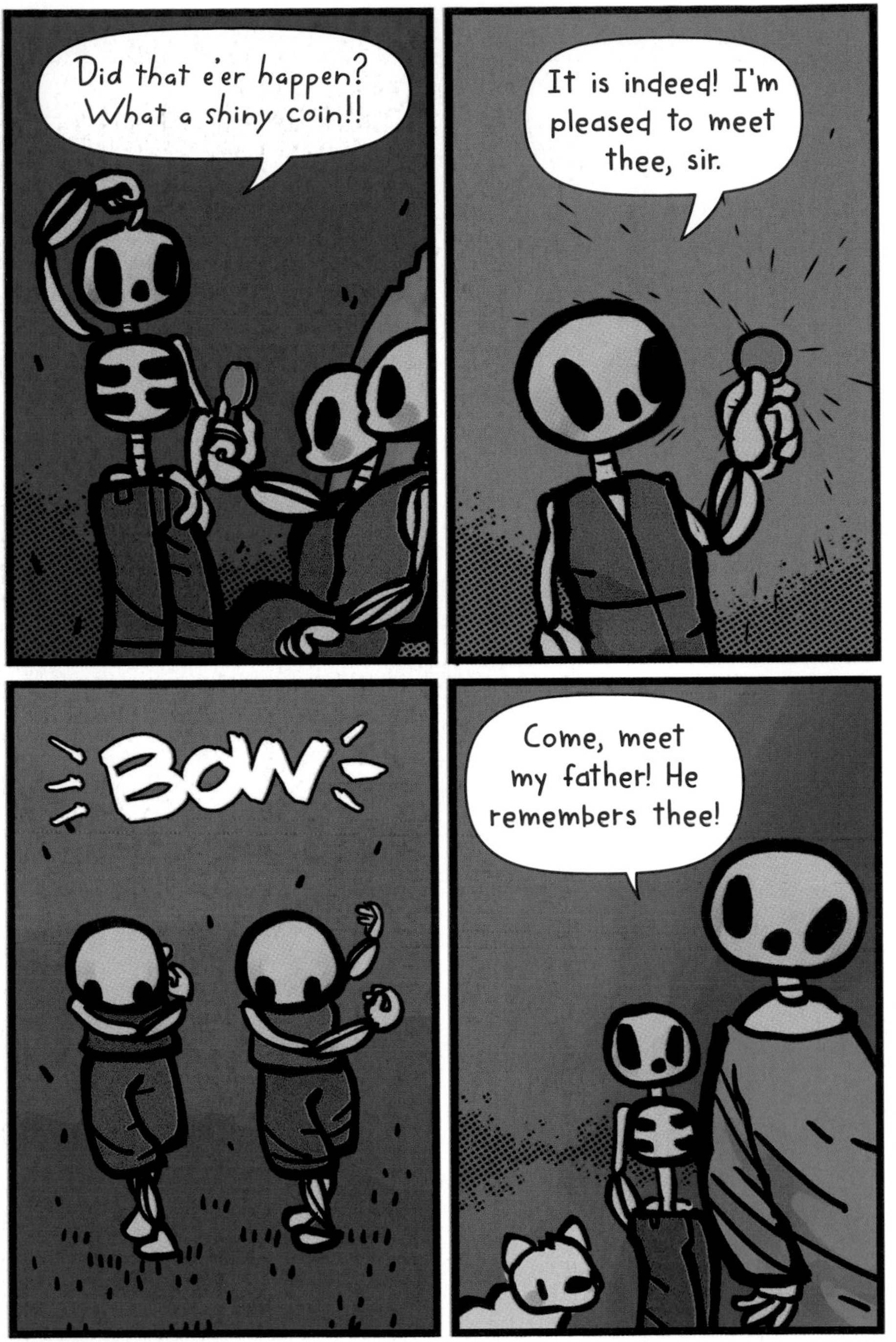
Did that e'er happen? What a shiny coin!!
It is indeed! I'm pleased to meet thee, sir.
BOW
Come, meet my father! He remembers thee!

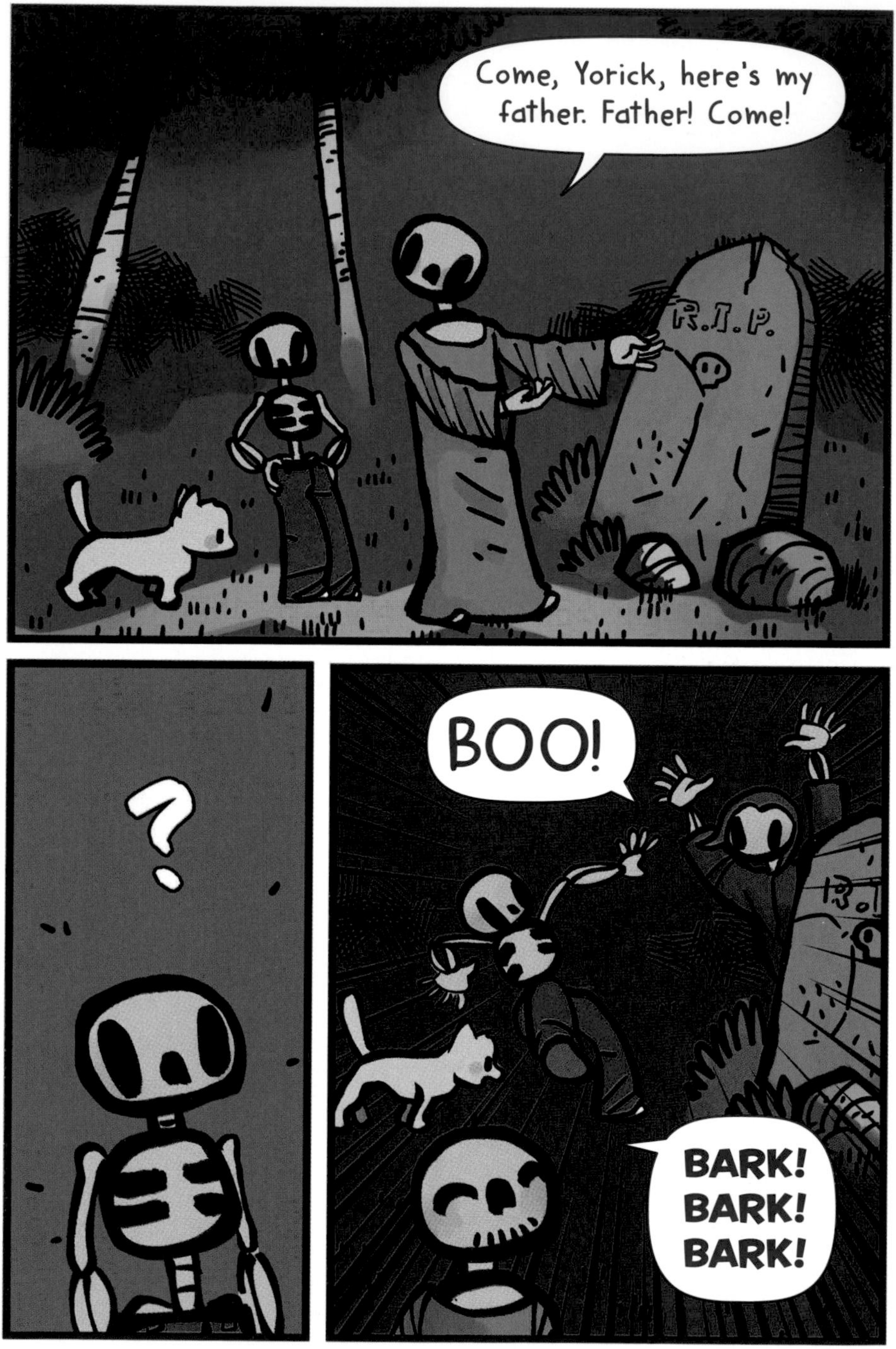

Come, Yorick, here's my father. Father! Come!
R.I.P.
?
BOO!
BARK! BARK! BARK!

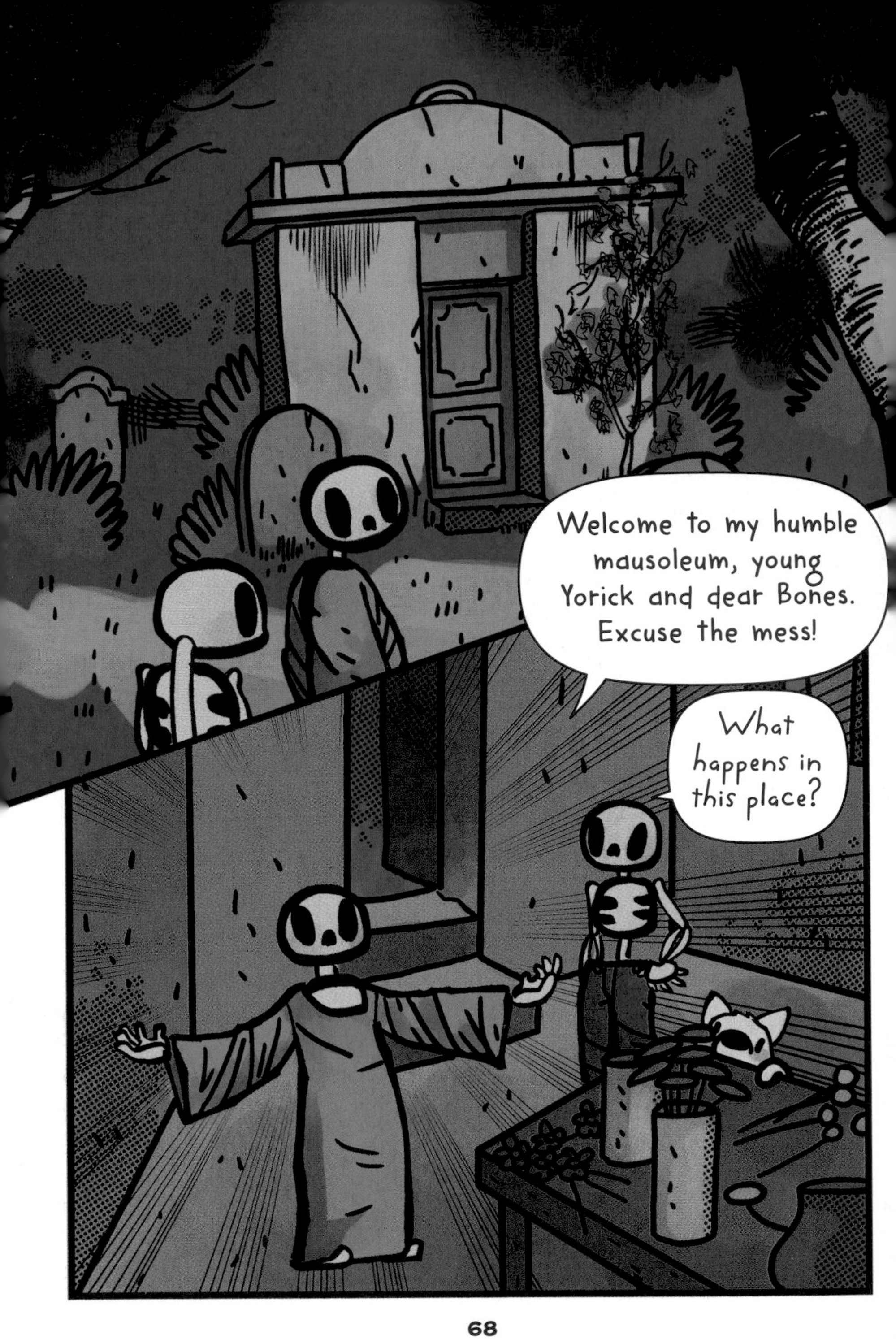
Welcome to my humble mausoleum, young Yorick and dear Bones. Excuse the mess!
What happens in this place?

69

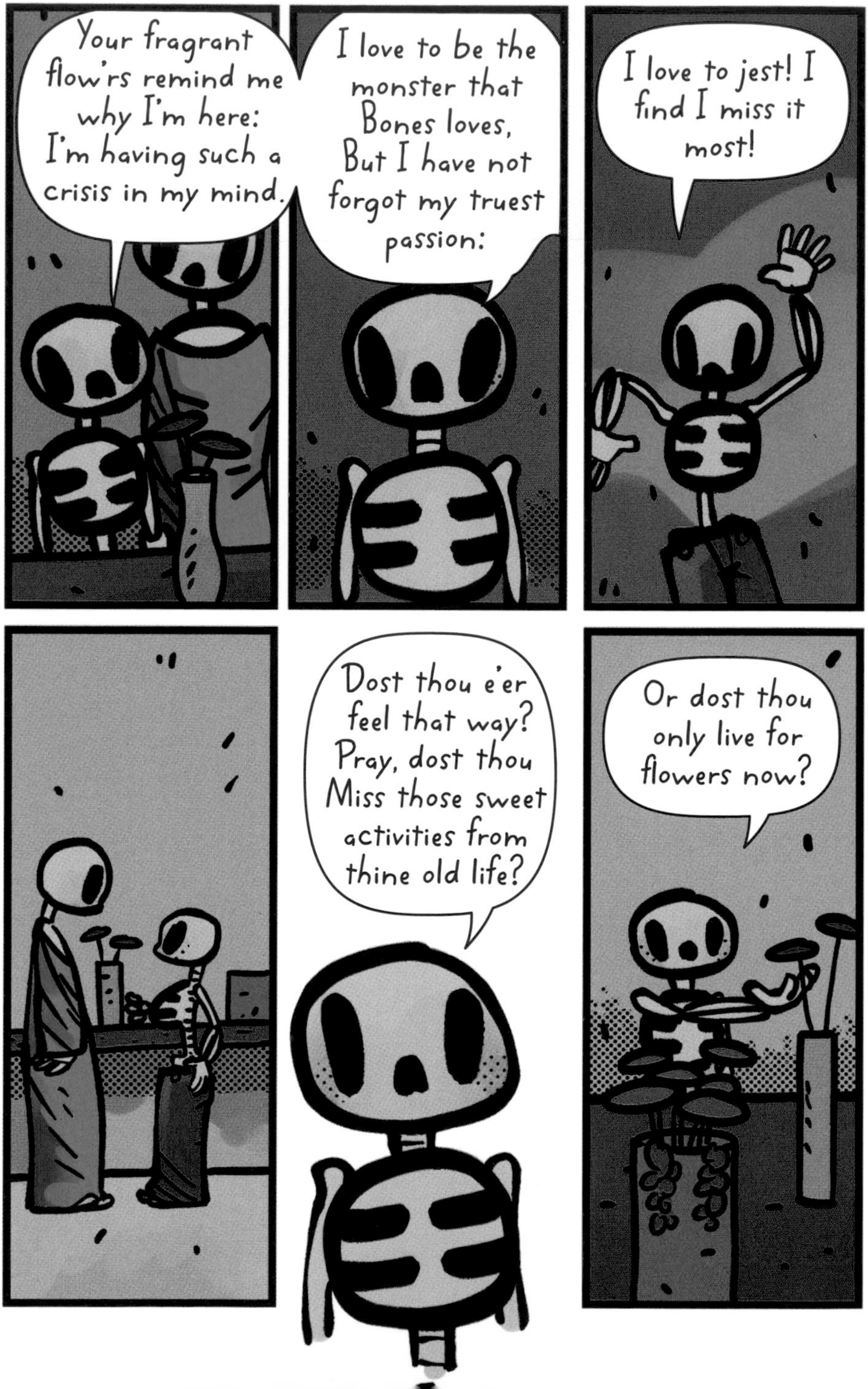
Your fragrant flow'rs remind me why I'm here: I'm having such a crisis in my mind.
I love to be the monster that Bones loves, But I have not forgot my truest passion:
I love to jest! I find I miss it most!
Dost thou e'er feel that way? Pray, dost thou Miss those sweet activities from thine old life?
Or dost thou only live for flowers now?

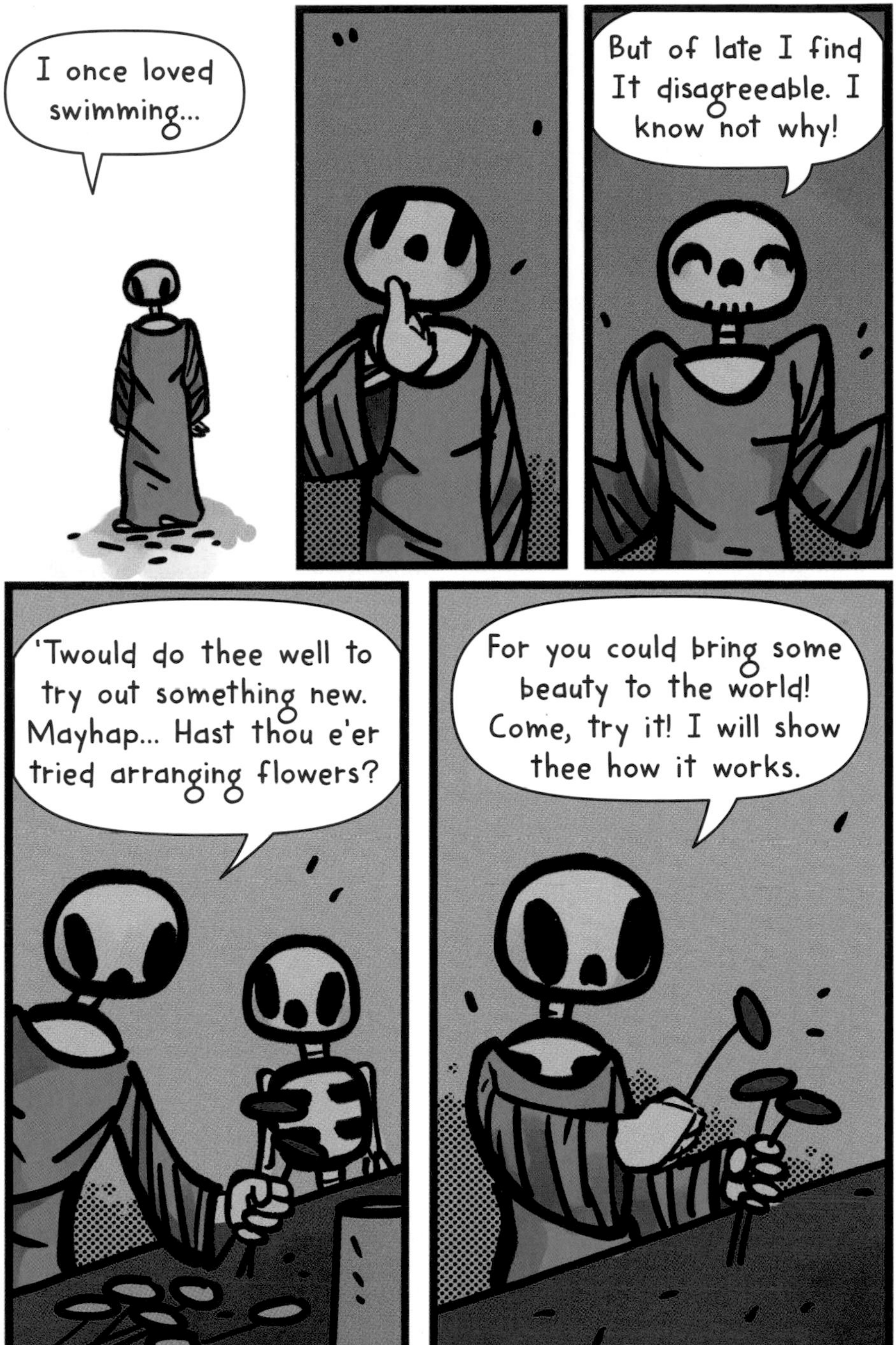
I once loved swimming...
But of late I find It disagreeable. I know not why!
'Twould do thee well to try out something new. Mayhap... Hast thou e'er tried arranging flowers?
For you could bring some beauty to the world! Come, try it! I will show thee how it works.

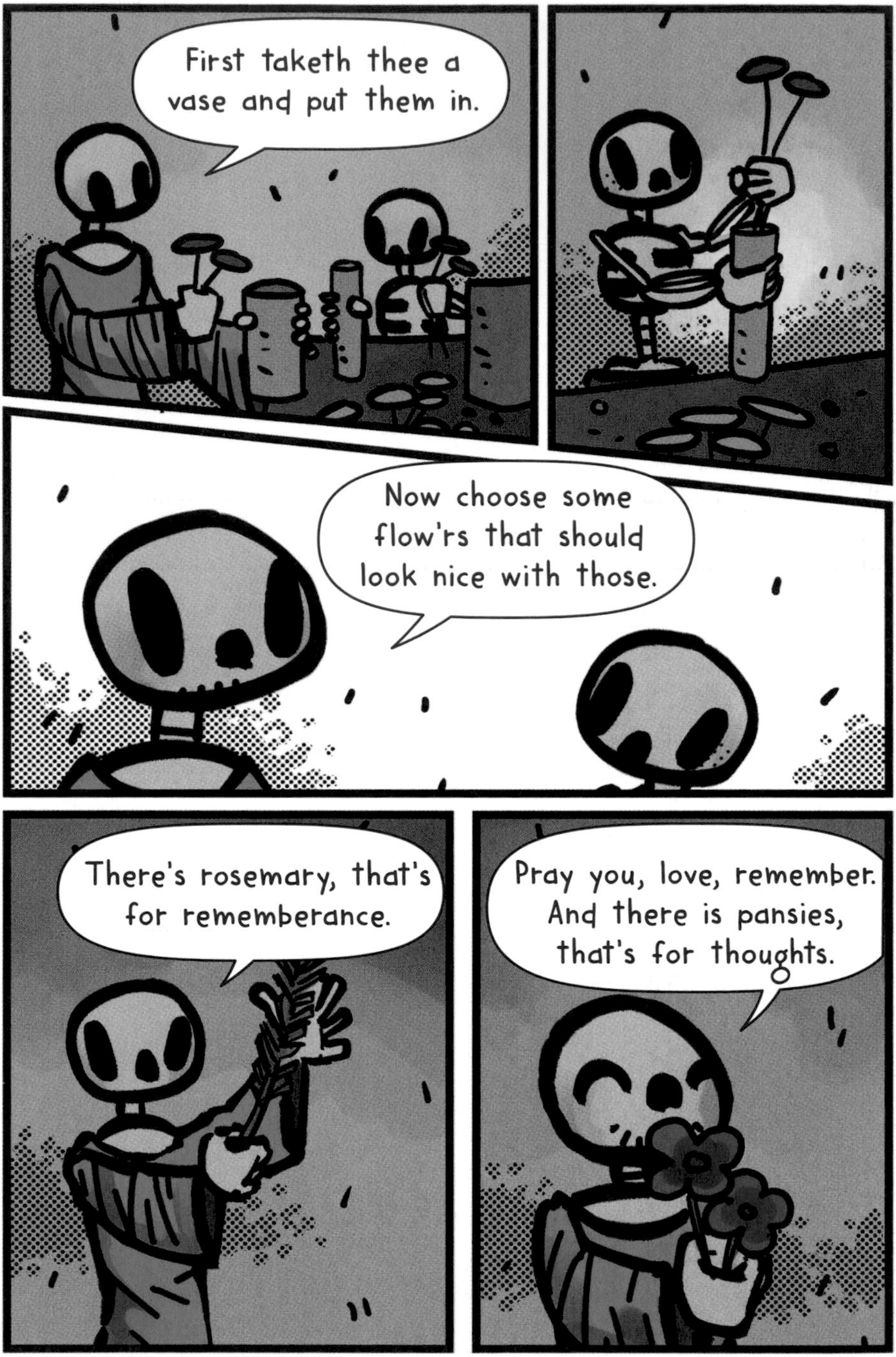
First taketh thee a vase and put them in.
Now choose some flow'rs that should look nice with those.
There's rosemary, that's for rememberance.
Pray you, love, remember. And there is pansies, that's for thoughts.

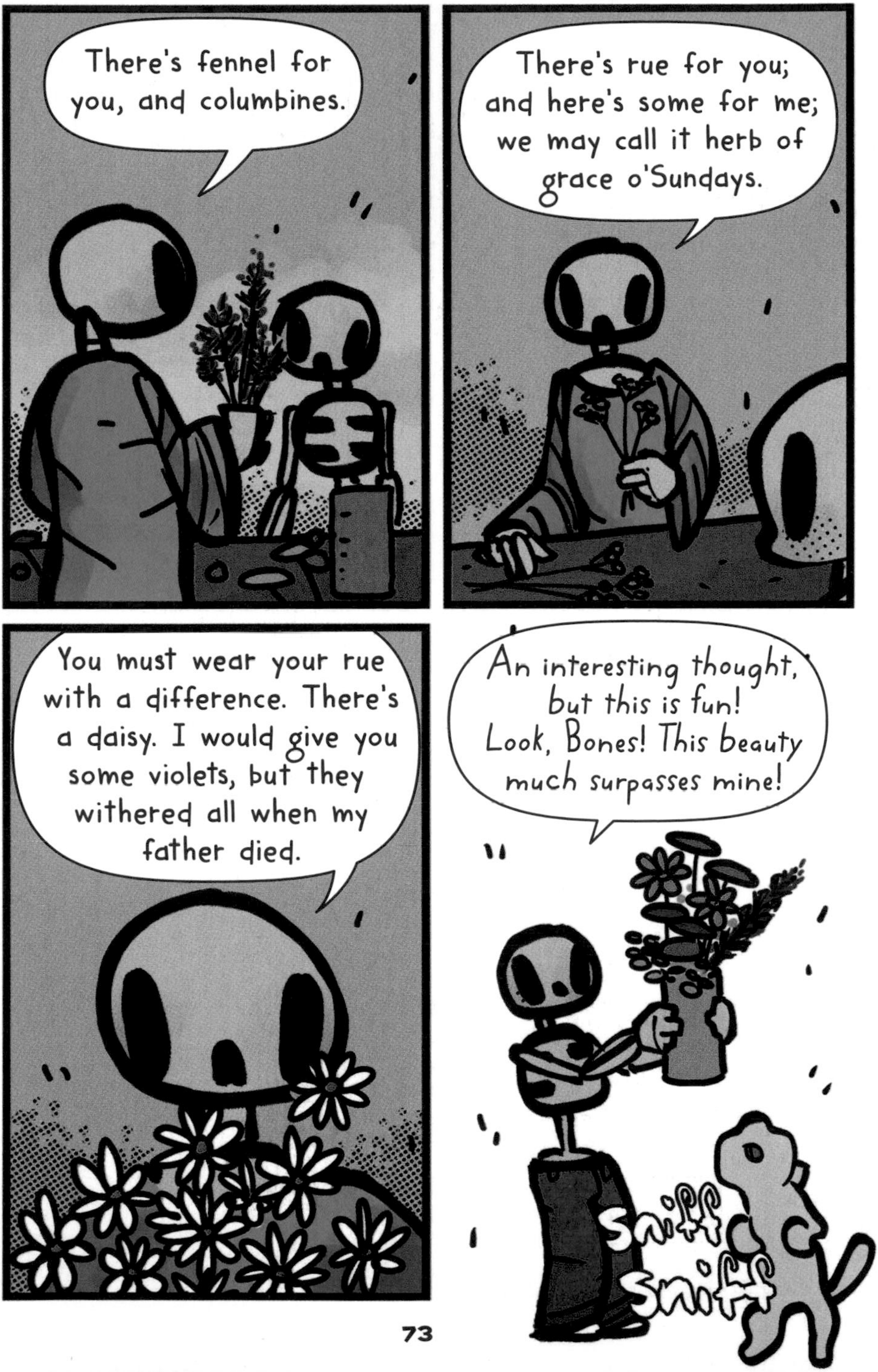
There's fennel for you, and columbines.
There's rue for you; and here's some for me; we may call it herb of grace o'Sundays.
You must wear your rue with a difference. There's a daisy. I would give you some violets, but they withered all when my father died.
An interesting thought, but this is fun! Look, Bones! This beauty much surpasses mine!
Sniff Sniff

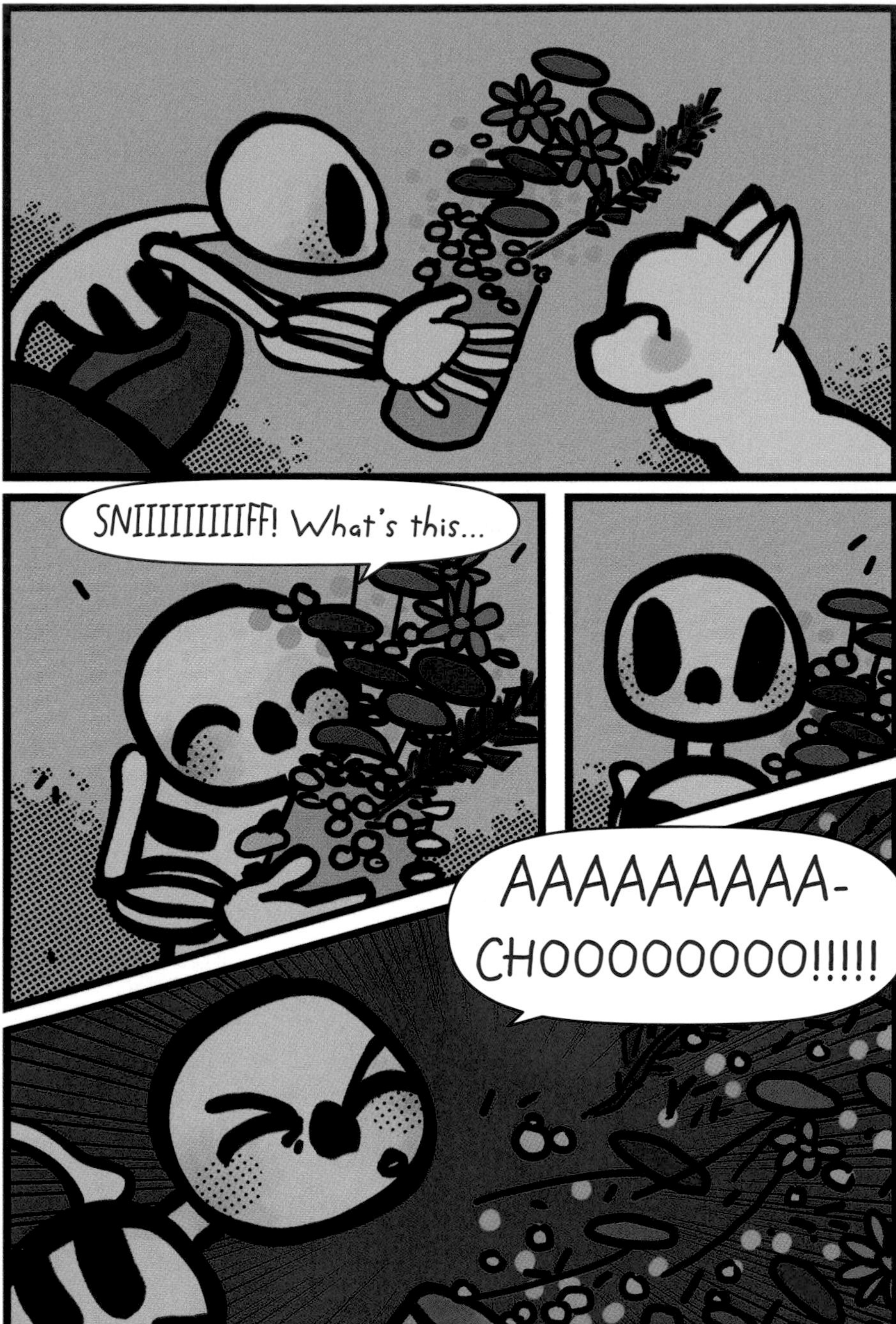
SNIIIIIIIIIFF! What's this...
AAAAAAAAA-
CHOOOOOOOO!!!!!

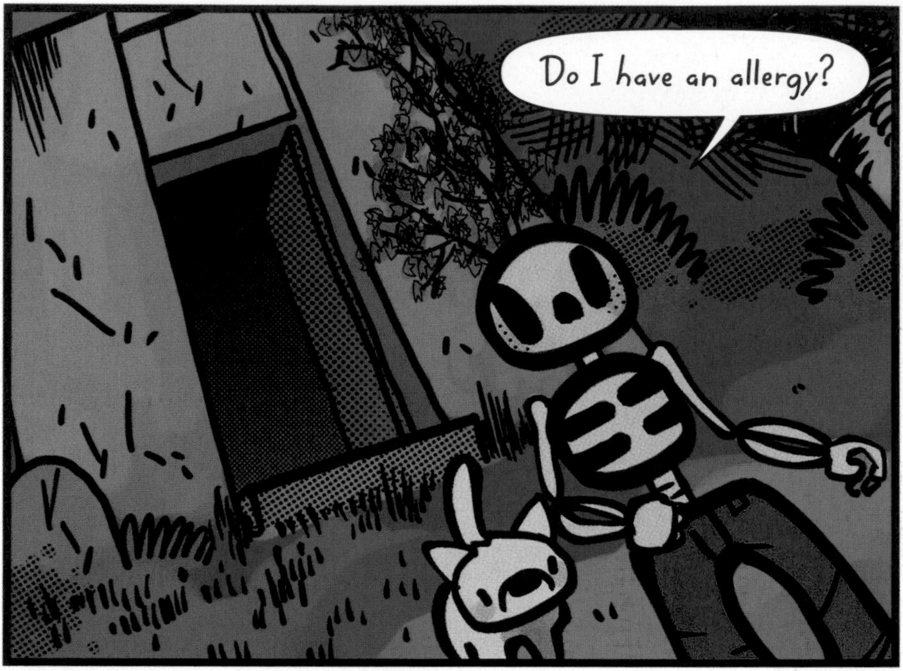
Do I have an allergy?

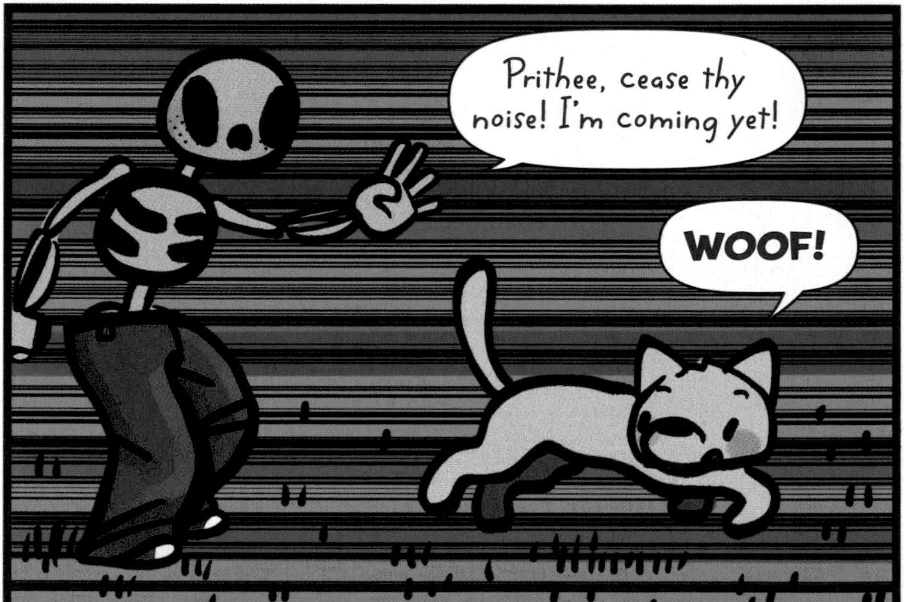
Prithee, cease thy noise! I'm coming yet!
WOOF!

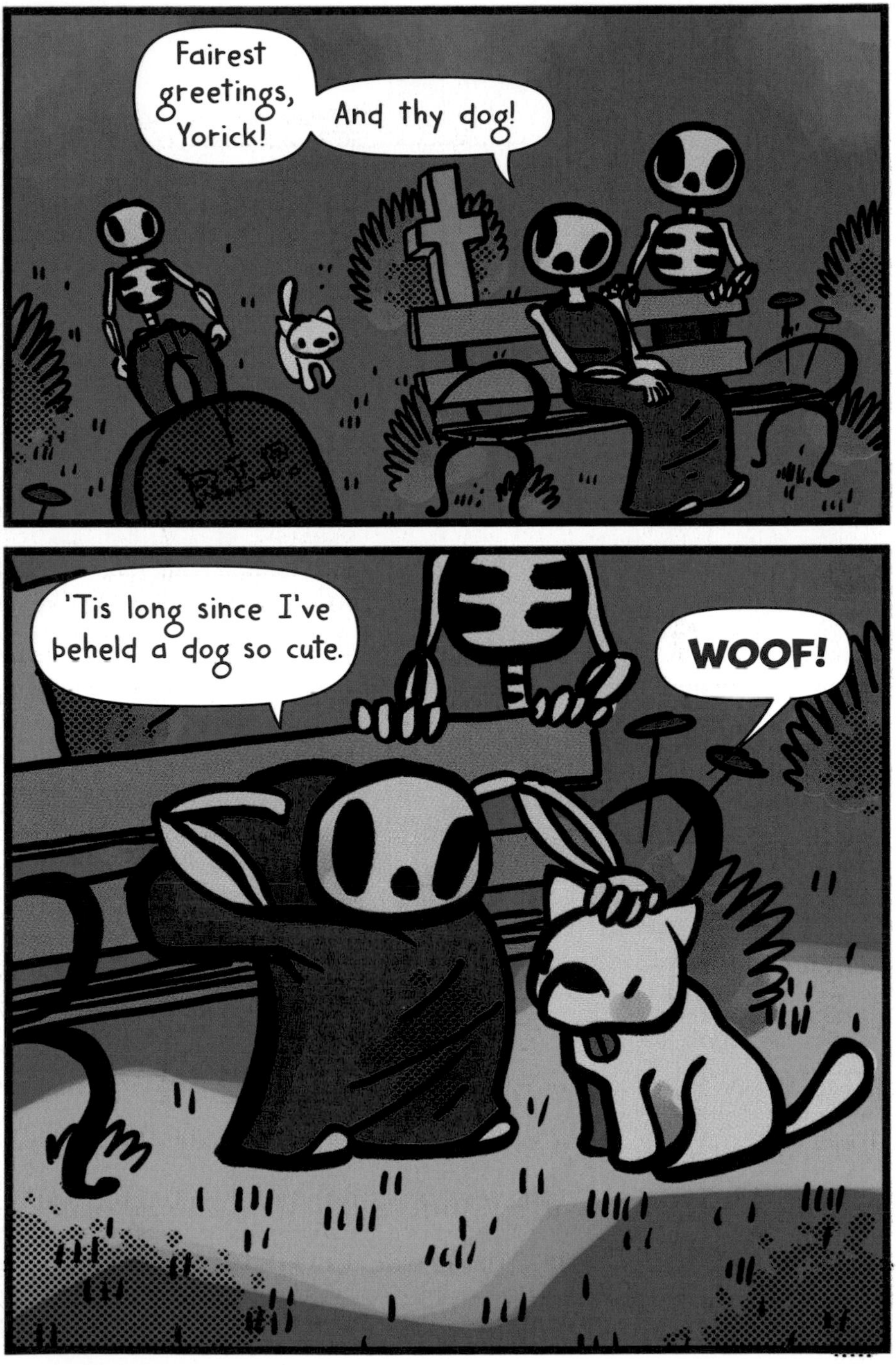
Fairest greetings, Yorick!
And thy dog!
'Tis long since I've beheld a dog so cute.
WOOF!

78

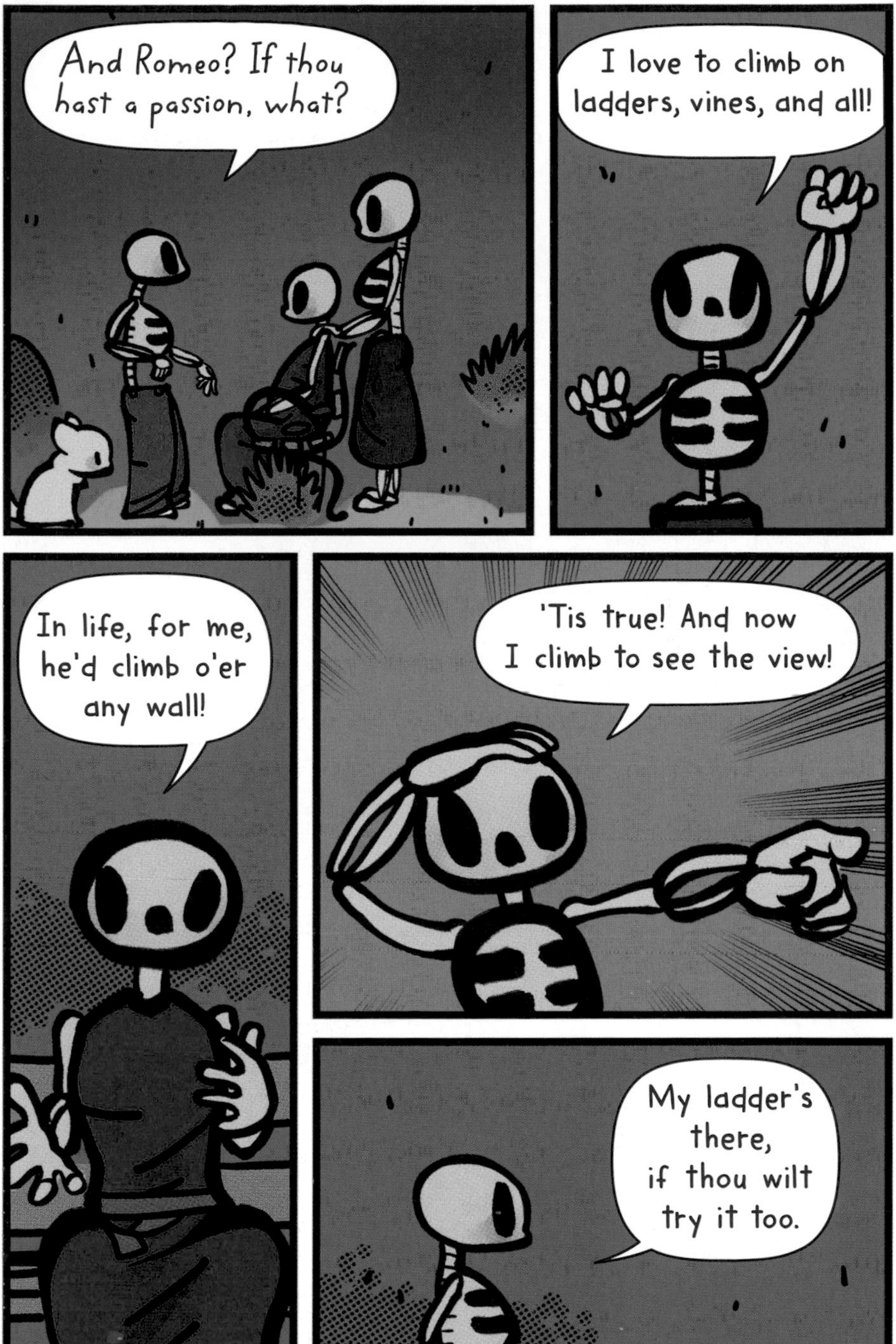
And Romeo? If thou hast a passion, what?
I love to climb on ladders, vines, and all!
In life, for me, he'd climb o'er any wall!
'Tis true! And now I climb to see the view!
My ladder's there, if thou wilt try it too.

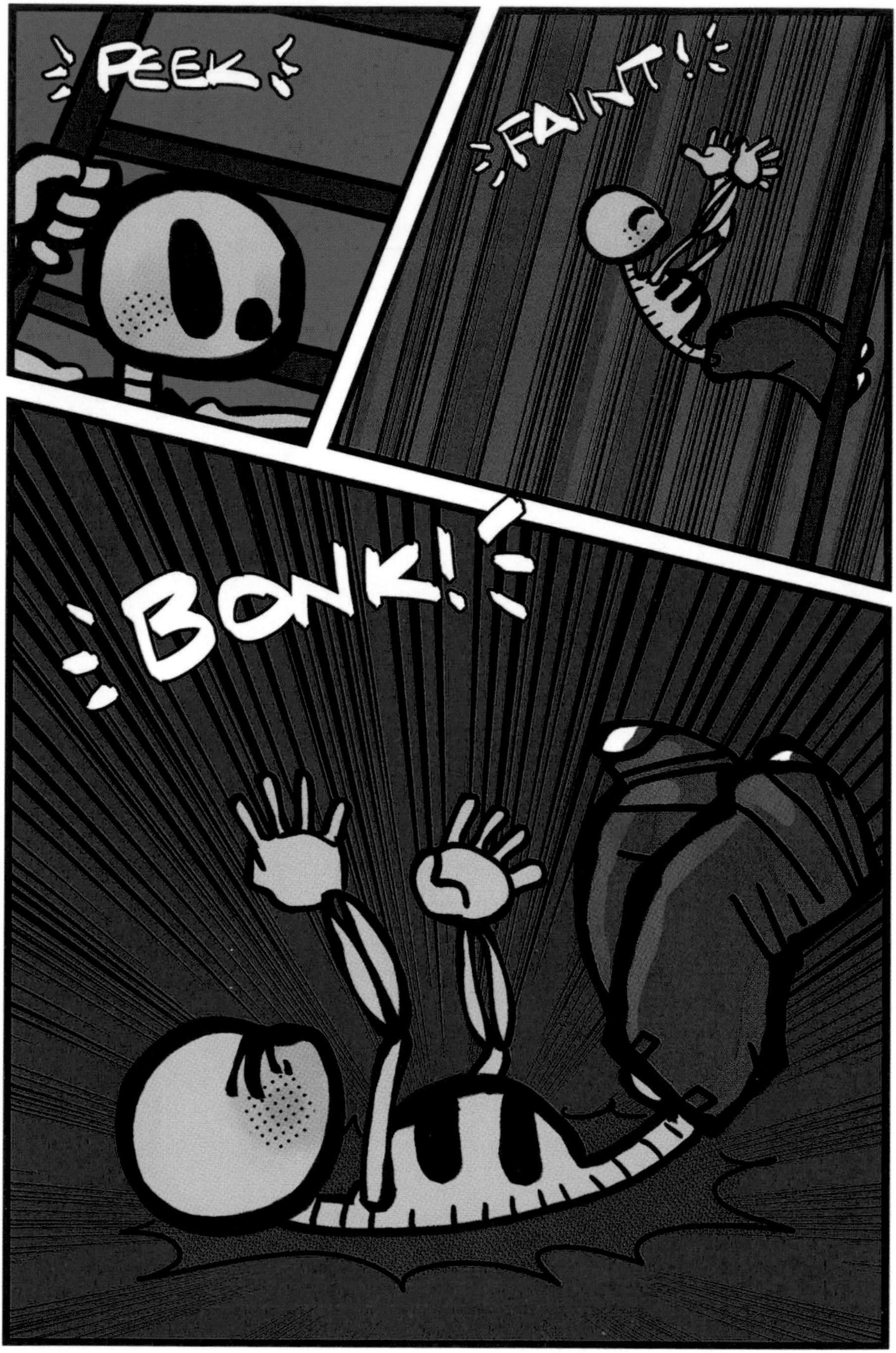
PEEK
FAINT!
BONK!

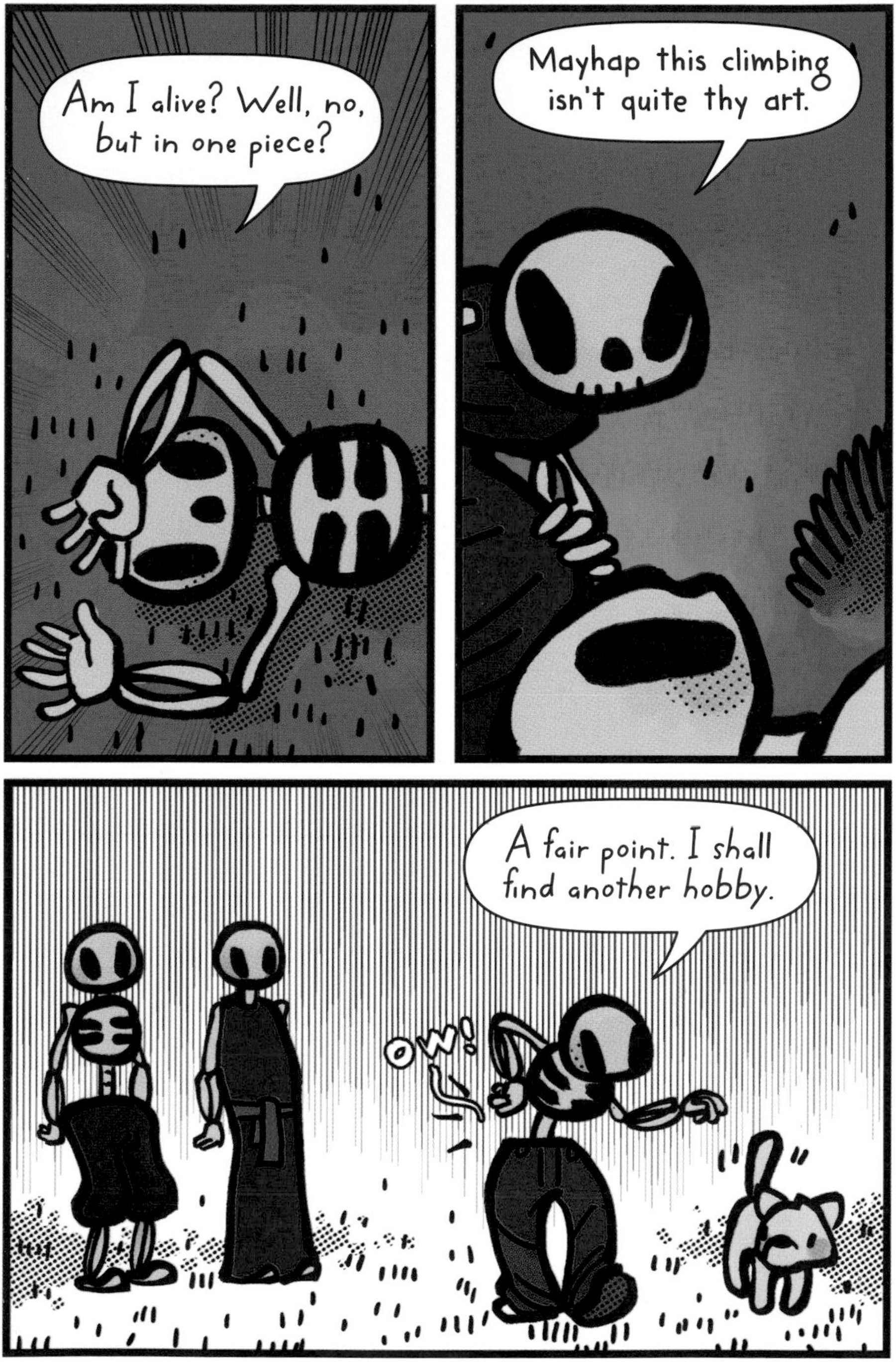
Am I alive? Well, no, but in one piece?
Mayhap this climbing isn't quite thy art.
A fair point. I shall find another hobby.
OW!

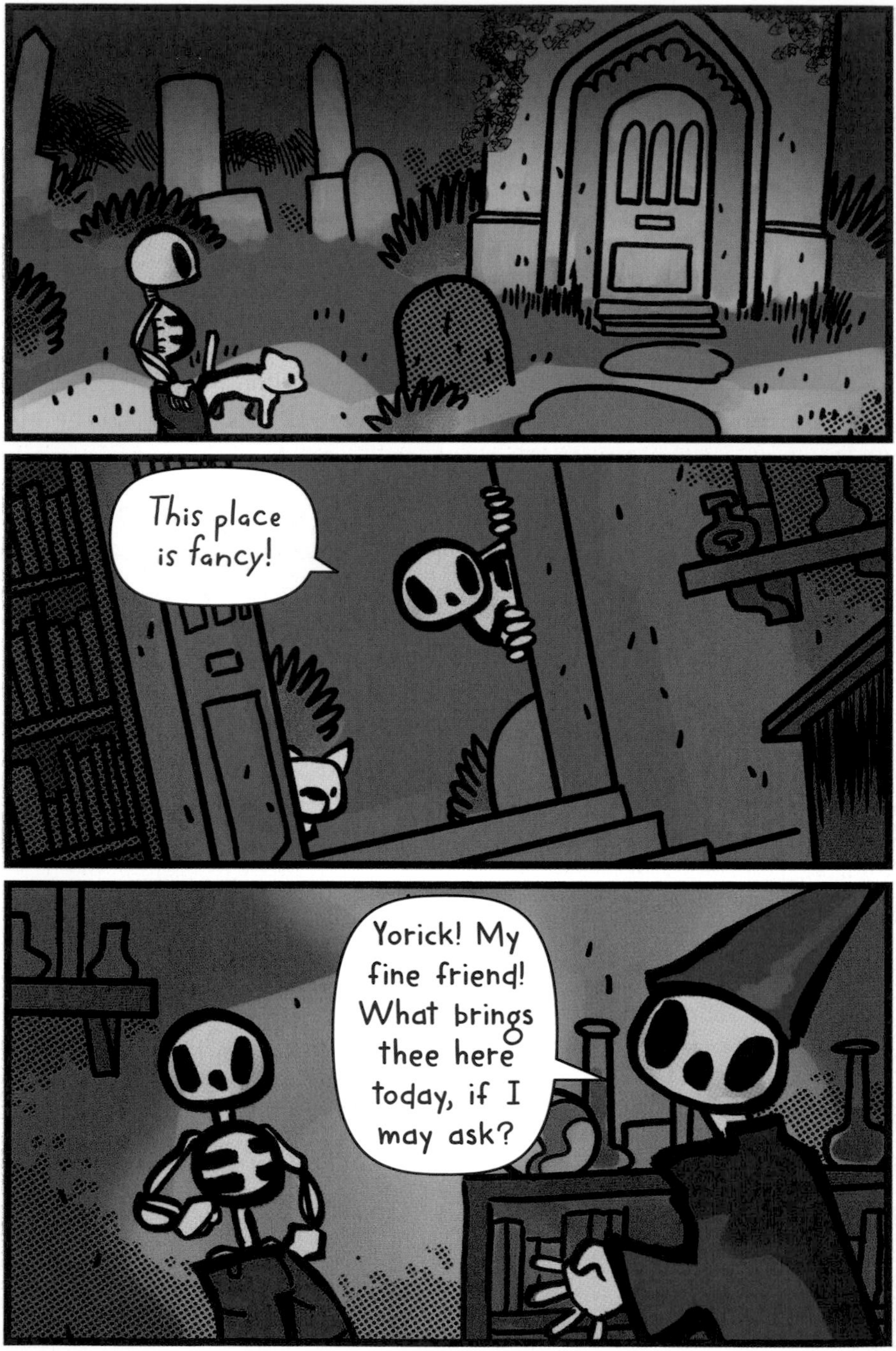
This place is fancy!
Yorick! My fine friend! What brings thee here today, if I may ask?

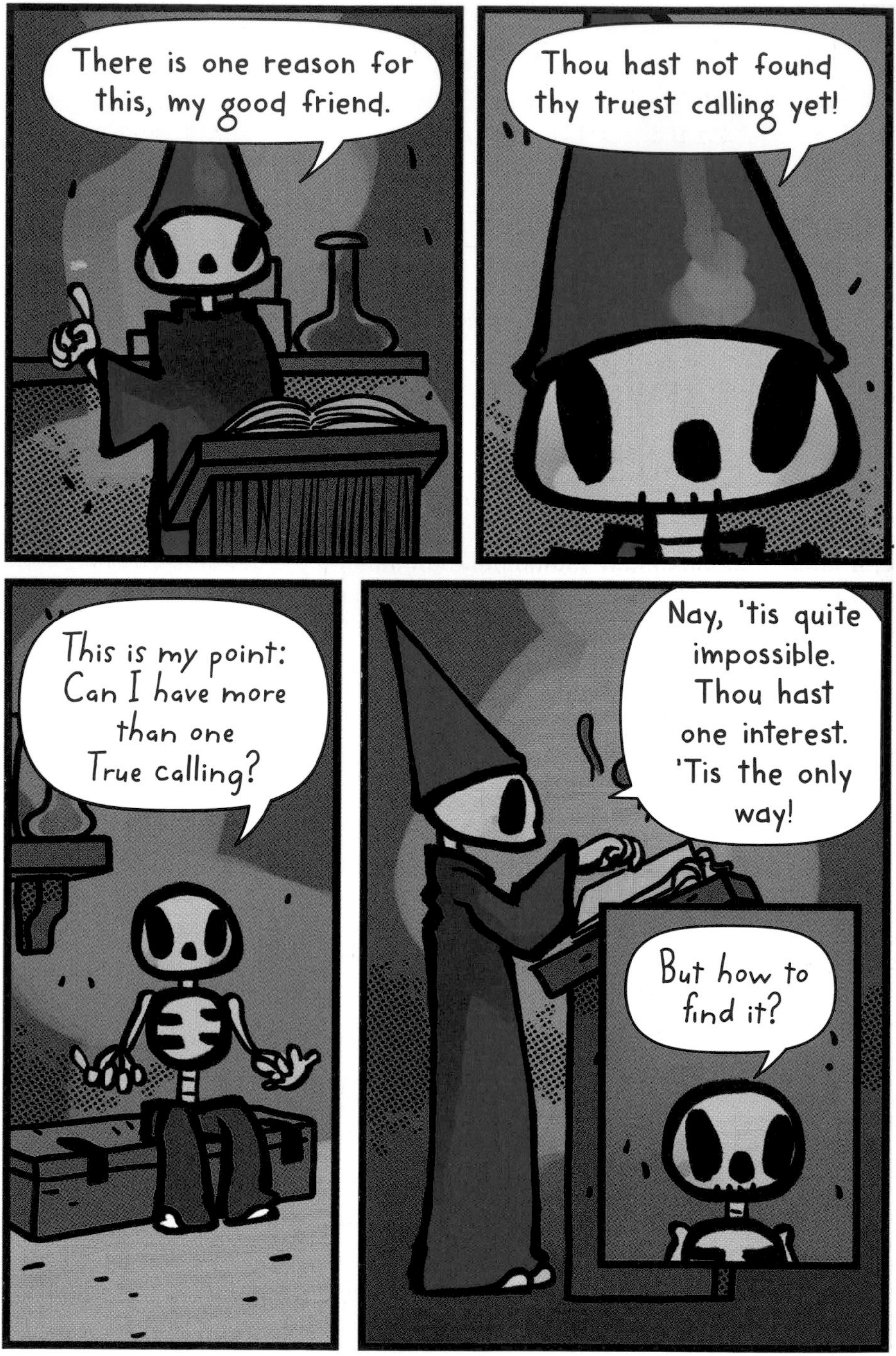
There is one reason for this, my good friend.
Thou hast not found thy truest calling yet!
This is my point: Can I have more than one True calling?
Nay, 'tis quite impossible. Thou hast one interest. 'Tis the only way!
But how to find it?

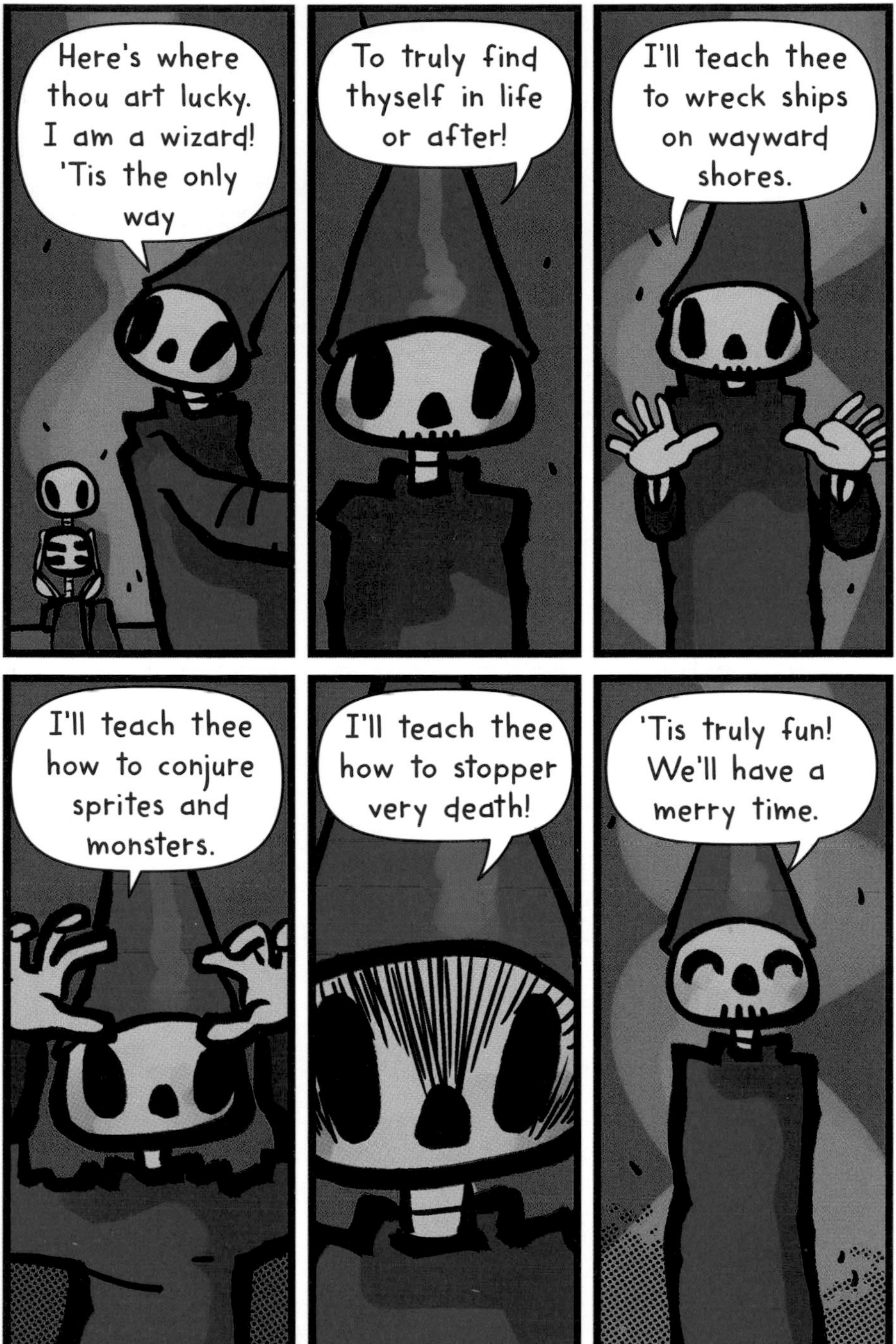
Here's where thou art lucky. I am a wizard! 'Tis the only way
To truly find thyself in life or after!
I'll teach thee to wreck ships on wayward shores.
I'll teach thee how to conjure sprites and monsters.
I'll teach thee how to stopper very death!
'Tis truly fun! We'll have a merry time.

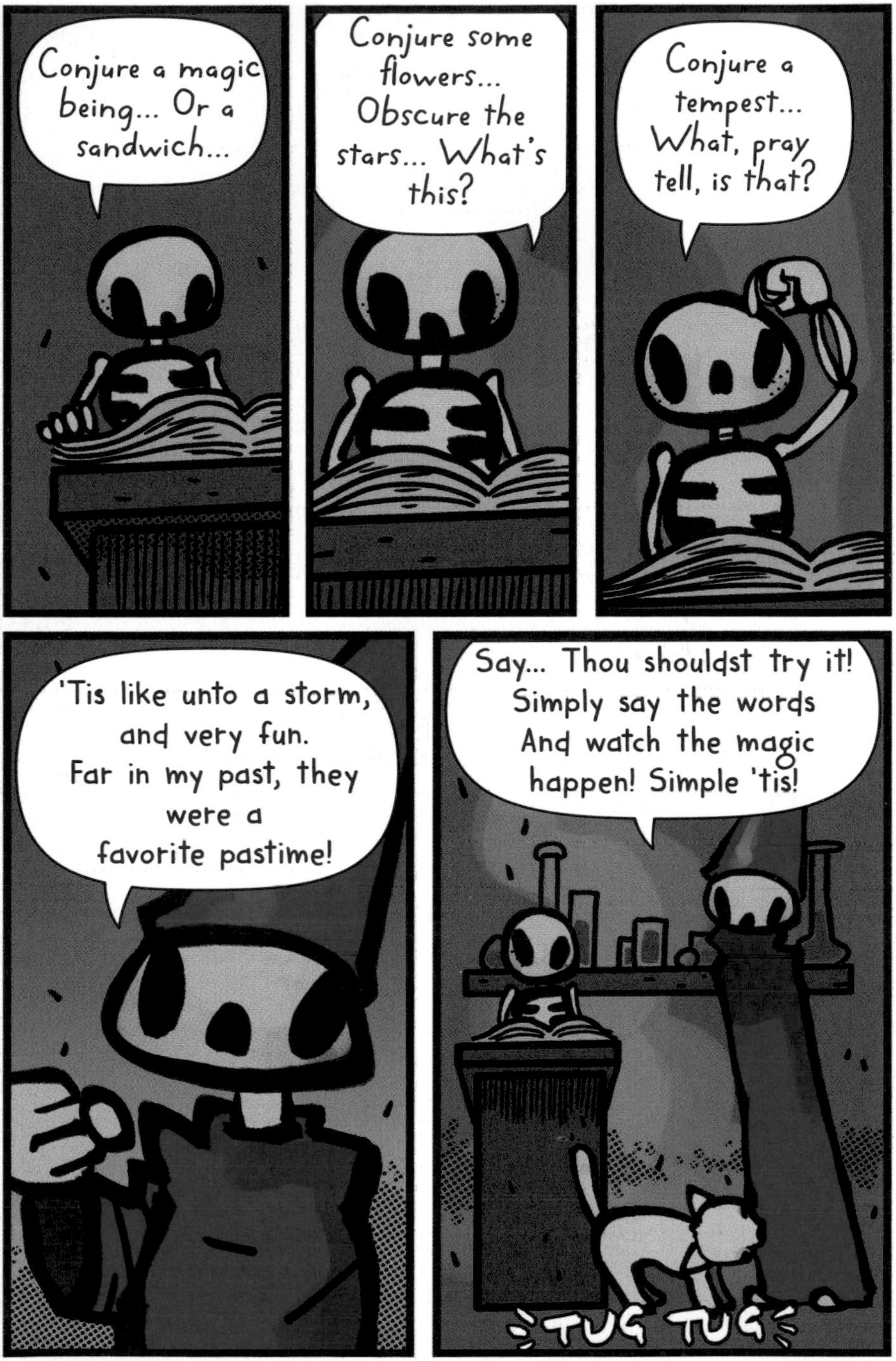
Conjure a magic being... Or a sandwich...
Conjure some flowers... Obscure the stars... What's this?
Conjure a tempest... What, pray tell, is that?
'Tis like unto a storm, and very fun. Far in my past, they were a favorite pastime!
Say... Thou shouldst try it! Simply say the words And watch the magic happen! Simple 'tis!
TUG TUG

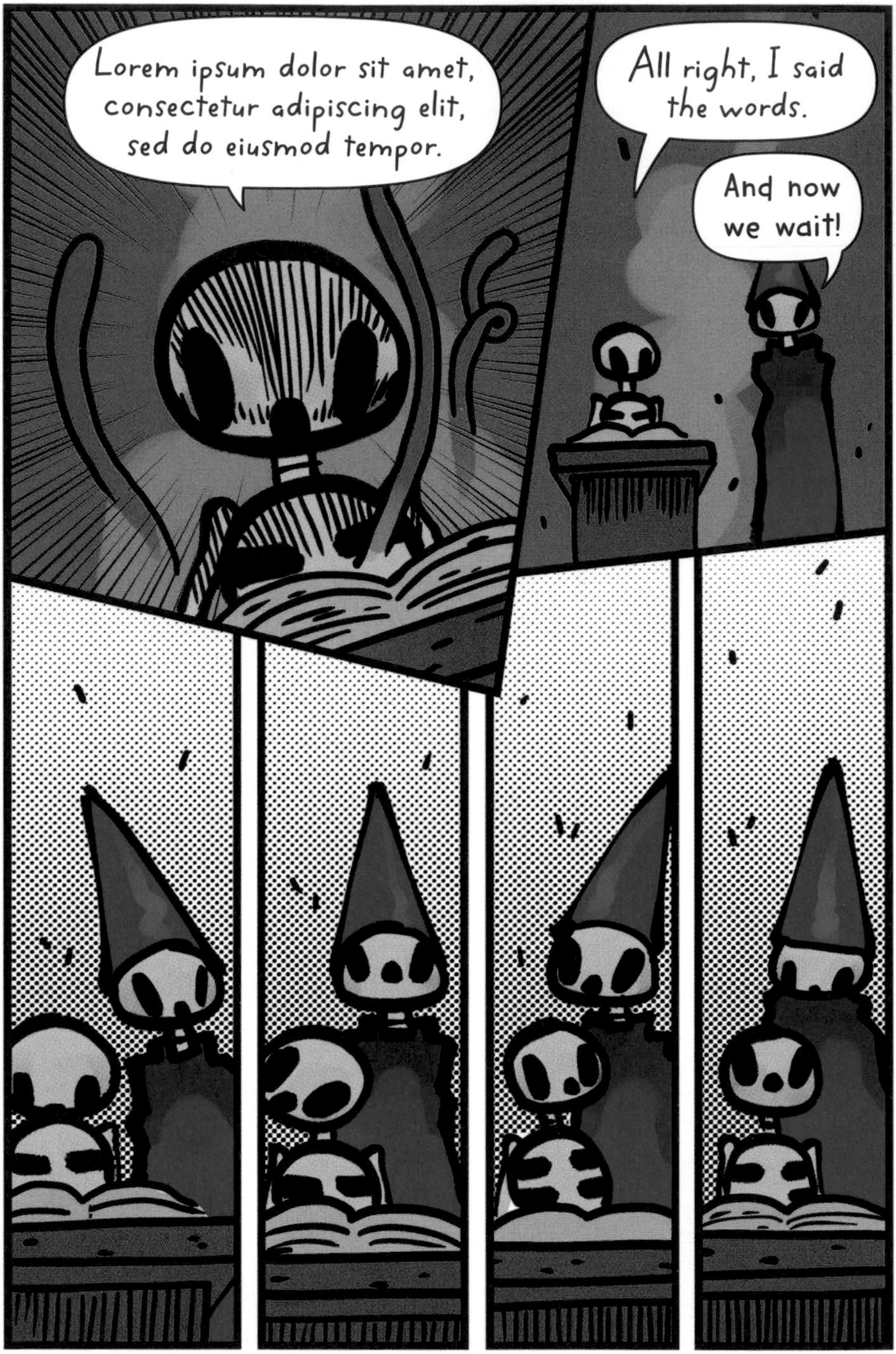
Lorem ipsum dolor sit amet, consectetur adipiscing elit, sed do eiusmod tempor.
All right, I said the words.
And now we wait!

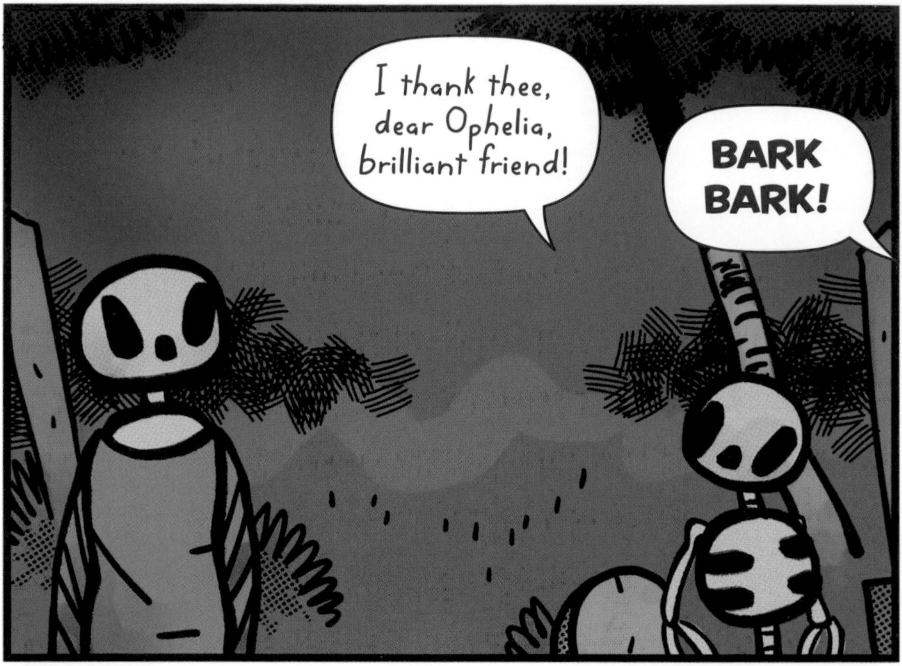
I thank thee, dear Ophelia, brilliant friend!
BARK BARK!

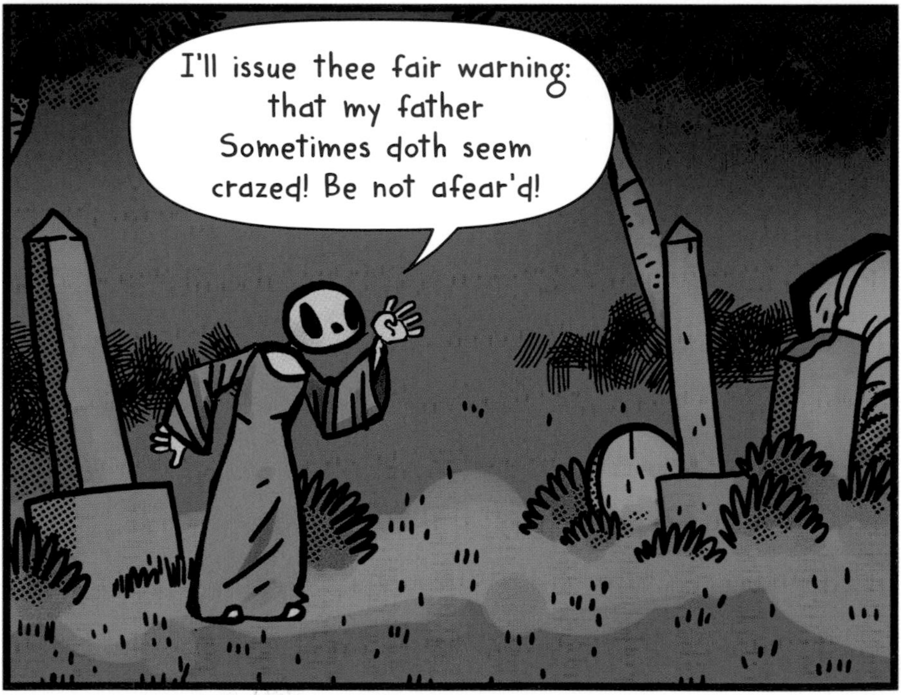
I'll issue thee fair warning: that my father Sometimes doth seem crazed! Be not afear'd!

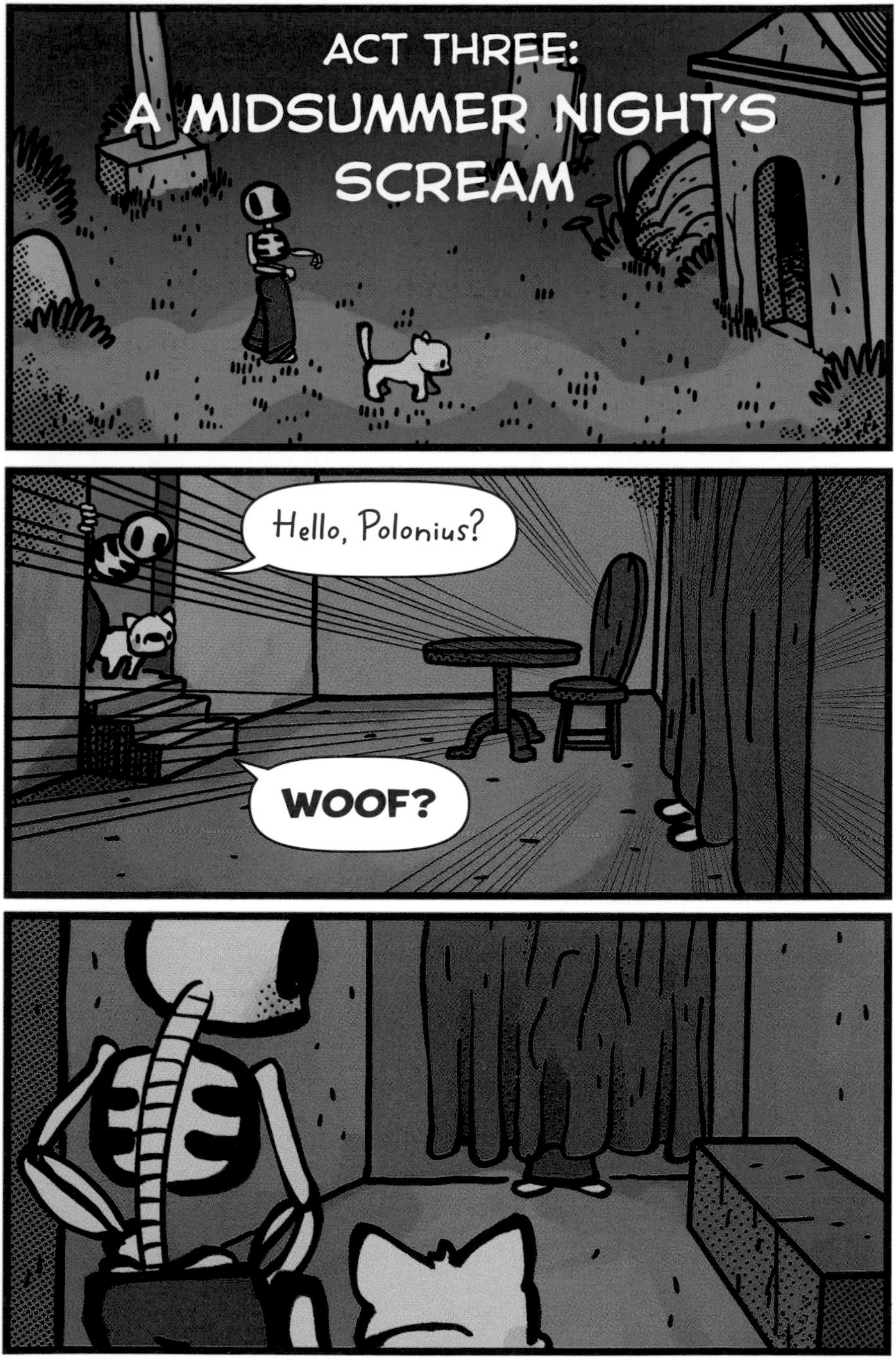
ACT THREE:
A MIDSUMMER NIGHT'S SCREAM
Hello, Polonius?
WOOF?

96

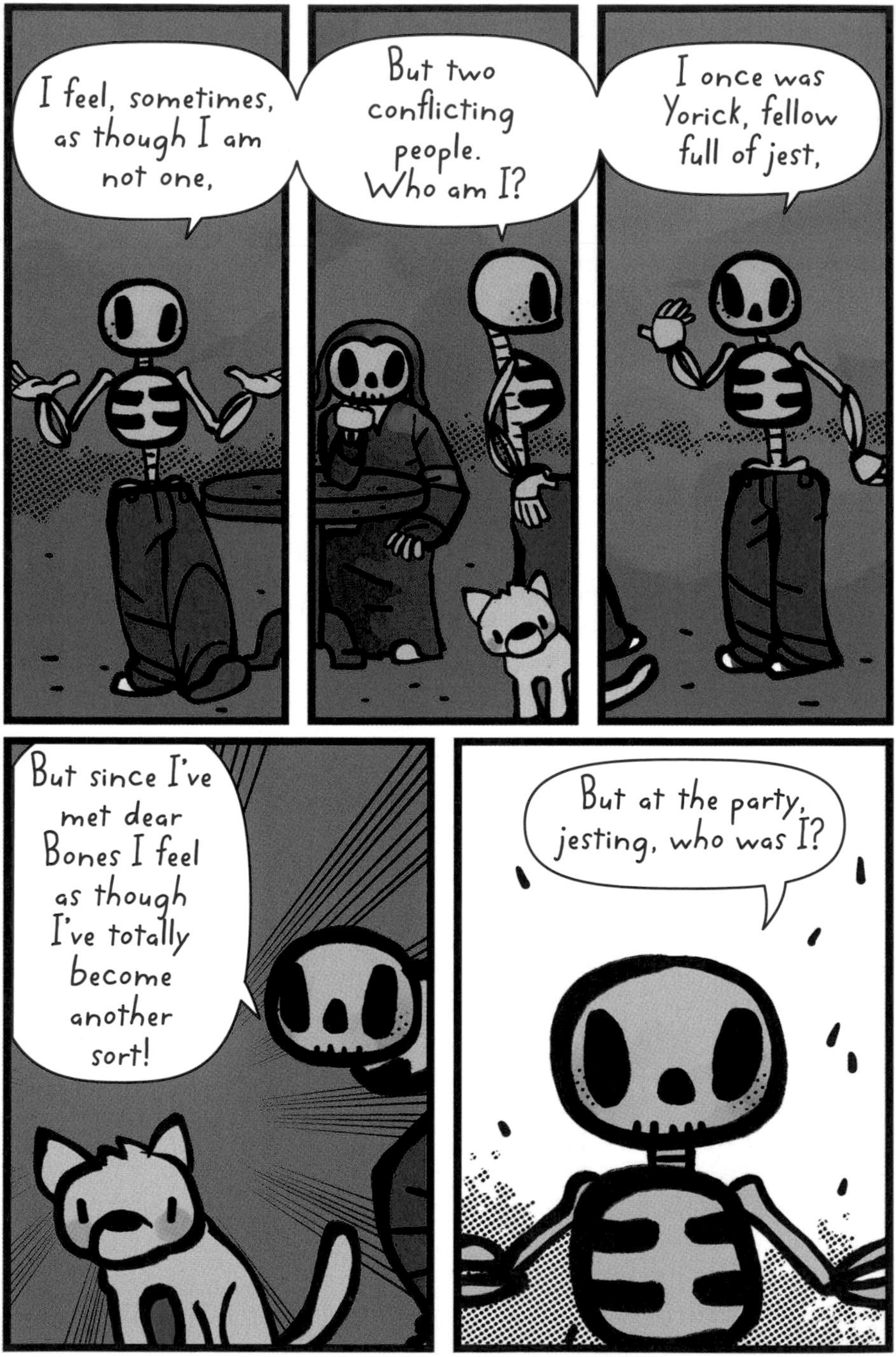
I feel, sometimes, as though I am not one,
But two conflicting people. Who am I?
I once was Yorick, fellow full of jest,
But since I've met dear Bones I feel as though I've totally become another sort!
But at the party, jesting, who was I?

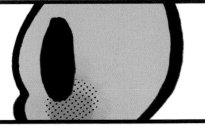

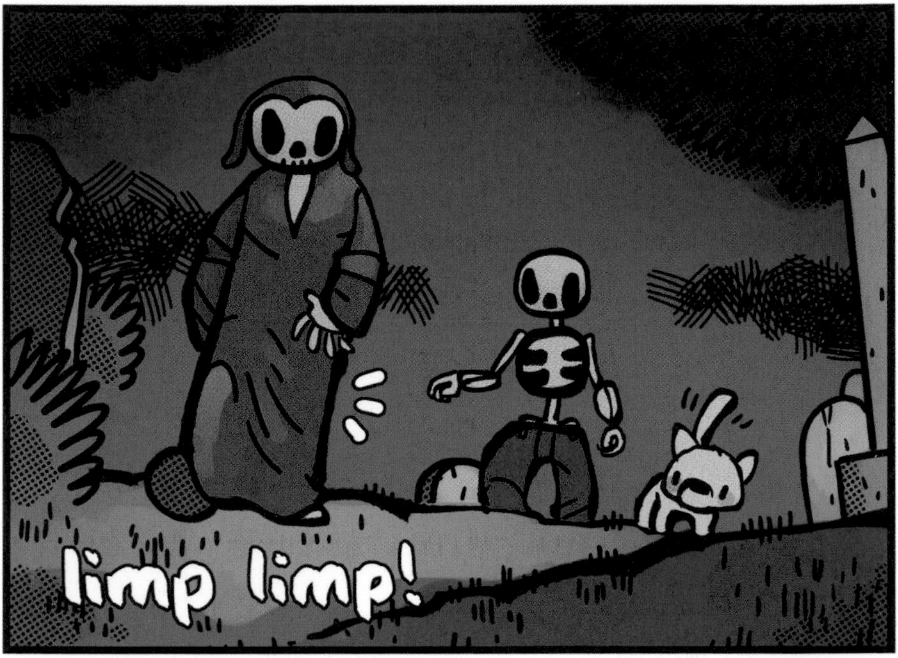
limp limp!

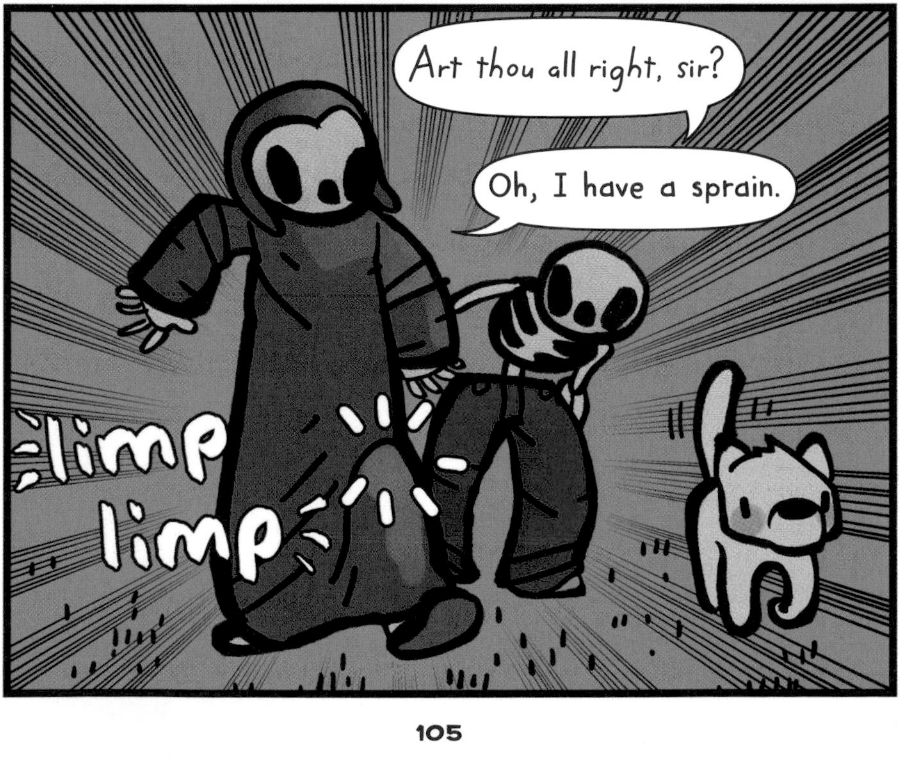
Art thou all right, sir?
Oh, I have a sprain.
limp
limp

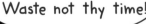

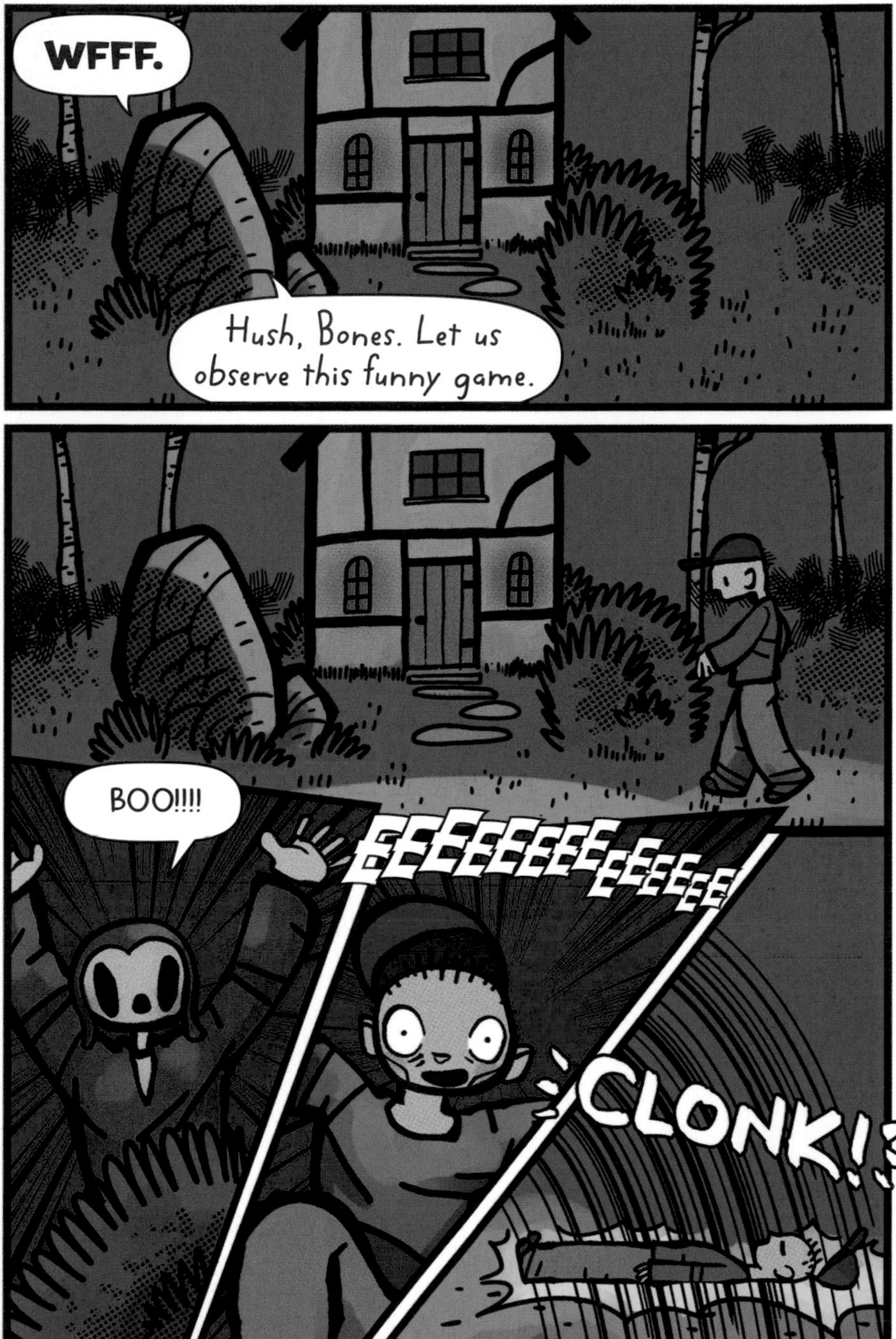
WFFF.
Hush, Bones. Let us observe this funny game.
BOO!!!!
EEEEEEEEEEEEEEE
CLONK!

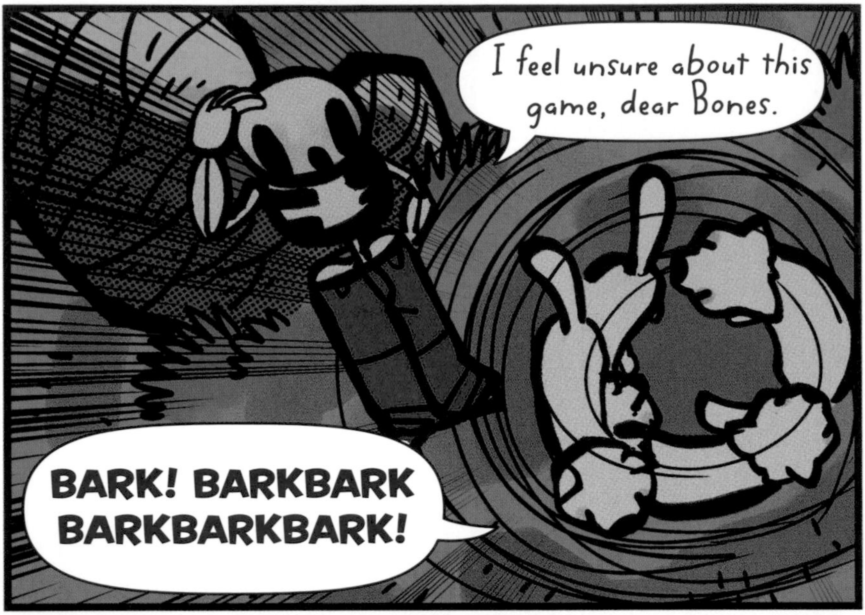
I feel unsure about this game, dear Bones.
BARK! BARKBARK BARKBARKBARK!

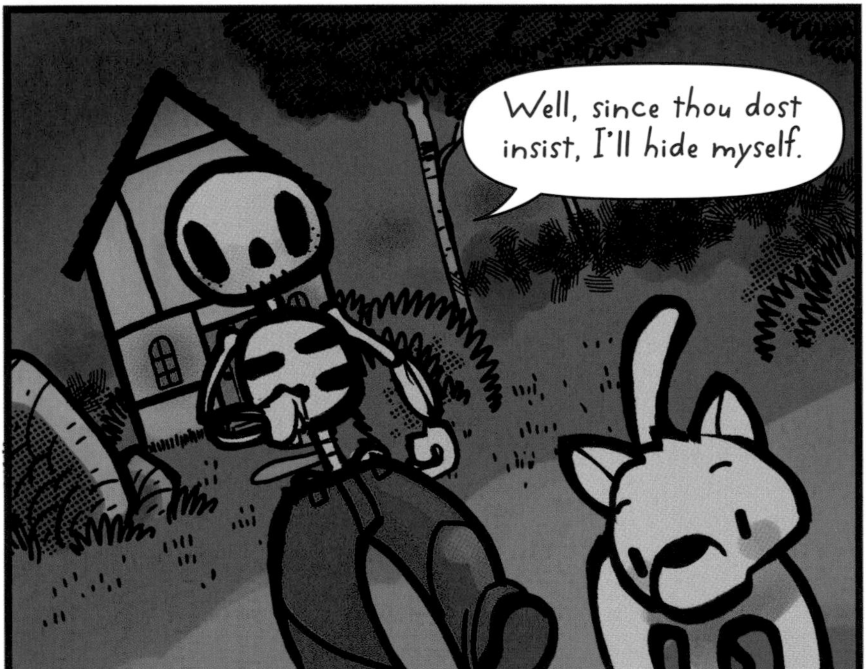
Well, since thou dost insist, I'll hide myself.

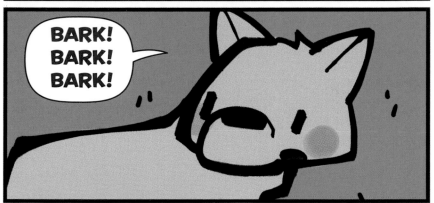

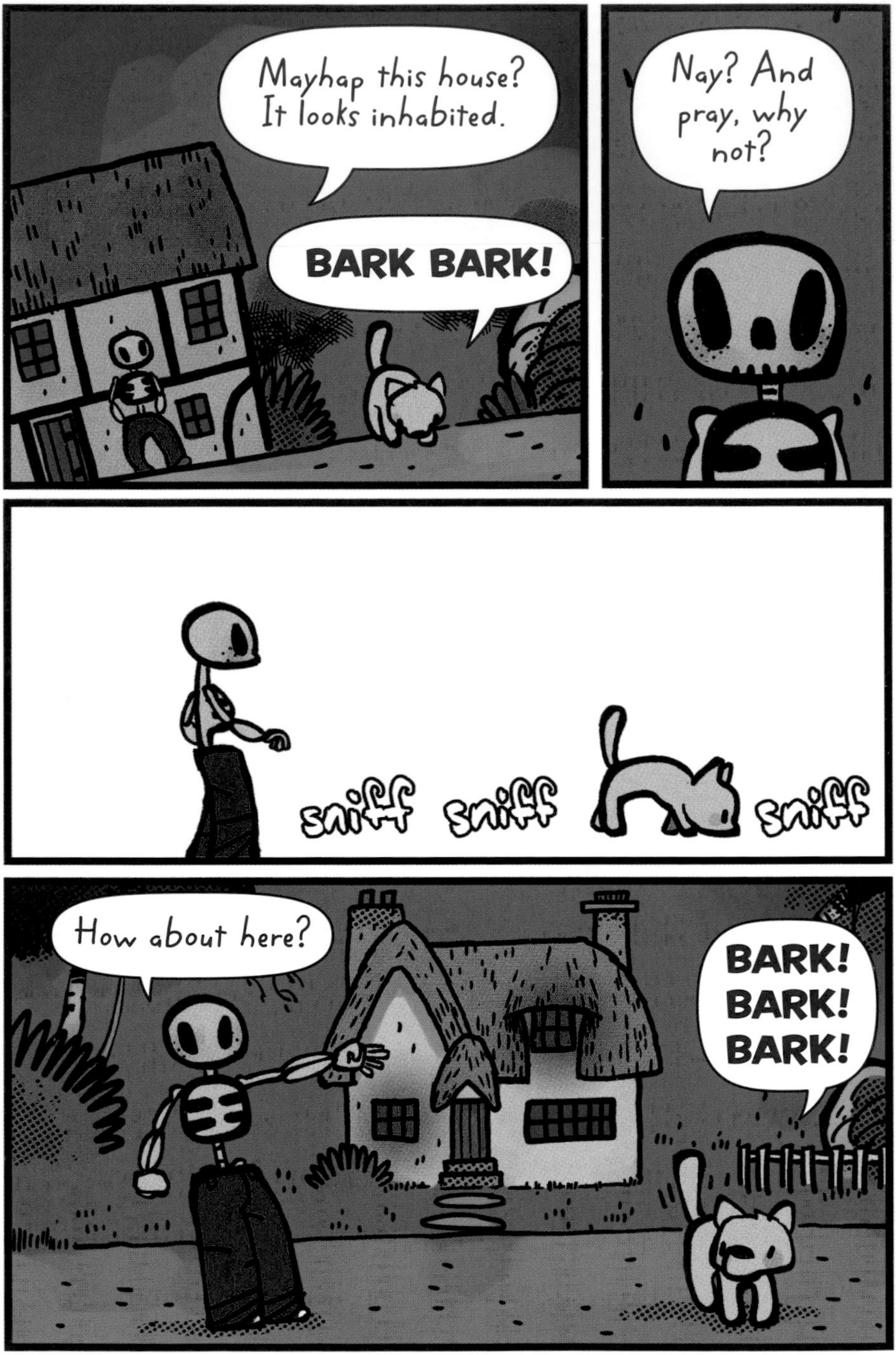
Mayhap this house? It looks inhabited.
BARK BARK!
Nay? And pray, why not?
sniff sniff
sniff
How about here?
BARK! BARK! BARK!

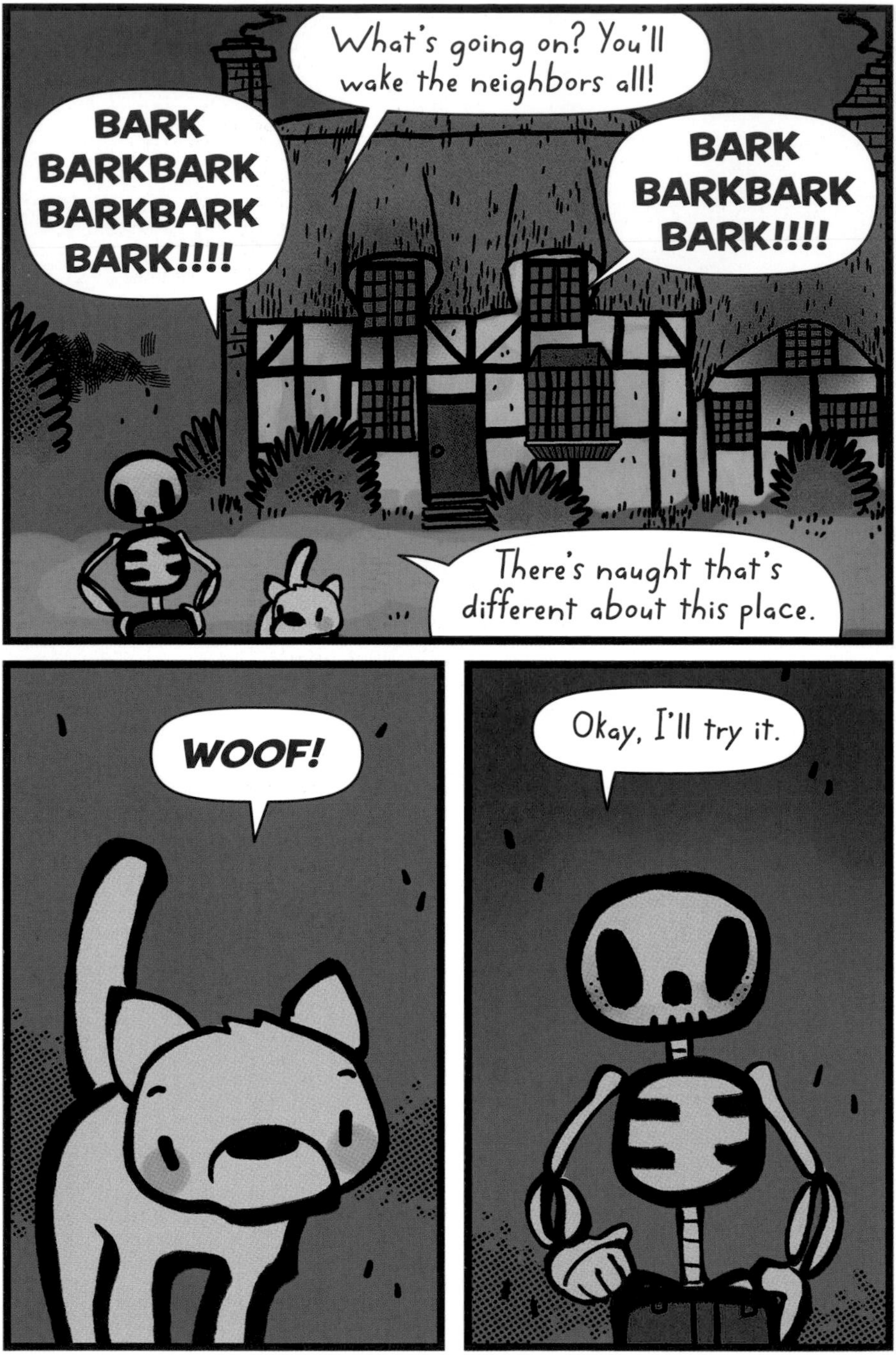
BARK BARKBARK BARKBARK BARK!!!!
What's going on? You'll wake the neighbors all!
BARK BARKBARK BARK!!!!
There's naught that's different about this place.
WOOF!
Okay, I'll try it.

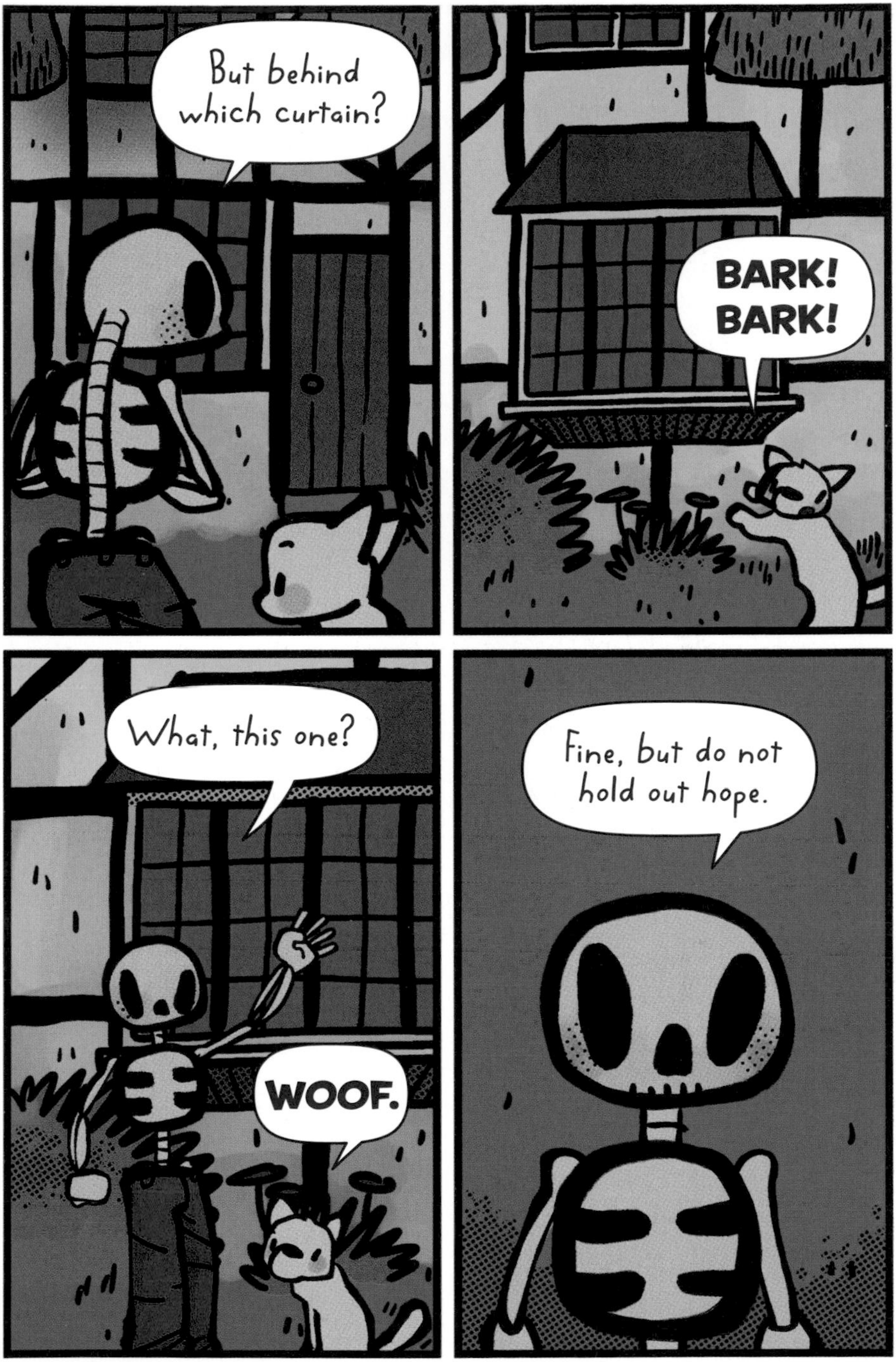

But behind which curtain?
BARK! BARK!
What, this one?
WOOF.
Fine, but do not hold out hope.

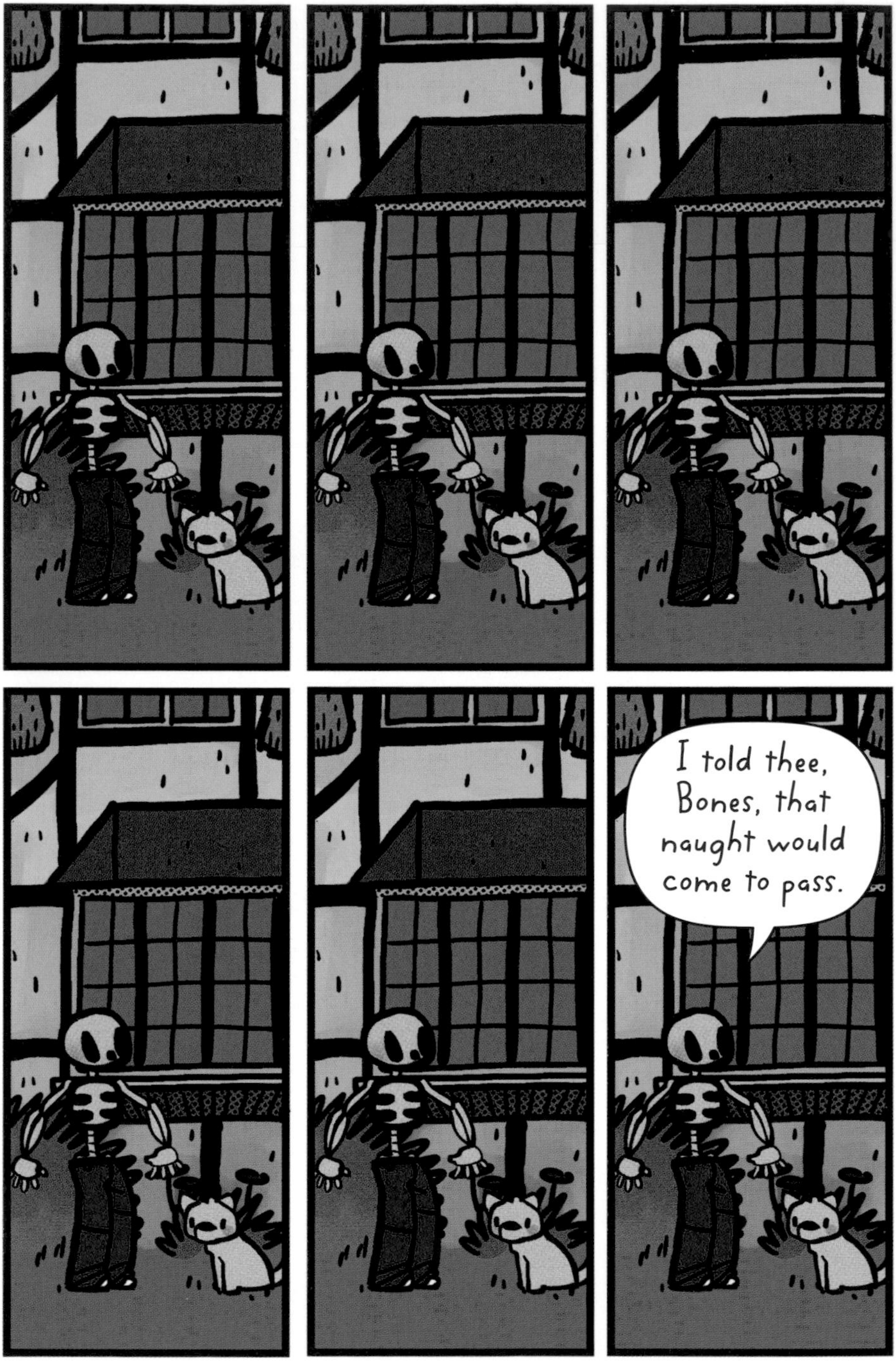
I told thee, Bones, that naught would come to pass.

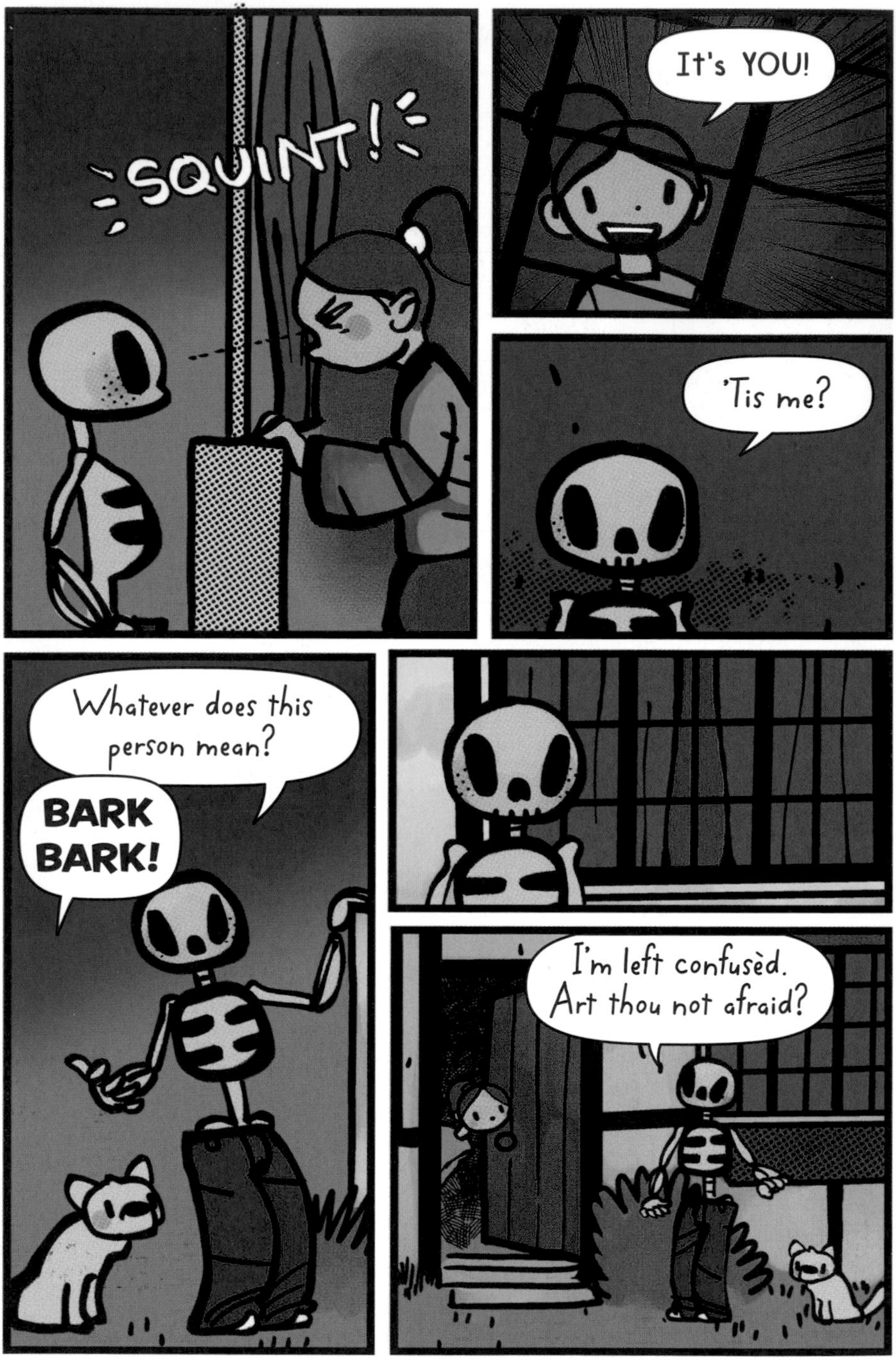
SQUINT!
It's YOU!
'Tis me?
Whatever does this person mean?
BARK BARK!
I'm left confusèd. Art thou not afraid?

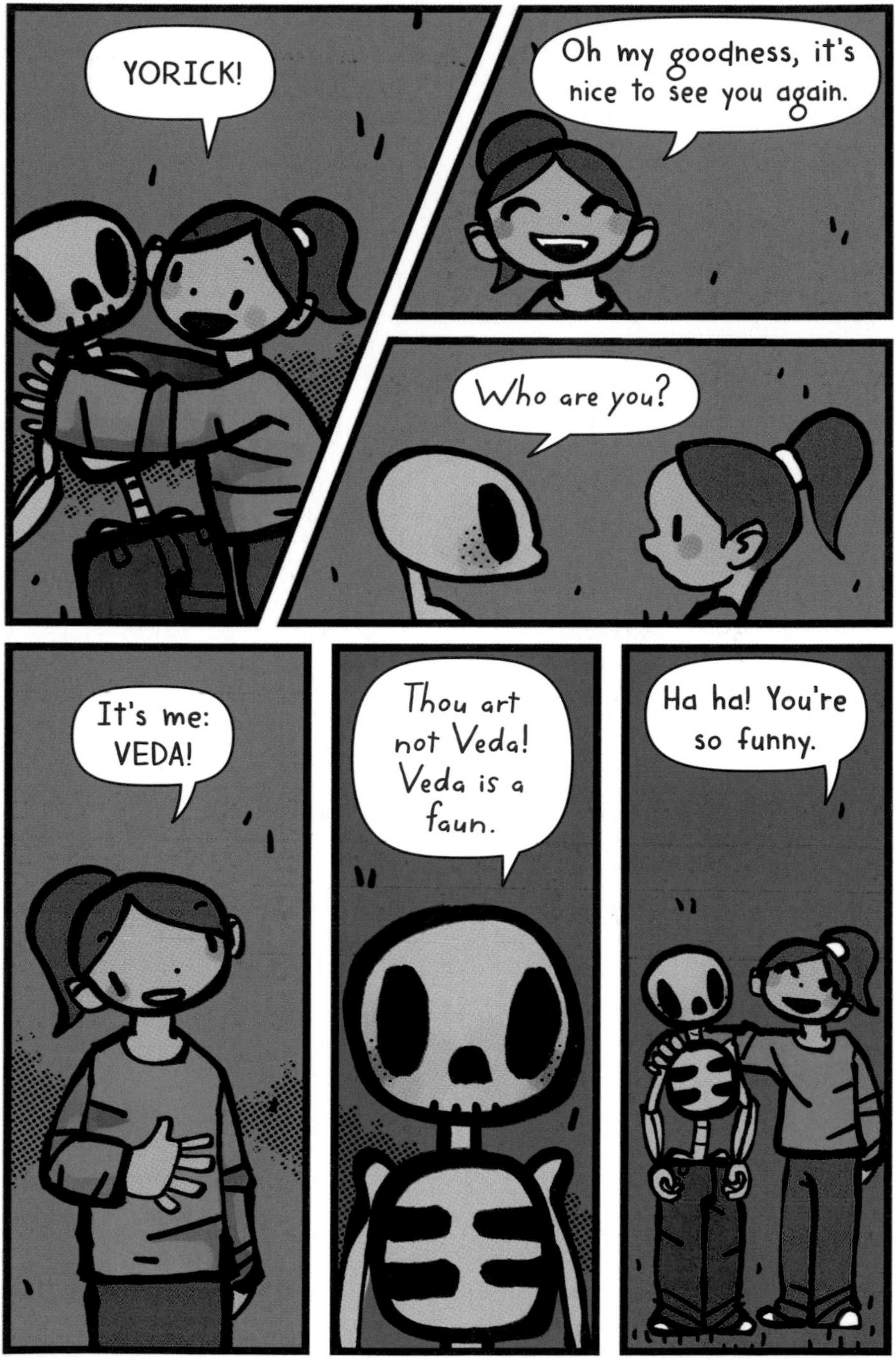
YORICK!
Oh my goodness, it's nice to see you again.
Who are you?
It's me: VEDA!
Thou art not Veda! Veda is a faun.
Ha ha! You're so funny.

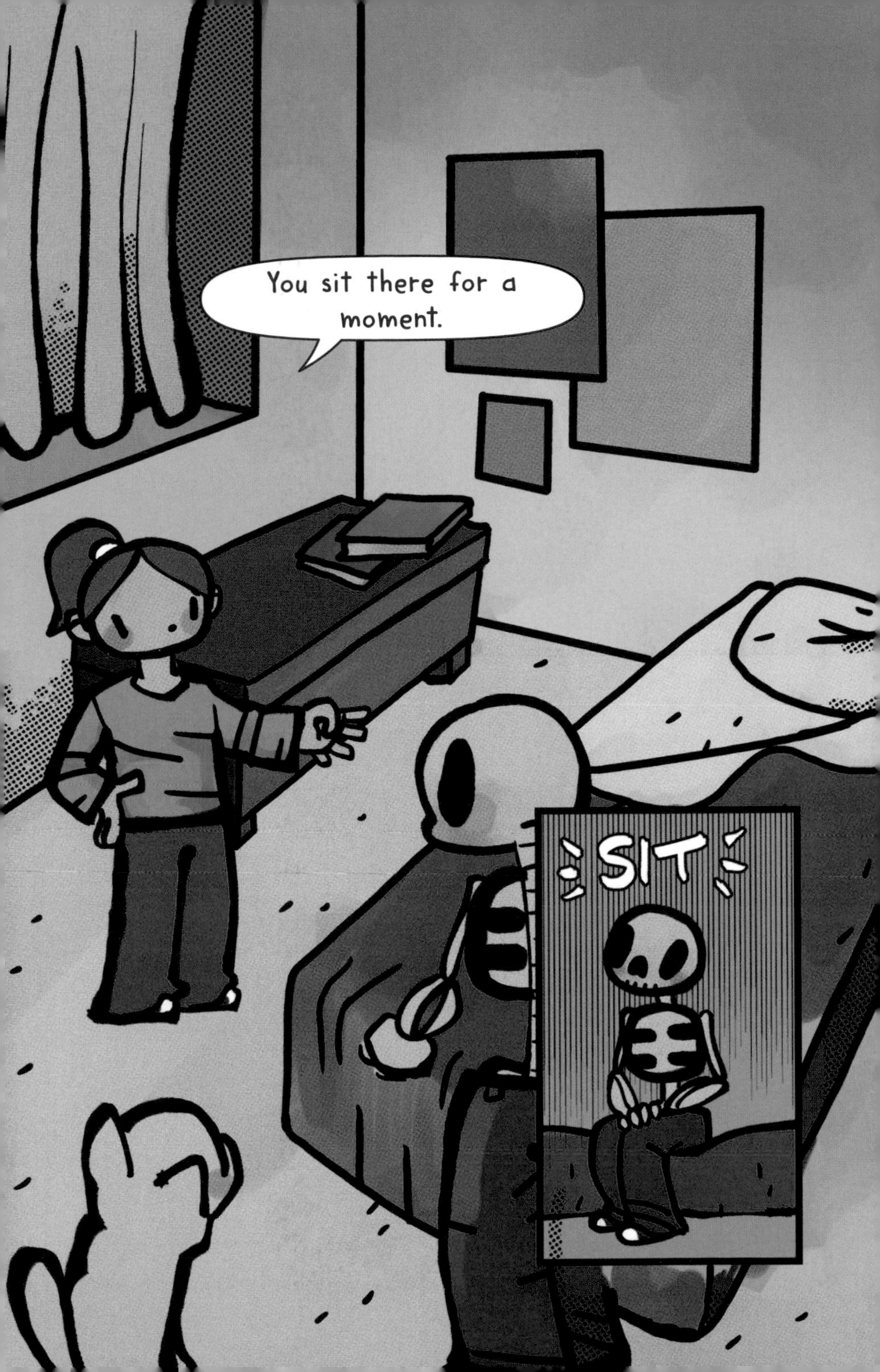
You sit there for a moment.
SIT

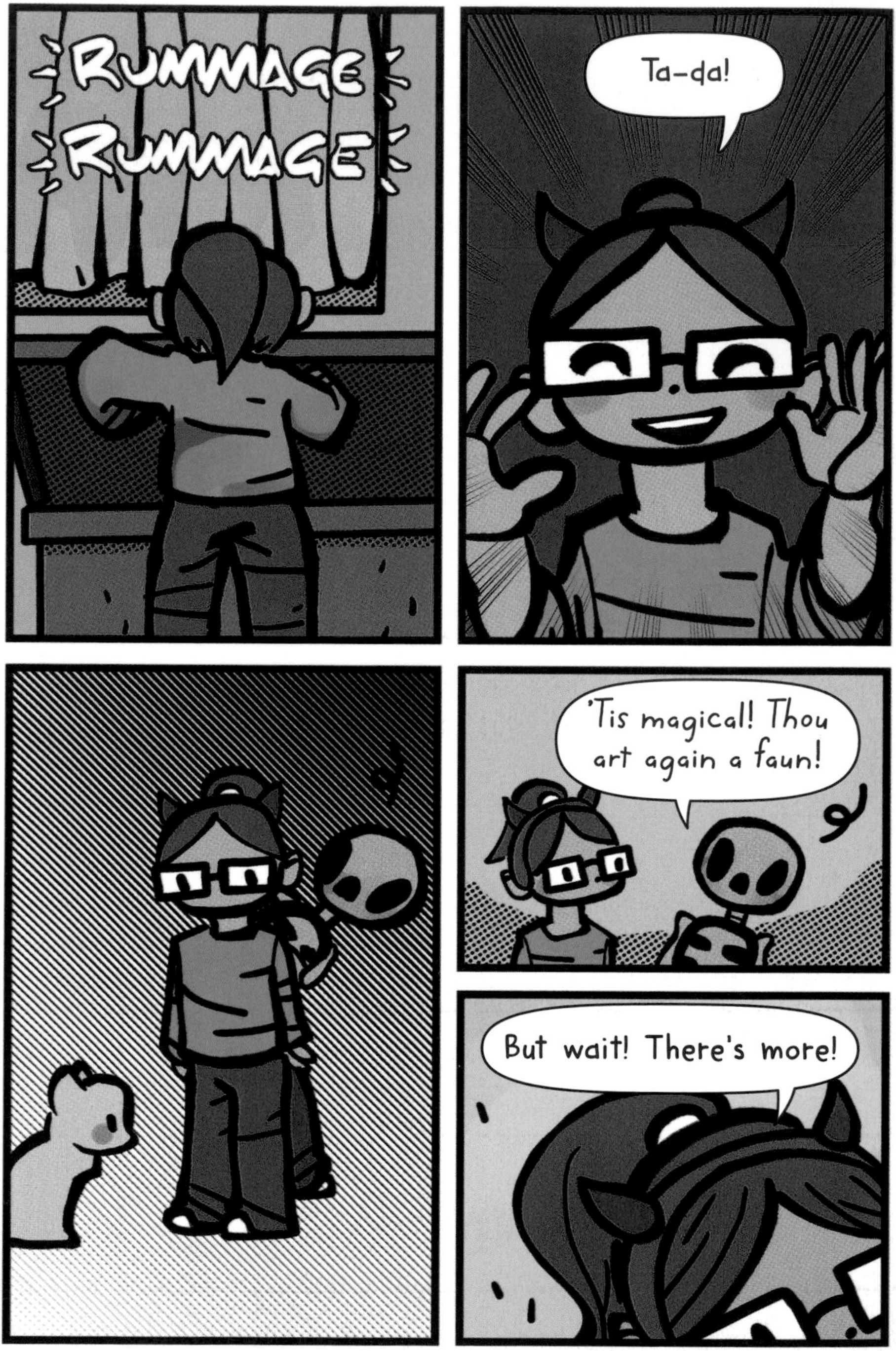
RUMMAGE
RUMMAGE
Ta-da!
'Tis magical! Thou art again a faun!
But wait! There's more!

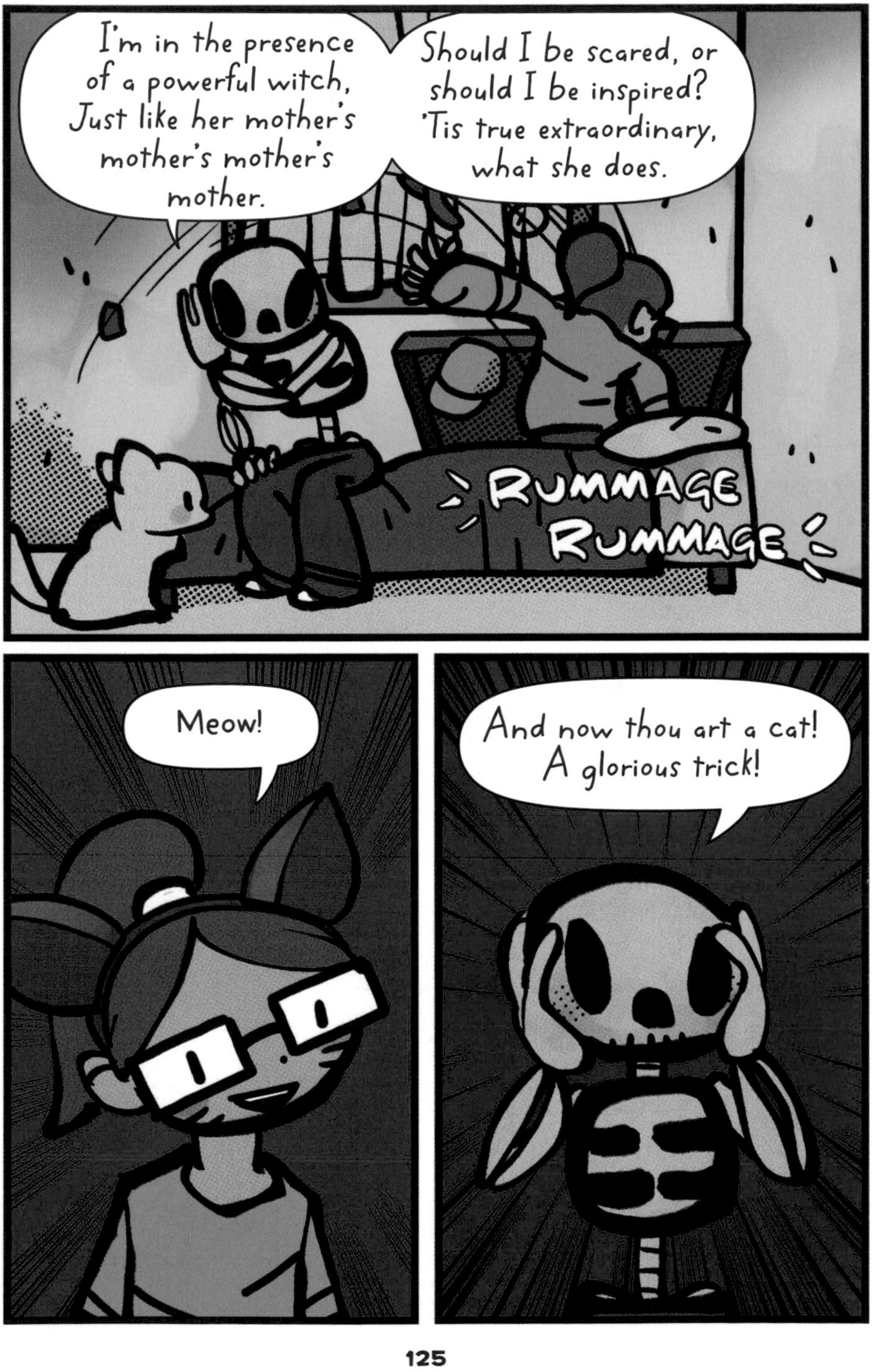

I'm in the presence of a powerful witch, Just like her mother's mother's mother's mother.
Should I be scared, or should I be inspired? 'Tis true extraordinary, what she does.
RUMMAGE RUMMAGE
Meow!
And now thou art a cat! A glorious trick!

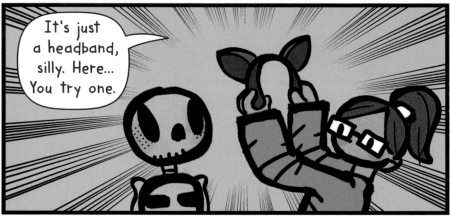

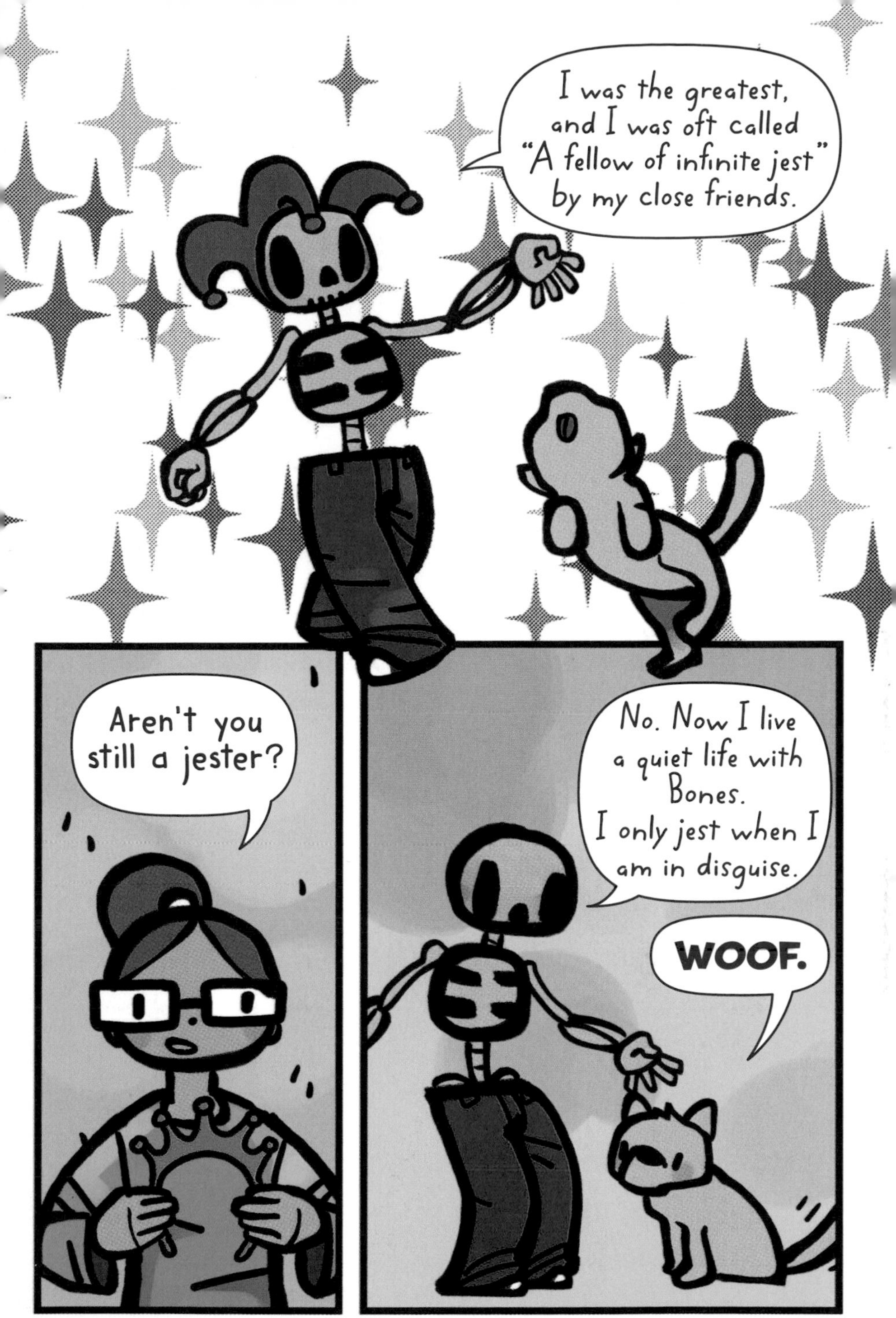
I was the greatest, and I was oft called "A fellow of infinite jest" by my close friends.
Aren't you still a jester?
No. Now I live a quiet life with Bones. I only jest when I am in disguise.
WOOF.

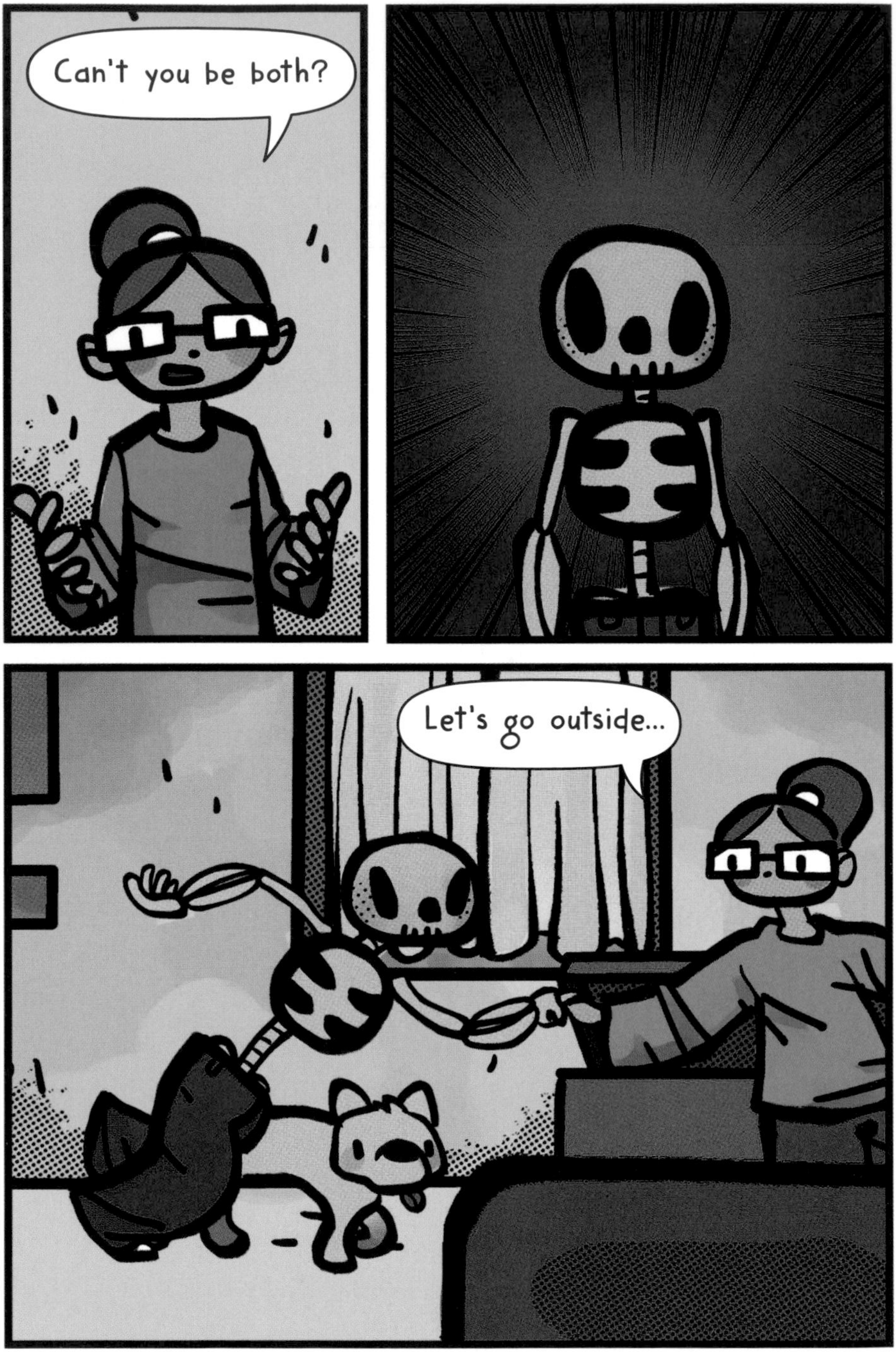
Can't you be both?
Let's go outside...

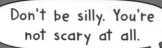
Don't be silly. You're not scary at all.

Alas! 'Tis kind of thee, but hast thou not Beheld my face, that very sight of death?

Don't be silly. I may have terrible eyesight, but that doesn't mean I can't see you.

I can see you just fine. And I like what I see!

Dost thou recall what once I said to thee— How I do hide a terrifying truth?

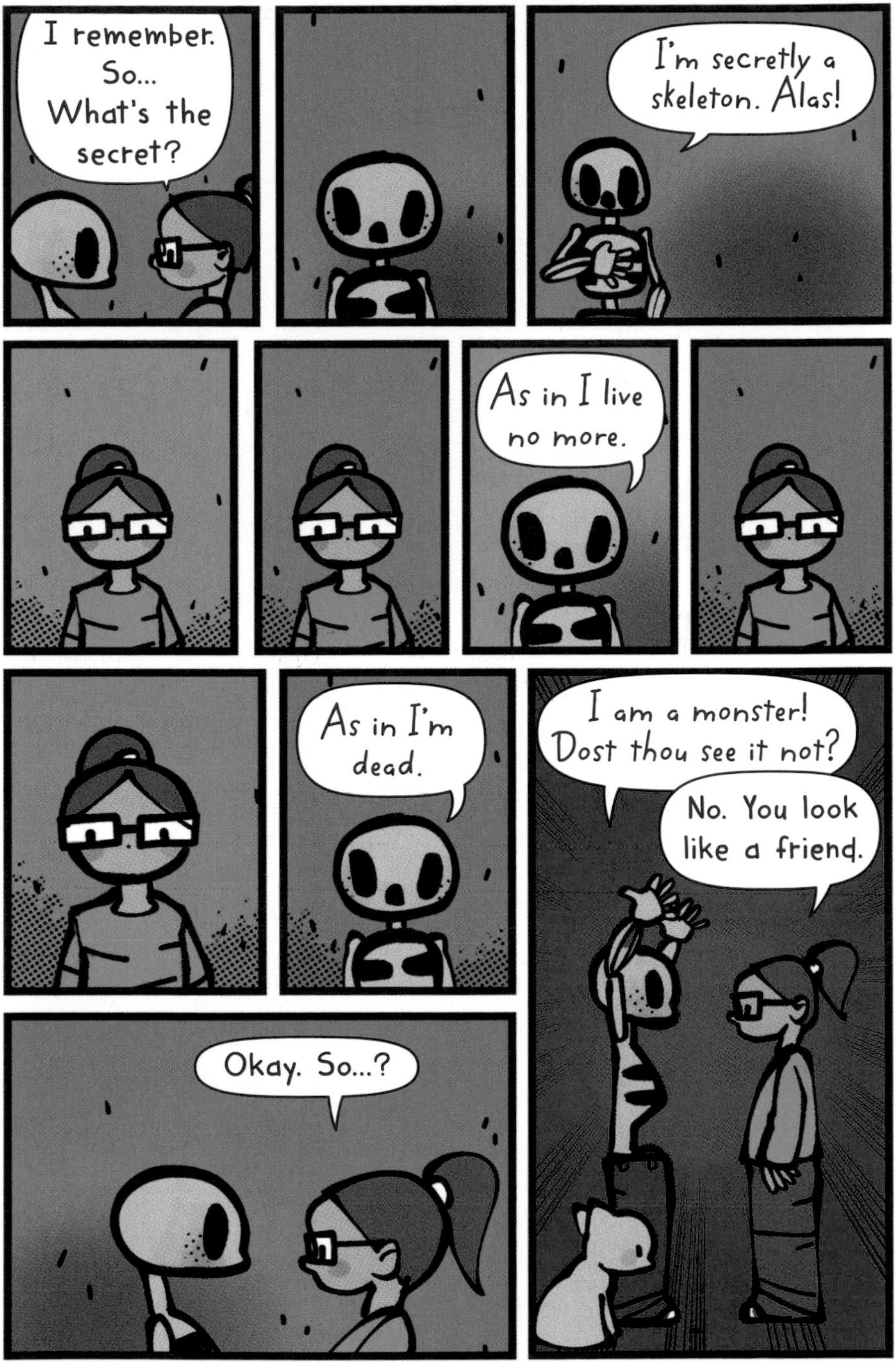
I remember. So... What's the secret?
I'm secretly a skeleton. Alas!
As in I live no more.
As in I'm dead.
I am a monster! Dost thou see it not?
No. You look like a friend.
Okay. So...?

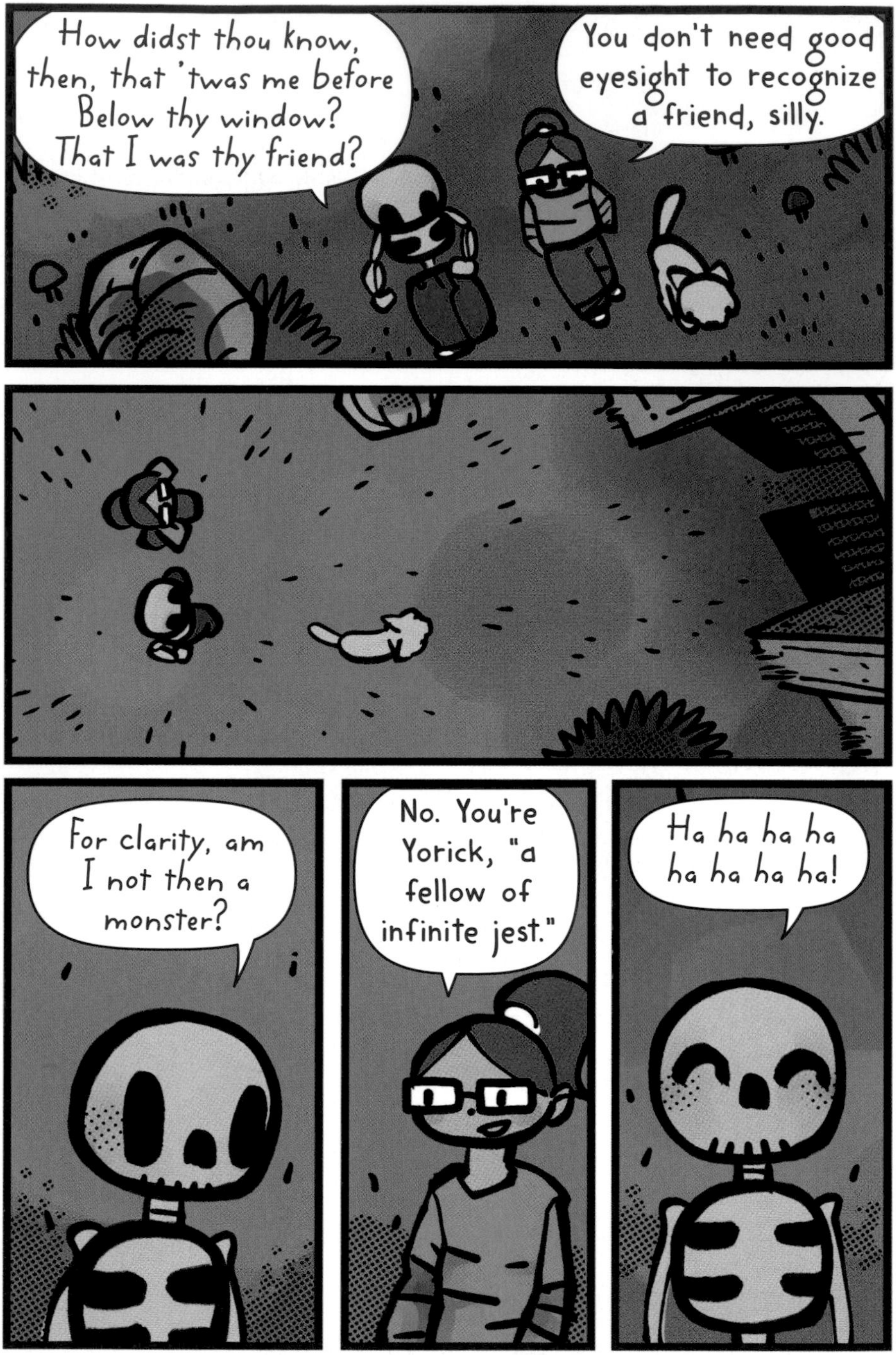
How didst thou know, then, that 'twas me before Below thy window? That I was thy friend?
You don't need good eyesight to recognize a friend, silly.
For clarity, am I not then a monster?
No. You're Yorick, "a fellow of infinite jest."
Ha ha ha ha ha ha ha ha!

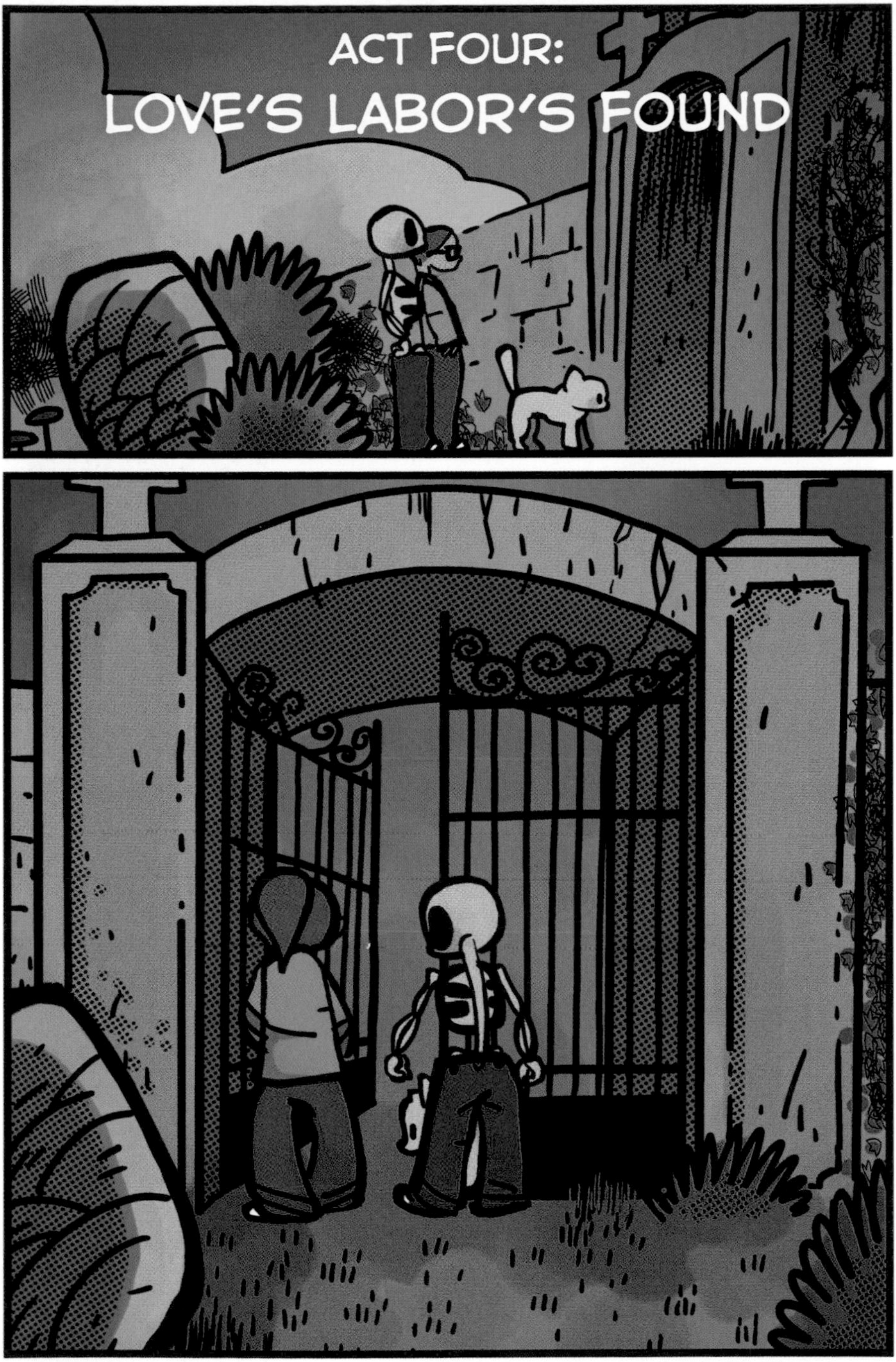
ACT FOUR:
LOVE'S LABOR'S FOUND

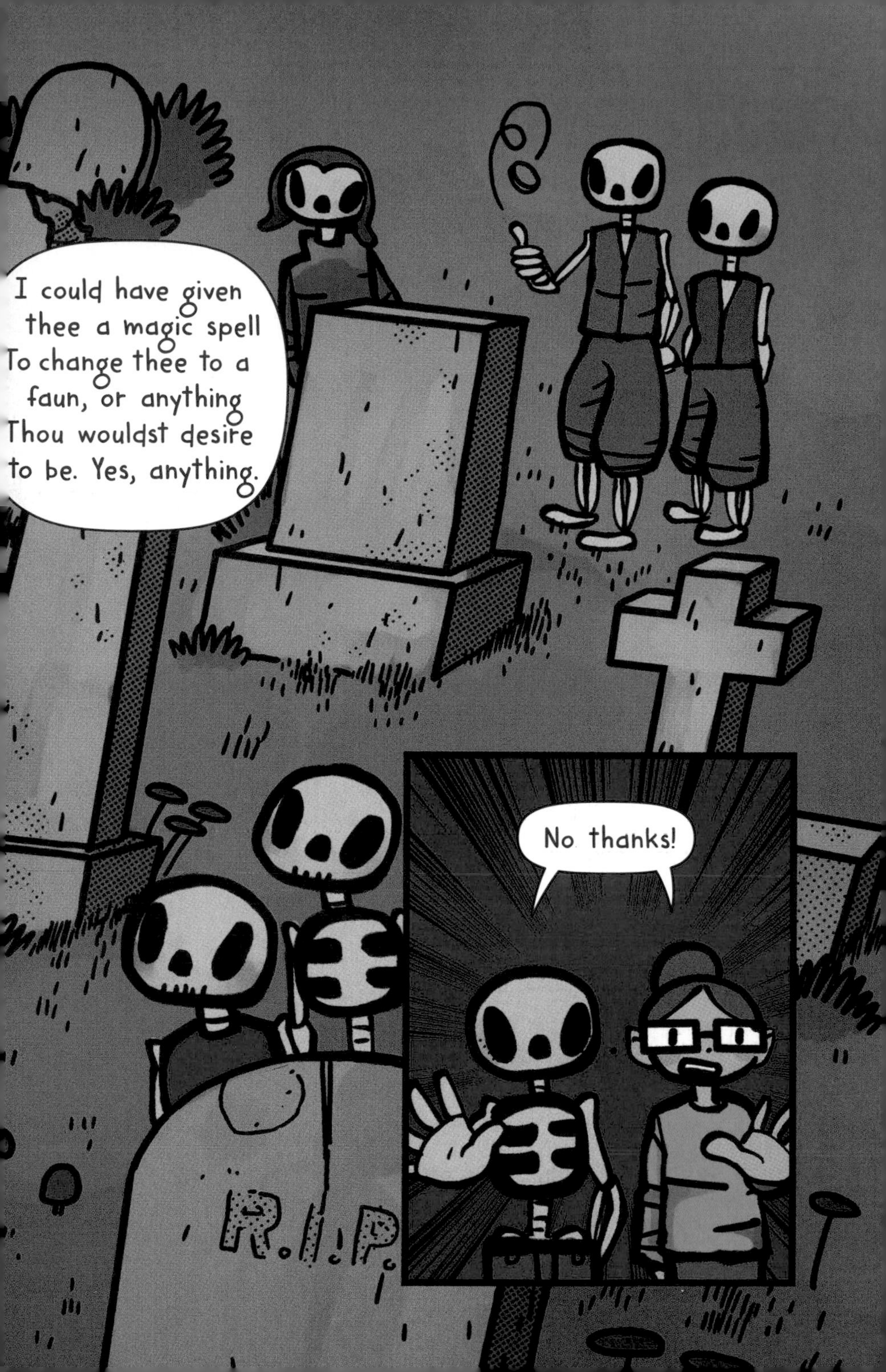
I could have given thee a magic spell To change thee to a faun, or anything Thou wouldst desire to be. Yes, anything.
No thanks!
R.I.P.

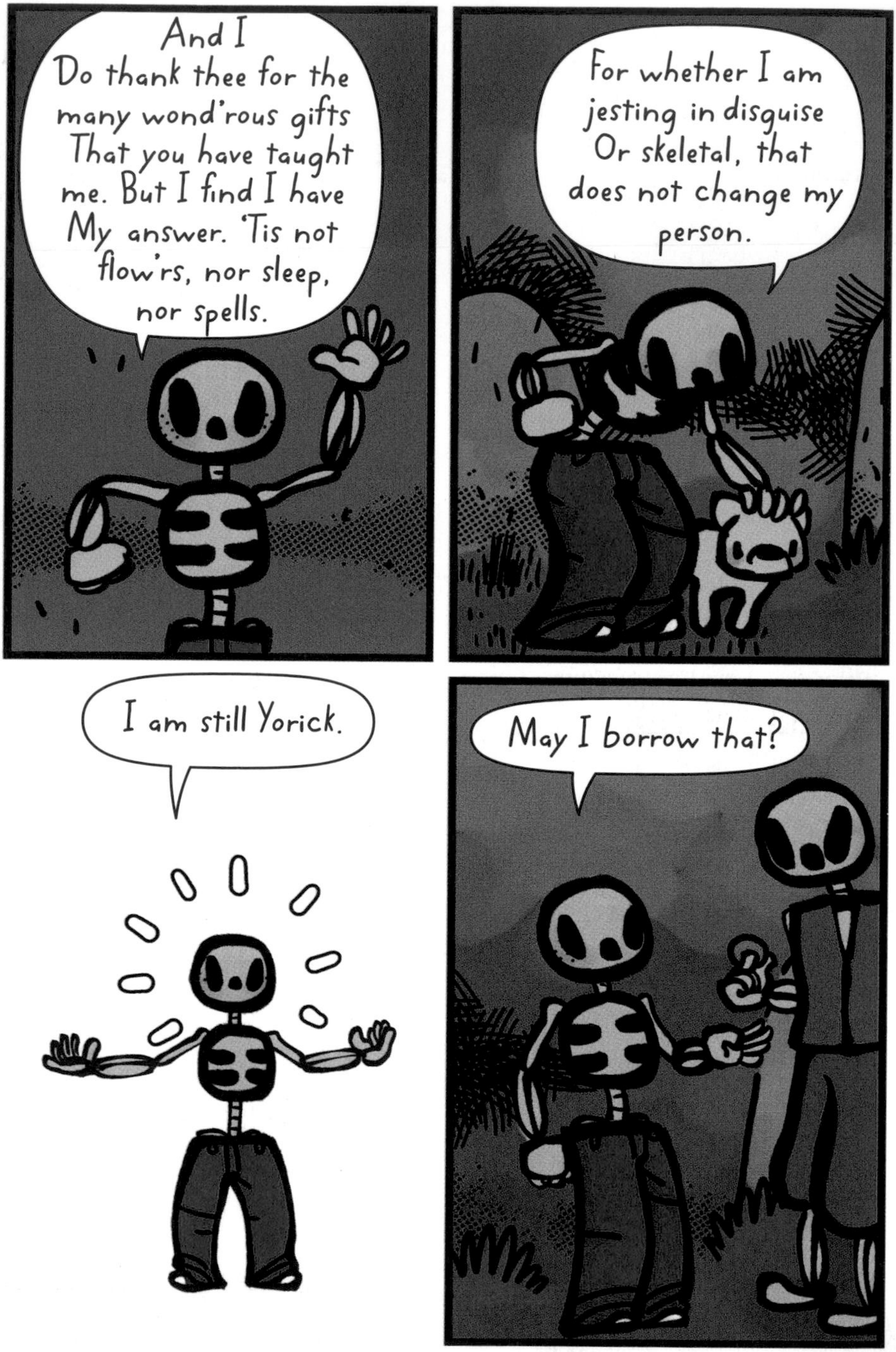
And I
Do thank thee for the many wond'rous gifts
That you have taught me. But I find I have
My answer. 'Tis not flow'rs, nor sleep, nor spells.
For whether I am jesting in disguise
Or skeletal, that does not change my person.
I am still Yorick.
May I borrow that?

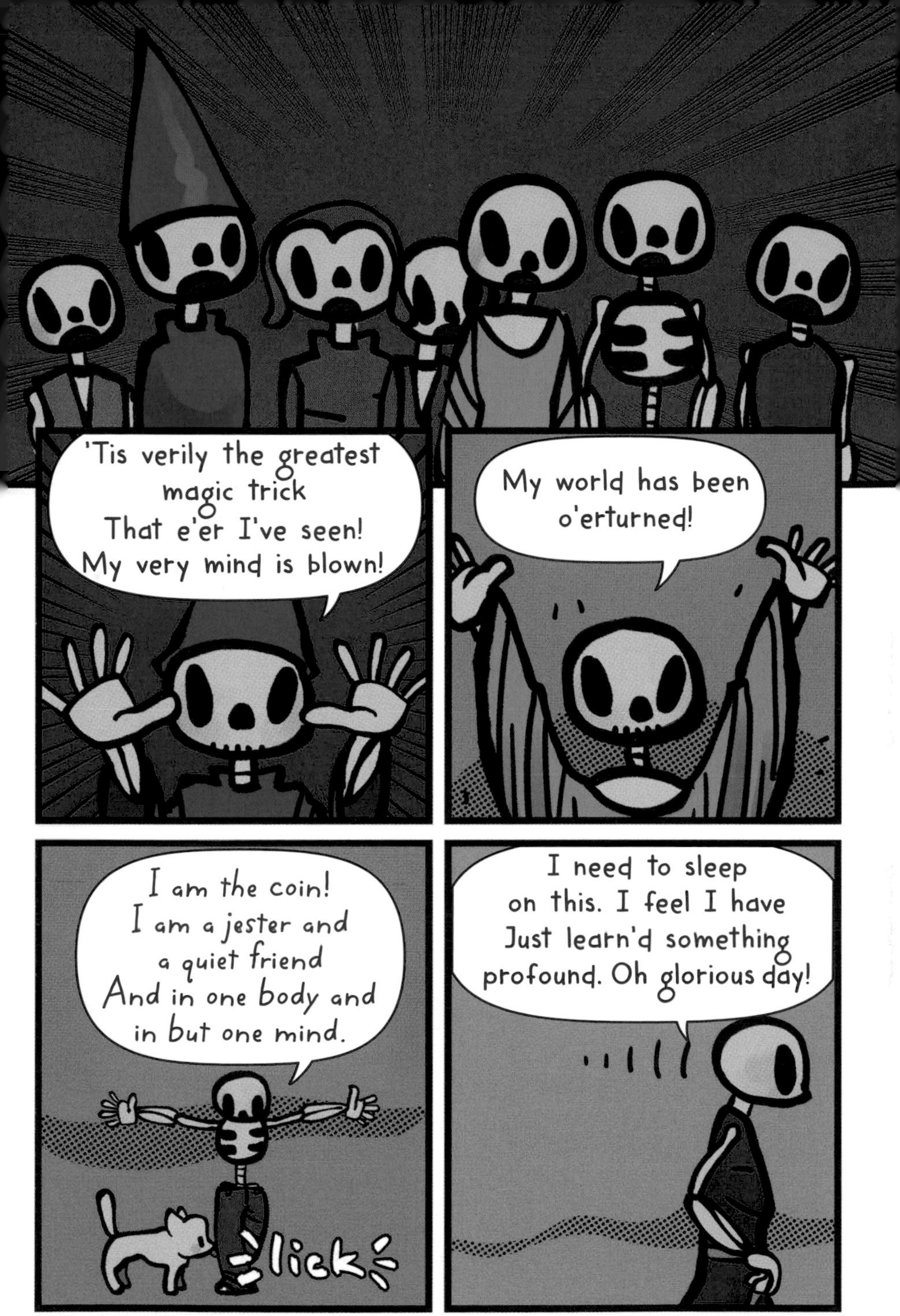
'Tis verily the greatest magic trick That e'er I've seen! My very mind is blown!
My world has been o'erturned!
I am the coin! I am a jester and a quiet friend And in one body and in but one mind.
lick
I need to sleep on this. I feel I have Just learn'd something profound. Oh glorious day!

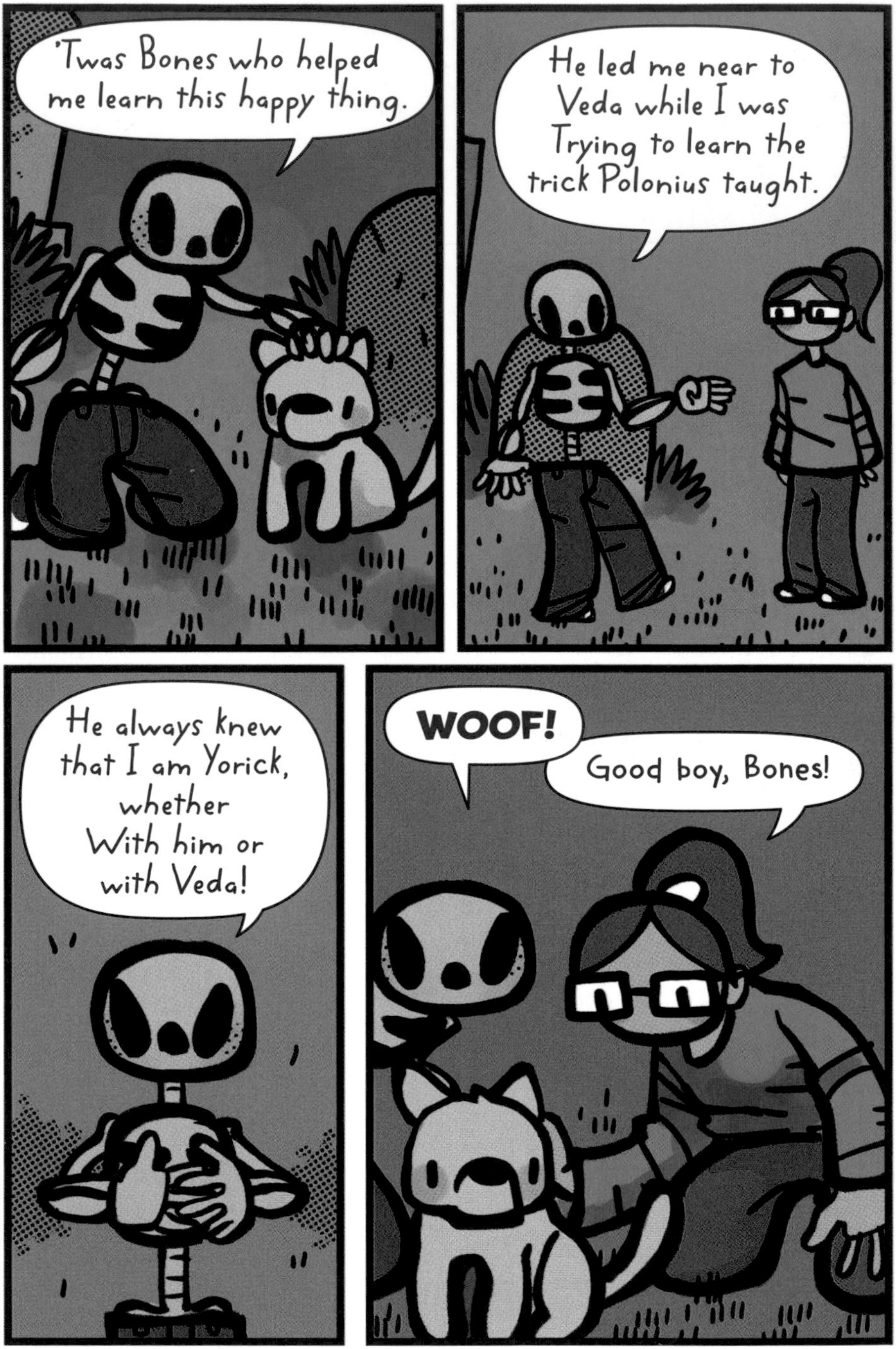
'Twas Bones who helped me learn this happy thing.
He led me near to Veda while I was Trying to learn the trick Polonius taught.
He always knew that I am Yorick, whether With him or with Veda!
WOOF!
Good boy, Bones!

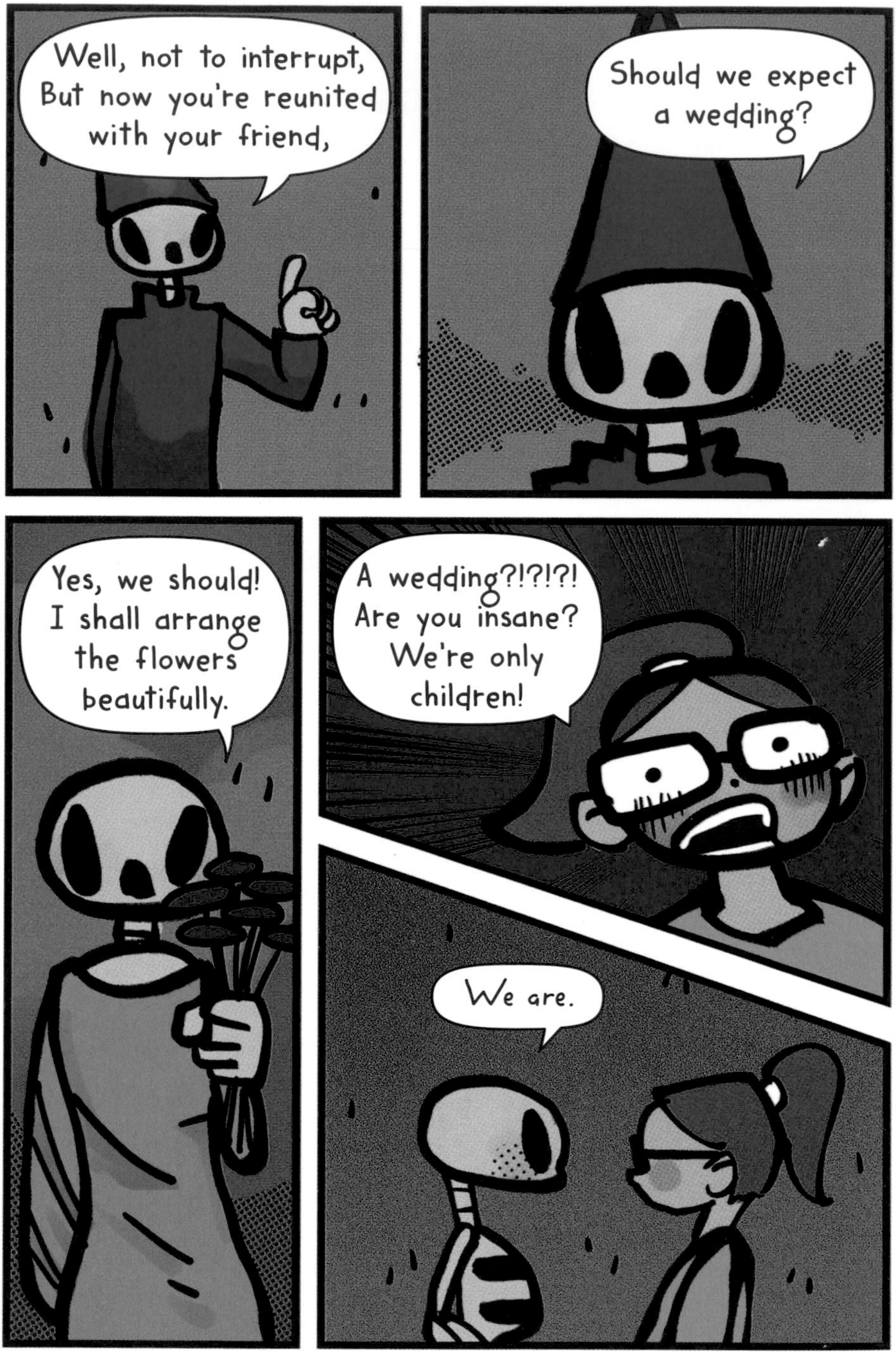
Well, not to interrupt, But now you're reunited with your friend,
Should we expect a wedding?
Yes, we should! I shall arrange the flowers beautifully.
A wedding?!?!?! Are you insane? We're only children!
We are.

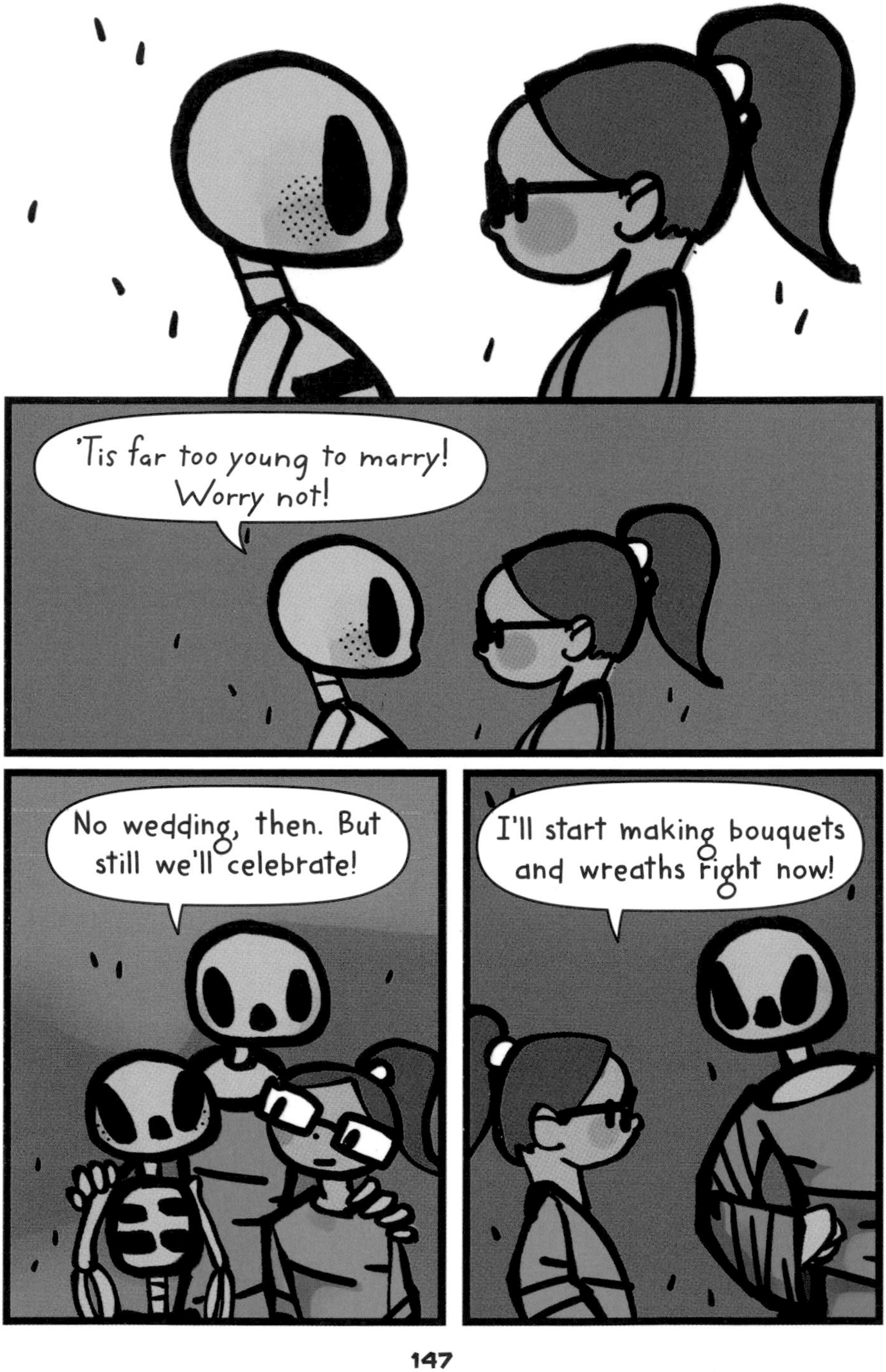
'Tis far too young to marry! Worry not!
No wedding, then. But still we'll celebrate!
I'll start making bouquets and wreaths right now!

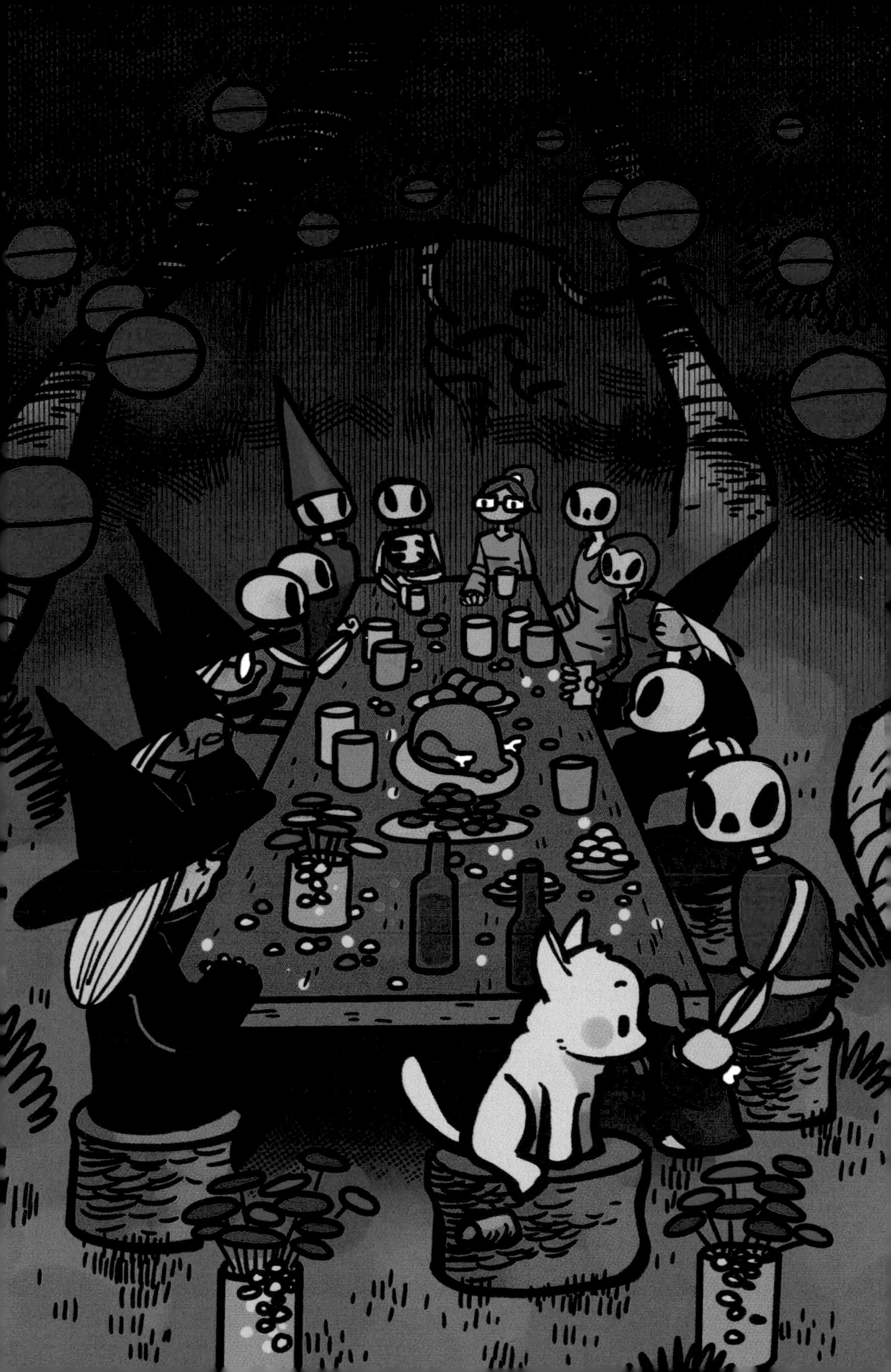

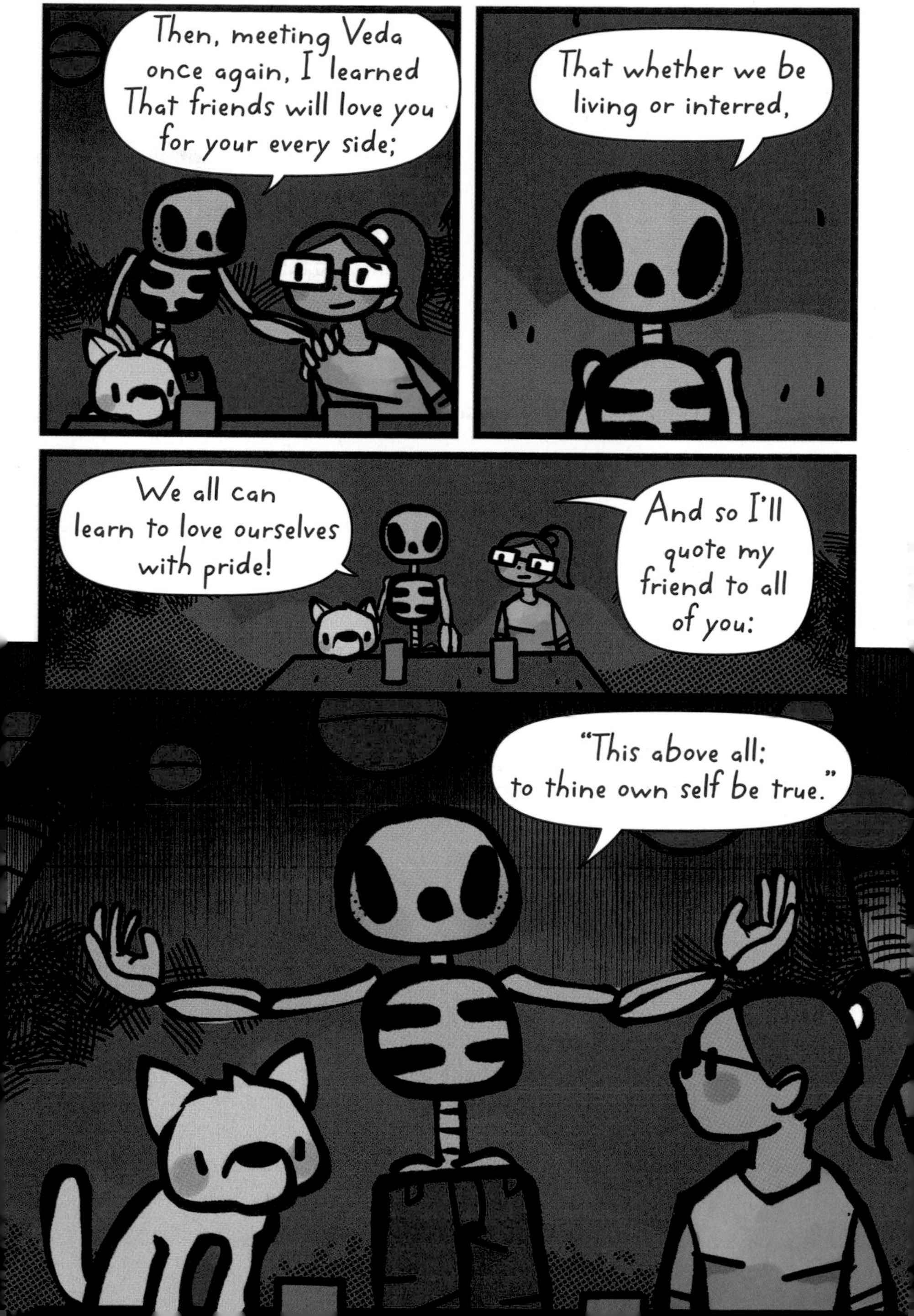
Then, meeting Veda once again, I learned That friends will love you for your every side;
That whether we be living or interred,
We all can learn to love ourselves with pride!
And so I'll quote my friend to all of you:
"This above all: to thine own self be true."

Acknowledgments

Jeremy

The first Yorick and Bones book was published during a global pandemic. This one was created during the pandemic. I would like to thank our AMAZING team at HarperCollins for their hard work and for keeping things on track during such uncertain times. I'm looking at you, Andrew, Erin, David, Bria, Maeve, and Shamin, and everyone else behind the scenes. Thank you to Krista, Scott, Joyce, Rebecca, Mme. Godel, Khalil, M. Brisebois, and M. Beattie for putting kids first. Your dedication to schools and children meant I was able to shift my thoughts regularly back into this book and that was only possible because of you. Thank you to these kids: Alev, Chloë, Esmé, and Hawk, for being early readers of book one—your enthusiasm carried into the creation of this second book. Theo, thanks for laughing at the right places when you finally read book one. And where would I be without you, Heather? Nowhere. Thanks for everything, but especially for being a cheering section when I most need it. And, finally, Hermione: my partner in crime, daughter, cowriter, coconspirator, and fellow Shakespeare nerd. What a joy to share this project with you!

Hermione

First of all, I need to thank Andrew Eliopulos, our amazing editor who made sure this book was awesome. Thank you, Andrew!!! I would also like to thank Paul and Susanne Moniz de Sà for all they taught me about Shakespeare and the theater, and my voice teacher, Wendy Nielsen, for being so supportive even though my writing has nothing to do with singing. Thank you to my friends for being amazing in general. Thank you to my brother for reading the first book even though he would "rather read a dictionary." And thank you to my mom for, you know, being my mom. Finally, I must especially thank my dad for making me part of this project that he's been working on for so long. It's an honor.